*Home safe at last . . .*

Dominique was as touched by the love in Julian's face as she was by all she felt for him. *Home safe at last,* she thought as she leaned against his sturdy chest and gratefully surveyed what was left of the weathered gray sanctuary. Vines covered its surfaces, and weeds sprouted through the cracks in the floor. The severity of her near tragedy became overwhelming and the tears that had been pent up through the ordeal and all the distress of the day's trauma erupted at last.

"Julian!" she cried. "Thank God for you, Julian!"

He took her chin in his hand and looked at her as if recording every inch of her face. She felt a longing to stay just as they were forever. A voice began to call to her from somewhere inside her head—something about Lizette. But the chatter was vetoed by the exquisite feeling of his mouth on hers.

Don't miss the next riveting saga from
HarperPaperbacks:

*The Sutcliffe Diamonds*

by Janet Quin-Harkin

And look for **BOYFRIENDS GIRLFRIENDS** —the romantic
new series by Katherine Applegate.

*#1 Zoey Fools Around*
*#2 Jake Finds Out*

Coming soon:

*#3 Nina Won't Tell*
*#4 Ben's In Love*
*#5 Claire Gets Caught*
*#6 What Zoey Saw*
*#7 Lucas Gets Hurt*

# THE
# JOURNEY
# HOME

## ZOE SALINGER

# HarperPaperbacks
*A Division of* HarperCollins*Publishers*

This is a work of fiction. The characters, incidents, and dialogues are products of the author's imagination and are not to be construed as real. Any resemblance to actual events or persons, living or dead, is entirely coincidental.

HarperPaperbacks   A Division of HarperCollinsPublishers
10 East 53rd Street, New York, N.Y. 10022

Copyright © 1994 by Madalyne Katz Whealer
and Daniel Weiss Associates, Inc.
Cover art copyright © 1994 Daniel Weiss Associates, Inc.

Produced by Daniel Weiss Associates, Inc.,
33 West 17th Street, New York, New York 10011.

First printing: April 1994

Printed in the United States of America

HarperPaperbacks and colophon are trademarks of
HarperCollinsPublishers

10 9 8 7 6 5 4 3 2 1

*Love and thanks to my darling daughter and muse,*
*Sabrina M. L. Katz-Eller . . . and to my dream*
*editor, Gail Greiner*

# VILLE DE FABIAN, FRANCE

## 1939

"Hold still, Jean!" Mimi shimmied her behind a few inches higher on the oak branch. "Just hold still one minute so I can finish this damn sketch!"

As much to annoy Mimi as to hide his smile, Jean turned his back to her and moved farther up the bank of the river where he was trolling for fish. "Why is it that you always bring such choice words back from the Paris gutters? Our lesson today is 'damn.' Can you spell 'damn,' children?"

Mimi laughed so hard, she almost fell from the tree. He had made his voice high and nasal. A perfect imitation of their Hebrew teacher, Rabbi Pelson.

Jean cast his line beyond the soggy weeds. "I can see it now. Rabbi Pelson asks his pet to recite the Hebrew alphabet: *Aleph, beth, gimel* . . . and instead of *daleth,* you slip in 'damn.' Now be quiet. You're scaring the fish."

Crunching as many twigs and leaves as possible, Mimi hopped off her branch and laid her pad on a rock. "You think you're a big deal because you're sixteen, don't you?"

Jean trudged farther upstream and cast again. "And you think you're a hotshot because you've been spending so much time in Paris lately." His own reminder that Mimi was beginning a whole other life in Paris, a life away from Ville de Fabian, was painful to him.

Too excited to catch the edge creeping into Jean's tone, Mimi trailed behind him on the riverbank. "Did I tell you what I saw at the cinema on Saturday? An American film—*Carefree*. With Fred Astaire and Ginger Rogers."

"I'm impressed," Jean said indifferently.

"It was so fantastic, Jean!" Mimi gushed. "Fred Astaire is a doctor and he tells Amanda— Isn't Amanda a beautiful name? I wish it were my name. If I ever have a daughter, I'm going to name her Amanda. What do you think?"

"Amanda's okay." Jean shrugged.

"Don't give yourself a stroke from all your excitement," Mimi said sarcastically. "Anyway, Fred is crazy as a bedbug. But extremely charming! He tells Amanda to eat seafood and whipped cream so she'll dream—"

"If you don't shut up, I won't catch a single fish."

But Mimi was too wound up to stop. "My father bought me a record of 'Change Partners'! The song from the movie! Why don't we go up and listen to it on the Victrola? I'll teach you how to do the Continental."

Go up to her house? What was she talking about? He hated going *near* her house. Especially

2

since Mme. Landau had proclaimed that she didn't want them spending so much time together. Because his family wasn't of their class.

Jean had been surprised when Giles, a Catholic boy at school, told Jean that he'd heard all Jewish people were rich. Most of the Jews Jean knew were dirt-poor. They'd been chased from too many towns to have regular jobs or put down roots. Like his own family, the kind of people who ate turnip soup all week to try to manage a decent Sabbath meal.

He'd never known a Jewish family as wealthy as the Landaus. He knew that Dr. Landau was considered one of the best doctors in Paris. But there wasn't an ounce of arrogance in Dr. Landau. If one of his neighbors needed help, he never accepted a cent. Rich or poor, gentile or Jew, Dr. Landau treated all people equally with expert care and warm concern. Mme. Landau, however, was another story—so snobbish, you'd think she was the Queen of Prussia.

"Just be quiet, okay?" Jean snapped.

As soon as Mimi realized that Jean's playful manner was gone, she was sorry she'd mentioned Paris at all. She used to hate going to Paris, because it meant being away from Jean. But the last few visits had been intoxicating.

Her parents had taken her to the theater almost every night. She'd been enchanted by the music of the sensational American performer Josephine Baker and by the lively buzz of people mingling in cafés. Fascinated by the sight

3

of lovers ambling arm in arm along the Seine. And those galleries full of Degas's wondrous ballet paintings, of Van Gogh's splendidly colored fields in Arles. They all danced in her imagination for days after she'd seen them.

She watched sadly as the muscles on Jean's face tensed. She saw this happen all too often these days. And she hated it. If Paris was going to be another barrier between them, she knew she'd grow to hate the city.

It maddened Mimi that the gap growing between her and Jean had nothing to do with them. Her mother! The woman's life was devoted to two things: collecting "appropriate" friends, from wealthy, prominent Jewish families, and making Mimi miserable by trying to keep her away from Jean.

"Jean Adler is not a boy of breeding, Mimi. He is not at home in refined society," her mother had said so sweetly, in a voice Mimi knew was an imitation of the Baroness de Rothschild, the model of French Jewish elegance. Once, when her mother thought she was out of earshot, Mimi heard her ridicule Jean's father. "A pathetic wandering Jew," she had called him. As if M. Adler were to blame for the persecution that drove him from country to country till he had finally found some peace in France.

Well, Mimi had news for her mother. She didn't give a damn about society. All she cared about was Jean Adler. And nothing her mother could do—none of her rules and none of her

4

rages—was going to keep Mimi away from him.

The minute her mother's car had left the driveway that morning, Mimi had raced toward the back door.

The Landaus' maid had dragged the broom across the kitchen floor as she tried to stop Mimi. "Just where do you think you're headed?" Marie demanded.

"To see Jean," Mimi said with an impish smile.

"You heard what your mama said when she left. You are *not* to be running off to see the Adler boy!"

"I won't tell, if you won't," Mimi had said, laughing. "Besides, we won't really be alone. Mama said that God watches every move I make."

Marie shook her broom at Mimi. "It isn't funny to be so disrespectful. You'll get in big trouble if you don't listen to your mother!"

"Marie, dear heart," Mimi cooed, as she backed down the kitchen steps. "You are in serious danger of turning into *un vieux machin*— a real fuddy-duddy! Keep this our little secret and I'll bring you back a negligee from Paris. Something—*ooh-la-la*—*exotique* and sexy!"

Mimi smiled to herself as she remembered how Marie's face had turned bright red. "Your mother is going to kill you!" she'd cried, shaking her broom.

*Mother!* Mimi thought in exasperation as she watched Jean gaze out over the water. How could anyone *not* understand how incredible he was? It wasn't just his rugged good looks. There were those dark eyes that flashed mischief one minute, then filled with profound sadness the next, causing Mimi's heart to ache. The overpowering electric charge she felt when she saw him—or even thought about him. And all the things she loved—sketching, riding, daydreaming about the future—they all took on a brightness when she did them with Jean.

Now Mimi watched Jean's tanned arms with pleasure as he teased the water with his line. She imagined his look of concentration. Suddenly she needed to look into his eyes. Had to know that she could make him smile.

"Jean, you're no damn fun anymore. Fishing is for old men. Let's do something fun. Let's go swimming."

Mimi rolled up her pants to her knees and tied her shirt at her waist to reveal her midriff. "Like my new suit?" she joked. "Damn pretty, *non?* It's the latest Deauville style. Come on, I'll race you across the damn lake."

"Shhhh!" Over his shoulder, Jean shot her an annoyed look. But she knew he was stifling a grin.

Mimi kicked off her shoes, wound her red mane into a knot and waded into the water. "Ah! It's so damn nice."

Seeing that Jean's stiff pose was falling apart delighted Mimi. She kicked some water in his direction.

"Cut it out, Mimi. What's that American expression you came back from Paris with last time? Beat it, kiddo. Twenty-five skiddoo!"

"It's twenty-*three* skiddoo, you clod!" Mimi erupted into laughter that Jean had a hard time resisting.

"I may be an old man, but you! You are an absolute child," he told her.

In response, she picked up a handful of pebbles and tossed them at the spot where Jean was trolling. "Twenty-three skiddoo, you damn fish! Swim for your lives!"

"That does it!" Jean called, tossing his fishing rod down as Mimi backed away. "You'd better run, you redheaded devil. Because if I get my hands on you, you're fish bait!"

"Is that so?" Mimi exclaimed, showing Jean an I-dare-you face before she took off up the hill.

But soon, to Mimi's joy, Jean had her trapped against the ancient grain mill across the path from her house. All at once the laughter stopped as Jean held her and searched her eyes, his expression one of confusion.

She leaned into his chest and smiled up at him. Touching his lips with her finger, she then tapped her own. "It's not nice to keep a lady waiting," she said in a voice as soft as that of her favorite film star, Simone Signoret.

Bending near, he watched her eyes close as she raised her face to his. Wasn't this, after all, where they had always been headed? The most natural thing in the world?

He brought his mouth softly to hers. In all the hours he had dreamed of this moment, in all the ways he had tried to fight those dreams, he never knew anything could feel so beautiful. "More," Mimi whispered, savoring this new magic rushing through her. She pressed her lips harder against his.

But a sudden cry shattered their delicious moment.

"Mimi! What do you think you're doing? How dare you! How could you disobey my orders the minute I turn my back!"

Startled, they looked up to see Mimi's mother glaring at them from across the path. Her Chanel skirt was gathered in her hand; dust covered her fine Italian pumps. Georges, the chauffeur, stood behind her, timidly holding an oilcan.

Jean tried to drown out Mimi's "Damn!" with a loud, guilty "*Excusez-moi*, Mme. Landau."

"You are *not* excused! If we hadn't turned back because of car trouble, heaven knows what I would have found going on here!"

"You'd better go, Jean." Mimi braced herself for war. Jean looked at her before turning down the path, a look that said nothing could take away the kiss they'd just shared.

"Start packing your trunk, mademoiselle," Mme. Landau commanded, her voice quaking with anger. "We're heading straight back to Paris in the morning. And that's where we're going to stay. You won't get another chance to defy me and sneak off with that—that Adler boy again!"

# CHAPTER ONE

## 1993. MANHATTAN

"Hey, gorgeous," a ponytailed taxi driver called to Dominique as she started across Fifth Avenue against the light. "Better look where you're going."

"Thanks," Dominique answered absently, backing up onto the curb in front of the majestic Metropolitan Museum. She was an art devotee, so the Met was one of her favorite hangouts in Manhattan.

But even the Met hadn't helped her shake the angry funk engulfing her since this morning's battle with her mother. *Not the best frame of mind to be in, girl, for crossing one of Manhattan's busiest streets!*

"Maybe the beautiful redhead needs a big, strong escort," called a messenger dressed in purple and black spandex. He let go of his bicycle handles to flex his muscles. "*I'd* sure like to look where she's going."

"Got that right," the cabbie chimed in. He turned up the volume on his radio, which was playing Garr Haywood and Dr. Hyde's "Let

Me," and mouthed the lyrics in Dominique's direction.

*Damn!* Dominique thought indignantly. *Spare me!* She would have loved telling them both to buzz off had her mother not been drilling her with all that noblesse oblige stuff since she was two. How young ladies of her rank were required to behave.

Dominique's looks, which everyone had raved about all her life—saying how much she looked like a model, et cetera, et cetera—had never been of much significance to her. And today, since she had gone to Central Park and the Met to do some sketching in old jeans and a faded T-shirt to *avoid* the usual attention, the ogles were especially irritating. As soon as the light changed, she sprinted across the street and jogged the next few blocks to her building.

Neal, the concierge at Camelot Towers, looked up from the *Daily News* on his desk. "Enjoyin' the spring weather, are you, Dominique?" he asked in his thick Irish brogue. Neal was a sweet old guy, but she wasn't up for a chat about the weather. The best she could manage was a Dial-a-Smile, as Dominique called the radiant face she could put on at will. A face perfected over years of charming all the phonies who buzzed around her parents' art gallery.

The elevator opened onto the floor of the Rappaport triplex. Mrs. Bard, the gentle, perpetually bewildered-looking housekeeper, called from the top floor. "That you, dear?"

Dominique waved to the woman at the top of the spiral staircase. "Hi, Mrs. Bard," Dominique called, hoping that she hadn't heard the morning's row with her mother.

Mrs. Bard started downstairs. "Your mother asked me to remind you . . ." She tapped her forehead to jog her memory. "Oh! Your parents will meet you at your uncle Nathan's at five for the seder."

Right! The first Passover seder. Dominique always looked forward to spending it at Uncle Nathan's and Aunt Eleanor's. She loved being with her cousins, Melinda and Zach. Melinda was a five-year-old cutie-pie, and Zach, three years older than Dominique, was going out with one of her best friends, Kaitlin O'Brien.

And Aunt Eleanor's sisters and their families were always there for the celebration. Every inch of Uncle Nathan's modest Upper West Side apartment came alive with a warm, crazy bustling that Dominique loved.

She just hoped that she and her mother could get through the evening without the whole family noticing the tension between them. *The old etiquette drills will get a real workout tonight*, Dominique thought sardonically.

Thanking Mrs. Bard, Dominique continued to her room. She dumped her backpack on her canopied bed, sat down beside it and took out her sketch pad to review the day's work.

There were several park scenes. The elderly

11

woman who sold balloons near the zoo. Young mothers pushing strollers at the playground. Kids dancing on Rollerblades on the other side of the Sheep Meadow. The museum pages were line drawings of eighteenth-century gowns. *Decent,* she thought, *but no magic.*

She tossed the book to her desk and stretched out on her peach satin comforter. The moment she did, a tiny calico cat hopped up from under the bed. He dropped the sockmouse Dominique had made for him and mewed his hello.

"Hey, Little Elvis," Dominique murmured, as the fur-ball headed for the crook of her arm.

He snuggled for a moment, then gazed up, gently butting Dominique's arm, until she understood that he wanted his head scratched. When Dominique obeyed, the cat closed his amber eyes and settled into his purring mode.

Dominique kissed the back of his neck. "Better keep oldsock-mouse handy, fella. After graduation you and I might just pack up and head for the border."

*Probably the only way I'd ever get my mother off my back!* Dominique thought. *And I could never leave this little guy behind. Especially with a woman who firmly believes he sheds just to annoy her.* Before Dominique had finished her thought, another voice yammered in her head. *Oh the poor little rich girl!* "Ms. Critic," Dominique called the voice, that uninvited guest always dropping by with a nasty remark. But the "poor little rich girl" snipe was a low blow.

Somewhere around her twelfth birthday, Dominique had started to wonder if something was wrong with her. Was she just an ungrateful brat because she felt so hemmed in by this best-of-everything life that her parents had created?

But by thirteen, she was convinced that something was madly out of kilter. People were going *hungry* and her mother was having riding boots made to order for Dominique in Italy! What was wrong with *that* picture?

Little Elvis adjusted himself along the curve of her back as Dominique reached for the silver-framed photograph on the night table. Taken when she was seven, it was one of her favorite pictures. She sat proudly astride a horse. A red ribbon was pinned to her vest, and standing beside her, wearing a grin as big as her own, was Grandmère Mimi.

She stared at the picture intently, remembering the day it had been taken. There had been a festival in Ville de Fabian, the small town in France where her grandmother lived. Dominique had been the youngest contestant in a horse show, and the judges had awarded Dominique a ribbon to encourage her early riding efforts. But Grandmère had made her feel as if it were an Olympic medal.

Until her mother, Amanda, had reminded Dominique that her posture was all wrong.

That she must not be lulled into a lazy attitude because of the easily won prize.

Once again, Mama had burst Dominique's happy bubble with her well-aimed shot. And would have snatched the happiness from the day, too, if Grandmère hadn't put together a scavenger hunt with the local children. How was it possible for a free spirit like Grandmère Mimi to have a daughter as rigid as Amanda?

Mama's message then was the same as it was today: to be a success, one must always be plotting the next move. And her next move for Dominique—after she graduated from high school in the spring—was N.Y.U.'s art administration program. Amanda had insisted that Dominique apply, and now Dominique was sorry she hadn't ripped up the acceptance letter before her parents had seen it.

Mrs. and Mr. Rappaport were an unbeatable team, whether in business or in running Dominique's life. Amanda, as direct as a sledgehammer. And Leon, subtle but irresistible. Like the good-cop–bad-cop teams on TV. One beat the convict senseless with a billy club. Then in walked the good cop, to soften the con up with coffee and a pack of smokes—or, in her father's case, ice cream. All so she'd break down and do what they wanted.

Everyone knew N.Y.U. had the best program of its kind for the business end of the art world. Terrific, if that was what you wanted to do with your life. Dominique, however, had other plans.

"Is it wrong to want success for my child?" her mother had said when Dominique balked at the idea.

True, all of Dominique's friends' parents wanted their kids to be successful. But none of them tried to run their kids' lives with the single-minded zeal of Amanda Rappaport. As they adored saying in *Elegance* and the other celebrity magazines, Amanda Rappaport had come from France with next to nothing—*save her single-minded zeal!*—and built Rappaport Fine Arts into an empire.

Amanda Rappaport was the same mighty force whether she was putting together a Cassatt exhibit or finding a ballet teacher for five-year-old Dominique. How she had insisted upon classes with Sandor Mikolov—the best teacher in the city! And true to form, Amanda expected Mikolov to give the same concern to Dominique's beginning exercises as he once gave to the famous Odessa ballet.

"Dominique, we have built this business for you, *non?*" her mother had said that morning over breakfast. "It is only right to prepare for your place in it. The way you are acting, someone would think Papa and I are trying to harm you!" Amanda's tiny, well-manicured hands fluttered in the air after she placed the china teacup back in its saucer. Sometimes Dominique heard the most charming silvery tones in her mother's voice, echoes of her French accent. But when they argued the accent got stronger, and the voice got even softer. Her mother's cool facade made Dominique want to scream.

Dominique held in her anger until the kitchen door had swung closed behind Mrs. Bard. Then she gave vent to her feelings. "I just want some say in how I live my life!"

Mrs. Rappaport clucked her tongue. "Now that you have come to your senior year, you feel you know everything?"

"I just want to know I've chosen my own life!"

Her mother clenched her teeth. A look Dominique hated. One Mrs. Rappaport wore before pulling a power play. "And what, *chérie*, is your brilliant plan?"

Dominique's turmoil pitched inside her. That was just it. She didn't have one. Not exactly, anyway. She just knew that there was something special she wanted to do with her life, even if she couldn't name it right now. Something that would make a difference in the world.

The *real* world. Not the empty world of celebrities, of wealth and power, of her parents' gallery. Dominique knew she at least had to *try* to find whatever that something was—or spend the rest of her life regretting that she hadn't looked. And there was no way that was going to happen to Dominique Rappaport.

"I'd like to do some research." Dominique speared at the bright mélange of berries on her plate.

"Dominique! *S'il tu plaît!*" her mother said in a barely audible voice, casting disapproving eyes toward the fruit. Dominique pushed her dish away, amazed once again at her mother's ability to whisper with the force of a roar.

Her mother continued. "You want to *find* yourself? This American idea of finding one-self, *c'est ridicule*! One becomes what one *makes* of oneself. You have a rare opportunity at the gallery. *And* support from your parents."

*As long as I live by your rules!* Dominique knew that she had to hold firm, she couldn't cave in. Either she broke free now or spent her life in the straitjacket of her mother's will. And though Donna Karan would be commissioned to design it, it would still be a straitjacket.

"That's just it, Mama. I want to make some-thing of myself, *by* myself. I don't want you and Papa to do it for me!"

Mrs. Rappaport glanced at her watch. "At ten thirty Baron von Hitzdorf and the baroness are coming to the gallery."

Infuriated by her mother's way of ending the discussion, Dominique muttered, "A very full calendar."

Her mother dropped her gray linen napkin onto the table. "Now you imply that you are not as important as my calendar. If my mama had cared for me one tenth as much as I care about you, I would be most grateful, *chérie.*"

"What's that supposed to mean? That Grandmère Mimi didn't care because she wasn't breathing down your neck every minute? Because she wasn't ordering annual portraits of you, the way you do with me?"

Amanda positioned a clip-on pearl earring higher on her lobe. "I have had portraits made of you, Dominique, because you are beautiful. Beauty is *à son avantage,* to one's advantage in life. It is your gift from Grandmère Mimi. Unfortunately, you also inherited her strong stubborn streak."

*Like you're not the most stubborn woman on the face of this earth,* Dominique thought. And, as for physical beauty, in Dominique's opinion it was just one more thing that the world made way too big a deal about. *If only Grandmère Mimi had been my own mother.* Even the simplest moments with Mimi had a splendid aura of adventure and spontaneity.

Dominique remembered Grandmère's face as she rocked her long ago and played with her fingers, singing "Clair de Lune." When she looked into Grandmère's eyes Dominique had seen such pure love, like a warm light she could feel shining inside herself. And then, looking up she'd seen her mother watching from the doorway. Amanda's eyes had such an impatient look, as if Dominique and Mimi's playfulness were a waste of time.

Now Dominique searched those same impatient eyes across the breakfast table. "Why do you always criticize Grandmère Mimi?" Dominique asked with frustration. "What did she do to you that was so terrible?"

Her mother's face took on a pinched, hurt look. But, as usual, she evaded Dominique's question about her problems with Grandmère.

"In France it is said that grandparents and grandchildren get on well because they have a common enemy. It seems I am *l'ennemie*. Because I try to ensure you do not make a mess of your life!"

Dominique put her head in her hands. Why was it that having a different opinion made her her mother's enemy? What horrible things had Grandmère done to earn the same dishonor? Things too awful for her mother to discuss?

Amanda stood and came around the table, patting Dominique's shoulder, as if that settled things. "You are so young. For now, take my word that my plan is best for you."

Feeling strangled by anger and frustration, Dominique watched her mother click away in her Ferragamo heels.

And now, as she replaced the horse-show photograph on the night table, Dominique felt the same sense of futility she had had that morning. *There's no way I can make her understand me. Every time I try, it ends in disaster.*

If Mrs. Rappaport knew her daughter had spent the day sketching, she would probably think Dominique was wasting her time. But her mother wasn't going to get the chance to crash the private party that took place in Dominique's head whenever she began to sketch. No one would.

As Dominique sat up, she saw the message light flashing on her answering machine. She pressed the PLAY button.

"Niki? I've got great news! Call me when you get back. If I'm not home, I'm jogging. Waffles for breakfast—you understand. Maybe I'll stop by later." Then, needlessly, the caller added, "It's me. Sara."

Dominique smiled. As if anyone else could have such a rapid-fire, breathless delivery as Sara Melnick. Most people were surprised that behind Sara's bubbly enthusiasm lurked a very serious student. And a gifted violinist as well.

On to the second message. "Hi, Niki. Kaitlin here. Where *are* you? Hiding out at the Met, no doubt. I've got to take my brother to the dentist—I know, I know, it's a glamorous life—so I'll talk to you later. *See* you later, actually. I'll be at the seder tonight at Zach's. Isn't that something? Bye, bye!"

Kaitlin O'Brien. Another unmistakable voice. Kaitlin, Sara and Dominique had been best friends since they'd started at Allwyn Prep twelve years ago. Usually, Dominique would return both calls quickly to see if she could catch them, but she didn't want to infect either of them with her current crummy mood.

The third caller was Dominique's other cousin, Melinda. Zach's five-year-old sister.

Dominique felt a wave of warmth as she listened to the little voice so full of urgency. "Hi, Niki. 'Member you said to call if I ever had a problem? Well, I have a problem. Mommy says I'm s'posed to sit at the *baby* table tonight. But I want to sit next to you at the big table. Call me back, 'kay?"

*This* call, Dominique returned at once. Smiling, she picked up the phone.

Zach answered. "Grand Central Station."

Dominique sighed. "Time for a new line, Zach."

"Yeah, finding a new one is a real priority," Zach responded with a solemn tone. "Soon as I finish studying for my psych exam, I'll dedicate my life to the search."

Dominique laughed and carried the phone to her window seat overlooking Central Park. Even though Zach was older than Dominique, they were more like siblings than cousins.

"I'm on a serious mission, myself," she said as she gazed down at the spring hubbub in the park. Hansom carriages clopping along the winding roads. Feverish Little League action in the ball field. "I'm returning a call from my favorite little cousin."

"Oh, right," Zach said with a laugh. "You're Melinda's lawyer. What's up?"

"Sorry, I must respect my client's confidentiality."

"Okay. But on the subject of confidentiality . . ." Zach lowered his voice. "It's not official yet, but

Kaitlin and I are tying the knot. I bought a ring and everything. Minuscule in size, big in spirit. We're going to announce it to the whole *mishpocheh*—the whole family—in one fell swoop. Tonight. Think I ought to spike the matzo ball soup first?"

Dominique laughed. "That might not be a bad idea, considering. No, but really, Zach. Congratulations! You guys have been dreaming about this forever, and I'm really happy for you."

She truly was. She had always felt that Zach and Kaitlin were an ideal match. They were both great athletes, they were the only ones in their crowd who ate pizza with anchovies, and they really did bring out the best in each other. Not to mention the fact that they glowed like a nuclear reactor when they were together.

"So you're not surprised?"

"Hardly. You guys were born for each other. And I have to say that if it were anyone else I'd say wait, but with you two, it would just be postponing the inevitable."

"All the same, this might cause an international incident," Zach said in a tense whisper. "But our minds are made up. I'm counting on you, cuz, to be on hand with the smelling salts."

The fact that Zach was only in his second year of college and Kaitlin was just graduating from high school would push both families' buttons—and hard. Dominique wondered what was going to upset them more—the age factor or the fact that Kaitlin came from an Irish Catholic family.

"Of course, Zach. You know I'm on your side."

"Said like a budding lawyer," Zach joked.

"Maybe I should consider it! Anyway, I'd like to speak to my client, Melinda."

"Sure," Zach answered. "See you later, cuz."

As she waited for Melinda to come to the phone, a tap at the door startled Dominique. A sandy-haired pixie stuck her head into the room. "Mrs. Bard let me in."

"Sara! You scared me!" Dominique said.

"Is it my fault I look like a gargoyle off the Dakota?" she said, referring to the architectural monsters on the landmark building across the park. Sara's manner of delivering comic lines with the most innocent face always made Dominique laugh.

"Waiting for Melinda to come to the phone."

Sara jogged in place. "Burning off the waffles—"

Dominique smiled and held up her hand as Melinda began to speak. "Hi, Niki," Melinda said. "Did you get my message?"

"Sure did, sweetie. And if I can't get your mom to let you sit at the big table, I'll sit at the baby table. Okay?"

"Mean it?" Melinda squealed.

"Sure do. But promise that we're not going to make a big fuss about the baby table in front of Danielle and Morgan. We don't want the little ones to feel bad. Okay?"

" 'Kay. I just crossed my heart, Niki."

" 'Atta girl! See you later, lovie."

23

Melinda answered with a kissing noise and hung up.

"You're amazing with kids, Niki," Sara huffed, still jogging. "My nephew Ronnie wants to marry you."

"What a doll. Too bad he isn't fifteen years older."

"*Tell* me about it," Sara said. "The guy situation—"

Dominique cut her off. "Wait a second, Sara. You left a message about great news. What's up?"

"Oh, right." The mini-alarm on Sara's watch beeped and she collapsed onto Dominique's floral chaise lounge. "I got the letter yesterday. But my mother misplaced it and—"

"Sara! Cut to the chase! The details, please!"

"Northeast Music Conservatory wants me and my violin!"

"*Yes!*" Dominique clenched her fist. "The best music school in the country! I'm so proud of you, Sara."

Sara grinned. "'Sara Melnick, Violin Virtuoso—'" Sara paused to come up with a funny ending to the headline, an old game of theirs. "'Friends Reveal Lurid Past!'" She sighed. "Don't I just wish."

"Cheer up," Dominique said. "Now that you're going to Northeast, maybe you'll have a lurid future. And I'll happily give the papers the whole disgusting story."

"From your mouth to God's ears!" Sara

clasped her hands in prayer. "But instead I'll probably become the nun Kaitlin dreamed of being before Zach came along. And I'm not even Catholic!" Sara suddenly sat up, her brown eyes opening wide. "By the way, Kait called this morning. She made it into Columbia. Great, huh?"

Dominique nodded. It seemed as if everyone was headed in the direction of their choice except her.

"Is your mom standing firm on the N.Y.U. deal?"

Dominique shrugged. "We'll see." Then, to get off the annoying subject, she asked, "What else is doing?"

Sara lit up. "Much as I hate to gossip, Zach and Kaitlin. Tonight—"

"They're going to announce their engagement!"

"Of course, you beat me to the scoop. But can you believe it?" Sara flopped back onto the chaise and sighed. "Still, I might as well face it, this is the closest I'll ever get to a wedding— being Kaitlin's bridesmaid. And then you'll fall in love—"

Dominique held her hand up. "Whoa! There's this rule about falling in love. You have to meet the guy first."

Falling in love was a fun fantasy, but Dominique's thoughts were not on fantasy at the moment. They were on getting the reins of her life away from her mother.

"None of those guys in your fan club even came close?"

Dominique shook her head. "You'd be surprised how fast the passion fizzles after a few wrestling matches."

"What about that handsome French guy? His family went skiing with you in the Alps this winter. What was his name?"

"Pierre. Pierre du Lac," Dominique answered. "Can't argue with the handsome part. My major childhood crush."

Dominique smiled to herself. After making her feel invisible all her life, Pierre had actually paid attention to her during their families' last annual joint vacation. Directed most of his dinner conversation to her, asked her to dance at the noisy Gstaad discotheque, gave her tips on her mogul technique. And every time she sneaked a look at him, she caught him watching her with a surprised twinkle in his eye. But in the almost constant presence of their families, they never had the freedom for much more than eye contact, intense though it was. Then, for Valentine's Day, he'd sent her a box of chocolate truffles, one of her passions. There was a note in the box that said he hoped he wouldn't have to wait until their next Rappaport–Du Lac family holiday to see her again. She had to admit that the note had delighted her even more than her coveted truffles.

Since then, they'd exchanged a few flirtatious notes, but nothing more had been said about their seeing each other before next winter. What would it be like, she wondered, to spend time with Pierre *sans* parents hovering nearby? Although she often had the feeling that their mothers—friends since their school days—secretly hoped that a romance would flourish between them.

Sara checked her watch. "Well, I think I made up for that waffle. Now I've got to get my last hot pretzel before we turn the clocks to matzo time."

Dominique laughed, walking her down the stairs. "Are your parents going upstate for spring break?"

"Not this year," Sara answered. "The house is being repainted, so we're staying in the city. You going someplace exotic, as usual?"

Dominique summoned the elevator. "No. My parents have to get ready for an exhibit."

"Good! We'll hang out together," Sara said as she stepped into the elevator. "Have a fun seder."

"You too," Dominique answered.

*A fun seder!* Dominique thought, as Sara disappeared behind the closing elevator doors. Between Zach and Kaitlin's engagement news and her problems with her mother, it promised to be a seder to remember, but it wasn't necessarily going to be *fun*.

# CHAPTER TWO

"Mmmm, smells good," Dominique said, as her aunt Eleanor opened the door.

Chicken stuffed with savory rice. The fragrant dill of the matzo ball soup. The *tsimmes*, an exquisitely spiced carrot dish. The aromas wafted deliciously in the hall.

"Oh, that's my new perfume," Aunt Eleanor teased.

Dominique laughed and leaned to share a warm hug with the small, smiling woman.

"Come in, Dominique. Let all who are hungry join our table tonight," Aunt Eleanor sang out, borrowing a phrase from the seder service. "That looks beautiful on you, sweetheart." She admired Dominique's violet silk suit with its decorative silver buttons. "But what doesn't?"

Before they could finish their greetings, a little creature squealing, "Niki's here! Niki's here!" dashed between them and attached herself to Dominique's waist.

Dominique kissed her cousin. "Missed you, sweetie-pie."

Aunt Eleanor peered down at her daughter with a sternish expression, to chide her for her manners. "Yes, and Melinda missed you so much that she nearly knocked us both out with one hug!" But the child was too aglow with adoration of her older cousin to even notice her mother's reproof.

Dominique bent to straighten Melinda's sash. "I want to ask your mom something in private," she said, winking. "Meet me in the living room in two minutes."

Melinda raced off in a flash and peered out from behind the bookcase, hazel eyes alive with dreams of the big table.

"Aunt El," Dominique said, "I know it's a huge favor, but, if I take responsibility for keeping Melinda on her best behavior, can she sit at the big table?"

Aunt Eleanor looked over at Melinda. "She's been *nudzhing* the life out of me all day."

"What if we sit near the baby table so I can keep an eye on the little ones?"

"What can I say?" Aunt Eleanor said, raising her hands in the air. "I'm a pushover. That's why these kids make chopped liver out of me."

Dominique laughed and embraced her aunt.

As Aunt Eleanor walked back into the kitchen, Dominique signaled Melinda. "You owe me a high five."

Melinda ran over and clapped hands with Dominique. Then she whooped a loud "Yippee! I'm sitting next to Niki!"

Dominique whispered in her ear. "Remember what I said about not making a fuss?"

Melinda clapped her hand to her mouth, then crossed her heart.

"Good girl. Now we can work on a plan to hide the *afikomen* so that your daddy will never find it."

The child giggled and twirled energetically away in the pink ballet shoes Dominique had given her for Hanukkah.

"Hi, Dominique," Uncle Nathan called. He paused on his way from the kitchen, carrying a tray of cold vegetables, to kiss his niece. "I heard you two plotting. I'm going to keep a very sharp eye on the two of you *and* the *afikomen*."

"I heard, too," Kaitlin chimed in, following Uncle Nathan with a bowl of fruit. "The *afikomen* is the matzo the kids steal from the seder plate, right?"

"Yup," Uncle Nathan said. "Some mysterious little gonif"—he winked in Melinda's direction—"will sneak off with the matzo and hide it. If I can't find it, I have to pay off the bandit to get it back."

"I'll never tell, Melinda." Kaitlin placed the fruit bowl on the glass table in front of the sofa and crossed the room to hug Dominique.

Kaitlin's shiny black hair, usually pulled into a ponytail, was in soft curls for the night. She wore a turquoise linen dress, which Dominique thought set off her aqua eyes beautifully.

31

"Stunning," Dominique whispered, squeezing her friend's hand.

Kaitlin smiled. "Happy Pesach!"

"Hi, cuz," Zach said, entering the room with two folding chairs on each arm and a bowl of nuts in one hand. He pecked Dominique's cheek. "Notice how Kait pronounced *'afikomen'* and Pesach like a pro?"

"Practice makes perfect. And hanging around you two, I sure get a lot of practice." Kaitlin picked an almond from the nut bowl Zach held and popped some into his mouth.

"Ah, young love!" Dominique said as Zach kissed Kait's fingers, surprised by a twinge of envy. Some day it would be great to be that much in love.

Dominique steadied the television tray as Melinda and her cousin Jackson ran by to grab some raisins. Plastic television trays. A metal fold-out dining table covered with a holiday cloth. Early Rappaport, Eleanor called her style of decorating, and Dominique loved it. It was cozy and relaxed, like the people who lived here.

As Zach set up the chairs, Kaitlin waved Dominique into the hallway. "Zach told you?" she said in a hushed voice.

"I think it's terrific!" Dominique said.

"All that praying for Zach to dump Mindy Kaufman in freshman year may not have been kosher," Kaitlin said with a smile, "but it finally paid off." Then a crease appeared at the center of Kaitlin's brow. The way it always did when she was nervous. "Nik, I'm worried about how the family will feel. . . ."

Dominique nodded sympathetically. "I know, but listen. Bottom line is, they're crazy about you. And even if they'd rather you waited, they'll get used to it after a while."

Kaitlin bit her lip. "But the religion thing—"

Zach came over and put his arm around her waist. "Will you chill, Kait? It's going to be fine."

Aunt Eleanor's sister, Aunt Selma, marched out of the kitchen, waving a wooden spoon. "Jackson, *tateleh*, help Morgan put her shoe on. And Danielle, *mamaleh*, don't fill up on nuts before dinner."

"Hi, Aunt Selma." Dominique exchanged hugs with the tall woman with silver-blue eyes.

"So, Kaitlin," Aunt Selma said. "You're enjoying?"

The Old World accent of Aunt Eleanor's sisters, and their devotion to homemaking, always tickled Dominique. "The *baleboosteh* squad," Uncle Nathan called them.

Kaitlin smiled. "Yes, I'm enjoying!"

"You'll enjoy later," Aunt Selma announced, beckoning the girls into the kitchen with a wave of her spoon. "Now I have jobs for you, if you don't mind, darlings."

"Careful. No enjoying, now," Dominique teased Kaitlin as they followed Aunt Selma.

Melinda skipped into the kitchen ahead of Kaitlin and Dominique. "Do you have a job for me, Aunt Selma?"

33

"*Ooo*, a big job, *mamaleh*! Stirring the *charoset*."

"*Charoset*," Kaitlin said, as if she were in a spelling bee. "Chopped apples and walnuts symbolizing the mortar the Israelites made when they were slaves in Egypt. Right?"

"Nice work, Kait," Zach said, setting up the children's table. "You're going to ace the written test later. At least I hope so; otherwise you won't get dessert."

Aunt Honey, a golden-haired member of the *baleboosteh* squad, shot Zach a look. "Stop with the joking, Zach. You're going to make that nice girl very nervous."

Zach and Dominique exchanged smiles, knowing the aunts wanted to make Zach's Irish Catholic girlfriend feel at home. They knew from their own youthful experiences how awkward it was to be in the minority. Suddenly plunked down in the middle of a world with different customs. The aunts felt it was their job to be Jewish ambassadors, to ease any strangeness Kaitlin felt. And in their collective opinion, Zach was teasing her too much.

"I stopped, Aunt Honey," Zach said, holding his hands up as if in self-defense. Then he whispered. "If I didn't she'd beat me black and blue with her wooden spoon."

"You're terrible, Zach. But you know that, don't you?" Dominique said as she reached past him for an apron.

Soon Dominique and Kaitlin were engulfed in the happy kitchen commotion. Under Aunt

34

Eleanor's supervision, they began cutting parsley for the *seder* plate, stirring the soup, preparing the egg for roasting in the oven.

Aunt Selma tasted the soup. "Something's missing."

"A little salt, maybe?" Aunt Honey offered.

Aunt Selma meditated over the pot. "No. Tomatoes."

"War of the worlds!" Dominique whispered to Kaitlin.

"Tomatoes in chicken soup? Whoever heard of such a thing!" Aunt Eleanor shook her head in disbelief.

"I know it sounds crazy. But Tanta Lily always put tomatoes in her soup." Aunt Selma took two tomatoes from the vegetable bin. "And Tanta Lily made the best soup."

"An angel," Aunt Eleanor said wistfully. Then she slammed the top on the pot. "But she made lousy soup."

In the cozy madness of Aunt Eleanor's kitchen, Dominique felt the envy she had known as a child. This home, which managed without servants, always full of Zach and Melinda's friends, was her idea of paradise.

She could see why some of her friends envied her life. She knew it looked good from the outside. Her home was definitely *not* Early Rappaport, but a reproduction of ornate First Empire French, with paisley tapestries and antique chandeliers. Her life was one of European holidays, yachting and ski weekends, and a wardrobe brimming with designer outfits.

But Dominique always cringed inwardly about such grandeur in a world so full of need. True, she had joined the synagogue's Youth Committee to raise funds for needy children, but there was so much more to be done. And it wouldn't get done at Rappaport Fine Arts.

From childhood Dominique had been trained to ascend to the royal throne, groomed to take over the gallery, whether she wanted to or not. And the most frustrating part of it all was that she adored art.

Dominique remembered being at the gallery when she was about nine. Paintings were lined up along the floor while her parents planned an exhibit. She had become enchanted by an oil painting by May Lee, a brilliant Chinese artist. It showed a family at a wedding. Such faint brush strokes and such muted shades, yet the work was so powerfully alive. It was as if Dominique could feel the spark of May Lee's vision inside herself. As if she had literally stumbled into heaven.

It was the way Dominique had sometimes felt in synagogue for Shabbat service. One moment she would be fidgeting with her prayer book, then suddenly she would feel deeply moved. She never knew what caused it—the rabbi's words, the cantor's song, or the sweetness of the sound of voices in prayer—only that all at once, she felt a warm glow inside.

Then, when she was about twelve, she had almost cried when she heard someone at a party refer to Van Gogh's passionate *Starry Night* as "the Six Million Dollar Van Gogh." And another ask how much money Rembrandt's innovative *Night Watch* might "go for."

The Dial-a-Smile she put on to endure those kinds of evenings with those kinds of people was never needed at Uncle Nathan's. "I feel bad about Nathan," Leon Rappaport had often said of his brother. "He's got a lot on the ball. If he only had more drive, he could have been so successful."

*Success,* Dominique thought bitterly. A commodity her parents seemed only able to measure in wealth.

Dominique felt a knot in her stomach as she heard Amanda and Leon Rappaport's voices in the small foyer.

"Sorry that we are late, darlings," Amanda warbled in her accent that always charmed, entering the room like a Chanel-suit-clad empress. "A cousin of Queen Elizabeth, Lady Bowes-Lyon, insisted to look at the Gauguin."

But Dominique had to smile at the sight of Aunt Eleanor bounding into the living room to scold Dominique's parents. Not at all impressed by the distinguished client or the artist—especially not on Passover. "So, again you're late!"

"'We pray . . . that we shall become infused with renewed spirit and inspiration and under-

37

standing. May the problem of all who are downtrodden be our problem; may the concern of all who are afflicted be our concern; may the struggle of all who strive for liberty and equality be our struggle.'"

As Uncle Nathan read the seder opening—words that Dominique had heard many times before—she was taken aback at how deeply moved she was by their meaning on this night.

Now, looking around the table as the family raised wineglasses for the kiddush prayer, Dominique felt a warmth for them, for all of life, fill her heart as she studied the words slowly: "May the problem of all who are downtrodden be our problem; may the concern of all who are afflicted be our concern. . . ."

She knew these were the words she wanted to live by. *Words that have nothing to do with art administration,* she thought, watching her mother fold the napkin in her lap.

Dominique coached Melinda and Jackson through the Hebrew reading of the Four Questions—traditionally read by the family's youngest—and then, before Uncle Nathan could continue with the seder, Zach cut him off. "Wait, Pop. I have a Fifth Question to ask Kaitlin."

"What's he saying about a 'Fifth Question,' already?" Aunt Eleanor asked. "I never heard of such a thing!"

Nathan shrugged and wagged his finger at Zach. "Don't you embarrass our guest with your *mishegoss!*"

But Zach held his course. "Please, everyone."

Dominique held her breath as Zach took a small black velvet box from his pocket, opened it and presented Kaitlin with a small but lovely diamond ring. An excited tremor coursed through the room. Then everyone hushed as Zach said softly, "I love you and I want to spend the rest of my life with you. So how about it, Kait? Think you can handle a lifetime with me, with an option to renew?"

Kaitlin nodded, wearing an expression between laughter and tears while Zach placed the ring on her finger amid applause and cheers of *"Mazel tov!"*

Melinda cried out. "Yippee! A wedding! Could I be the flower girl? Please! Please! Pretty please!"

Dominique whispered, "Zach has more to say, sweetie." Melinda zipped her lip, but continued to jump up and down until Dominique calmed her.

Then an uncomfortable silence filled the room and Aunt Eleanor looked as if she was trying not to cry. Dominique reached for her hand, wondering if Zach was right to spring his news on them so publicly.

"Mom, Pop, you probably think we're too young, but you were both younger than we are when you got married. And in my opinion—and the opinion of everyone who's ever known you—you've had a wonderful life together."

The family looked at Uncle Nathan and

Aunt Eleanor, and they looked at each other and nodded.

"But we're not getting married so young. We intend to be a little more sensible than you wild and crazy kids," Zach added with a twinkle.

Dominique marveled at his knack for making everyone relax and saw the relief in his parents' faces when they realized he and Kait weren't rushing into marriage.

"We're waiting until Zach is out of college," Kaitlin said. "Which means that I'll be in my second year at Columbia."

"Oh, no!" Melinda piped up. "How old will I be then? Will I still be able to be a flower girl?"

"You'll have a very special place in our wedding," Kaitlin told her with a damp but happy smile.

"And maybe I ought to say a few words about the fact that we have different religions," Zach continued.

Dominique searched the eyes of the guests. All were holding their breath to hear what he had to say on this very charged topic.

"Our family has already had some examples of mixed marriages that have worked out great," Zach said. "Uncle Abe and Aunt Marie, for instance."

Dominique smiled. Zach was in top form. Uncle Abe, one of Aunt Eleanor's brothers, lived in California. He and Marie had the same kind of loving bond that Zach and Kait had, one that transcended any differences.

"As you always said, Pop, there's good and bad in all kinds of people. Well, I just found the best one for me, and we intend to respect each other's faith. Share our differences rather than let them separate us. And as for the children—once we have them—we intend to expose them to both religions and let them make their own choices when they're old enough."

Dominique's father went to Zach and clapped him on the back. "Eleanor and Nachum," he said, calling Nathan by his Hebrew name, "I'm proud of this *boychik* of yours! He's got some *kupp*, some head, on his shoulders."

*And I'm proud of you, Papa!* Dominique thought. Though he was committed to the same fast track as his wife, Leon Rappaport had a gentler, more easygoing style.

"What about me, Uncle Leon?" Melinda said. "Do I have some *kupp* on my shoulders?"

The room erupted into laughter as Leon lifted his niece in the air. "You've got a *kupp*, *shayneh maydelah*—beautiful girl—that could run the country!"

When the room quieted, Kaitlin spoke again. "I want you all to know how happy I am that Niki introduced me to Zach. And how happy I am that Zach introduced me to this wonderful family."

Dominique winked at Kaitlin. For all their worries, both Kait and Zach were going like gangbusters.

"I've loved being with you all tonight," Kaitlin added. "I love Zach and I look forward to being part of this terrific *mishpocheh*!"

"For that," Zach added as the crowd laughed, "you get to skip the written test. Mom, see Kait gets two pieces of honey cake for dessert."

"I'm so happy for you both," Dominique said, her own eyes beginning to fill.

Throughout the dinner, Dominique kept thinking how good it was to know that a love as beautiful as Kaitlin and Zach's really could exist in this world. Best friends as well as romantic partners. *That's the kind of relationship I want someday!*

When the family began to clear the table for dessert, Dominique felt her mother's cool hand on her arm.

"Come with me for a moment, darling. I have something wonderful to tell you."

Feeling both curious and apprehensive, Dominique followed her mother into the master bedroom.

"Close the door, *chérie*," Amanda directed. She rearranged the pile of coats the guests had left on the bed, clearing a place for them to sit.

"What is it, Mama? What's so important that it couldn't wait?"

"I have a surprise!" Amanda teased coyly. "How would you like to spend spring break in Paris?"

# CHAPTER THREE

"Paris! The City of Light." Dominique closed her eyes as the car turned into the Eighty-first Street transverse to cross Central Park. Images of the Eiffel Tower, the Louvre museum, the Paris Opéra whirled in her head.

And while she was there, she'd be able to see Grandmère Mimi in Ville de Fabian. Have her darling grandmother all to herself for the first time in her life!

Then there was Pierre. Ah, Pierre! Amazing how she had been discussing him with Sara just that afternoon . . . wondering what it would be like to get to know him better.

Paris and Pierre! Dominique smiled to herself. *As Aunt Eleanor would say, "So what could be bad?"*

"Monday, Leon, we will have the appointment for the reporter of *Art Today*. On Tuesday, Lord Thornton . . ."

Her mother's business chatter, which usually drove her up a wall, was muffled by the cancan music now playing in Dominique's head.

But then Mrs. Rappaport leaned toward her

and said, "While you are in Paris, it would be so nice, Dominique, if you phoned the Bonets. They have asked to see a photo of the Degas we're getting next month," Mrs. Rappaport told her husband. "And, Dominique, you will stop in at the Schlumbergers' to get a photo of the Picasso and bring it to René Dupont, *oui*?"

Dominique felt some air escape from her happy Paris bubble. "I thought this was supposed to be a pleasure trip."

"I'm certain it will be, darling. But it is smart to be killing two birds with the same stone, isn't that so?"

"Look, Mama . . ." Dominique was considering a smart remark about doing in the whole damn flock when she felt her father's hand on her arm. He gave her an understanding glance and put his finger to his mouth.

"Also, darling," Mrs. Rappaport continued. "It has been forever since we have seen Grandmère. Her letters, they are so brief. She does not like to talk on the telephone. And she refuses to fly to us in New York. Maybe you will find some time to see her, *non*."

"Of course! I'd love to see her!" Dominique's smile was back in place. She still felt a magical bond with her grandmother. When she was a child, her parents had had to pry her away from Grandmère Mimi at the end of each visit.

"Grandmère can be difficult," Mrs. Rappaport began.

*Like you aren't*, Dominique thought sarcastically. She tuned out her mother's riff on what a character Grandmère Mimi was. No negative comment Amanda Rappaport could make about Grandmère Mimi would bring Dominique down. *Grandmère Mimi, all to myself. Yes!*

Dominique loved it when people pointed out how much she was like her grandmother. And there was something poignant behind Mimi's eyes that made Dominique wonder about her early days. She had picked up whispers that Mimi had some great secret, something from her past. . . . Maybe this trip, she'd find the missing pieces to the puzzle of Grandmère Mimi and Mama's troubles.

Even more pressing, Dominique thought, was the puzzle of her own life. Instinctively Dominique felt that Grandmère could help. If there was anyone who could help her make sense of this powerful yearning for a meaningful direction in life, it had to be Grandmère Mimi. She was the only one who had ever really understood what Dominique felt. The only one who ever really *listened.*

In the lobby of their building, Mrs. Rappaport patted Dominique's hair and sighed as they waited for the elevator. "This beautiful hair, so fiery red and thick."

Dominique rolled her eyes. *Any second she's going to start in on how damn* magnifique *my cheekbones, how aquiline my nose! Why does she always have to be fawning over me? And who else has a mother who speaks about her in the third person when they're standing a foot apart?*

The door opened into their penthouse apartment and Mrs. Rappaport added, "We must get the appointment for the trim of the hair tomorrow."

"*Oui*, Mama," Dominique said, hurrying to her room, her mother's Franglais now driving her up the wall. "Tomorrow we get the appointment for the the trim of the hair."

Inside, Dominique kicked off her shoes and glanced at her answering machine. One message. She pressed the button.

"*Bonjour*, Dominique! This is Pierre who is speaking to you in such poor English." Dominique smiled, happily surprised at his voice, relishing his accent many times more than her mother's.

"It gives me happiness that you will come to Paris, *non*? I am looking forward to you having many pleasant times *avec moi*—with me? *Oui*? You will, *s'il tu plaît*, let me know the time of your arrival so I may have the pleasure of meeting your plane. I hope that this idea is pleasing to you as well. *Au revoir!* Good-bye for now!"

"Little Elvis!" Dominique laughed, as she picked up the cat and hugged him. "This trip has the definite possibilities!"

An hour later Dominique sat in her bedroom window seat and stared out across the park, lit only by the traffic snaking across it and the occasional gas-style lamp. This window seat was her favorite spot in the apartment. She had sat there in so many different moods, on so many different occasions.

When she was six and home with chicken pox, she spent long hours looking for the horses on the trail. Trying to spot Snowball, the horse she rode on each weekend lesson. Since she couldn't have her lesson that week, Dominique filled an entire tablet with pictures of Snowball.

When her father came home from work each day he stopped in to visit her. She remembered how she pointed to the people in the park. Asking him, as if he knew, what they were doing outside that day.

Good old Papa. He would listen to her questions and nod with such serious attention. He'd look down into the park for a long time, then make up funny stories. Clear his throat and say in a thoughtful voice, "That fellow on the bike is Mr. Hymie P. Chenkel. He's on his way to work at the Left Shoe Store. If you need a left shoe, they have the best selection in town."

He could always take time to relax and make her laugh. But Mama could never relax. The little wheels in her head kept clicking away at ninety miles an hour. "Saturday, the ballet lessons . . . Straighten your posture, *chérie* . . . Have you finished your homework . . . The trim of your hair . . ."

And now those wheels were hammering out the message that managing the Rappaport gallery was Dominique's own personal Manifest Destiny.

47

*And just exactly what is it that you want to do with your life, Dominique?* Ms. Critic asked.

*I don't know,* she answered. *But I'm sure not giving in to her plan without making a damn good search elsewhere—even if I have to turn the world upside down!*

Friday she had been desperate enough to ask Mrs. Brant, Allwyn Prep's college counselor, for help. Big mistake. "With your grades and lively mind, dear," she'd said, repeating what she'd spouted at the beginning of the term, "you'll have a clear field at whatever you choose. The problem in choosing seems to be that you're just so good at everything!"

*Terrific,* Dominique had thought. *A fortune cookie would have been more helpful.*

One of her parents' clients had suggested decorating. "She has a natural flair!" Mrs. Bridgeport said. *That might satisfy some of my artistic drive,* Dominique mused. *But then I'd be stuck with the same phony clientele, fussing over their second home in the Hamptons and their third in Aspen. The ones Mama fusses over at every gallery opening. Aargh!*

She thought about how much fun she had being around kids when she was a counselor last summer. She had directed a production of *Guys and Dolls* and never laughed so much in her life. *What about teaching? Nope. Too much bureaucracy.*

*I know! I'll be a decorator to kids! Rich kids with plenty of allowance money to throw around!*

*Get serious, now,* she chided herself. *The clock does not take time out for joking.*

Her father's familiar knock on the door interrupted her brainstorming. "Still awake, Dominique?"

"Yup. Come on in, Papa," she called.

Mr. Rappaport poked his distinguished bald head into the room, grinning his Papa Bear grin. He looked behind him comically. "Want to make sure I'm not being tailed. Don't tell your mother—I'm cheating on my diet tonight, and I'll give you half my ice cream."

As he walked into her room, Dominique noticed that he had spotted her sketch pad. Usually she kept it out of her parents' sight. The last time he'd seen it was when she'd done her Snowball series, and he'd been genuinely impressed. But over the years, her art was the only way she had of designing her own private world. And she was going to keep it that way. But in her rush today, she'd forgotten to conceal it.

"Ice cream? Sure. No, wait a second, what flavor is it?" Dominique asked, scooping up the pad along with a stack of magazines and depositing the whole pile in the magazine rack.

Mr. Rappaport stared into his bowl. "Crazy Mixed-Up Mocha. Nuts, fudge, cookie chunks. Everything but garlic."

"No garlic? But, Papa, you know how much I love garlic on my ice cream." The cheerful banter with her father was always an oasis from her mother's uptight manner. If only the woman could learn to chill out a little bit.

"So." Her father sighed, joining her on the

window seat. "What's going on in that clever *kupp*, sweetheart?"

"Maybe you'll think I'm turning into a nut job, but here goes. I want more than anything to do something *special* with my life. Something important. And I get all balled up inside because I don't know what it is."

"Most people feel that way when they're young. That's why it's important to put all that energy into one direction and go for it. Otherwise you can make yourself *meshugge*—really a nut job. And you'll end up nowhere fast."

"It's not like I want to search forever. But I just want to find a purpose, something I can really care about. Something right for me. Something—" Unable to find the right words, Dominique broke off, feeling foolish.

Her father nodded. "What you want, sweetheart, is to find something that makes your heart sing."

Yes! "Exactly! Something that makes my heart sing."

"Bubbe Sadie told me at my bar mitzvah, 'Leon, mine *boychik*, may you find in life what makes your heart sing.'"

His Bubbe Sadie imitation always got a laugh out of Dominique. "So did you find it? Does the gallery make your heart sing?"

Her father put his ice cream bowl on the bookshelf beside the window seat. "Sometimes. Not every single day. When you're eighteen you think something's wrong if your heart isn't

50

singing constantly. But constant singing gets as boring as having Crazy Mixed-Up Mocha three times a day."

"Sorry, Papa, but I'm getting too old for ice cream analogies. What I'm trying to say is, for me, going into the gallery business would be like"—Dominique searched for a comparison, then raised her hands in surrender—"like eating *vanilla* three times a day."

Her father smiled. "But how can you say that when you haven't even tried?" he asked thoughtfully.

"A major gut feeling."

"If Mama and I push, it's because we want to make sure you get started in a good, sound direction. Sure, we have a wonderful life now. But we've worked very hard for it. And we were happy to save you from the hard times we had. Your determination is wonderful, angel. But one of the disadvantages of your advantaged life is that you don't realize how tough life can be."

Dominique groaned. "I'm supposed to feel guilty now, right? Because you two worked so hard to make a good life that I'm not sure I want?"

"It's late, sweetheart." Her father stood. "Let me just say this. Your mother wouldn't give you such *tsuris* if she didn't love you. If she *nudzhes* too much, it's always out of love."

"So I have to go along with her plan or she'll *nudzh* me to death? That doesn't seem like a good enough reason to make a life choice."

51

"And why do you say no before you've even tried? What makes you so sure it won't make your heart sing?"

Dominique mimed tearing her hair. "Okay, so maybe you're right. Maybe art management will be the best career for me. But I want to feel like *I'm* choosing it. No offense, but Mama has planned every single step of my life. From the minute I could walk, there was Sandor Mikolov for ballet. Hebrew school twice a week. French lessons Saturday morning. Fencing in the afternoon. I picked up a crayon and—boom!—she put me in art classes at the Ninety-second Street Y. In third grade, I began piano lessons. Then back to the Y for gymnastics and origami." Dominique leaned back against the window in fatigue. "I just want to make some choices of my own before I'm ninety."

Her father looked at her for a long time, then nodded his head. "Tell you what. Take your trip to Paris. Take a friend. Take two, if you want. Tell them to tell their parents it's my treat. Have yourselves a ball. Get all this teenage turmoil out of your system. When you come back, if you have a realistic plan, we'll consider it."

Dominique jumped to hug him, but he hadn't finished his speech. "But if not, you'll let our wisdom prevail. You'll register in the fall at N.Y.U. and have a rotten, miserable life in the Rappaport sweatshop."

Dominique hooked her arm through her father's and narrowed her eyes. "Level with me, Papa," she said as they walked toward her door. "I have a funny feeling that Mama and Odette have been cooking up this match between Pierre and me since we were born."

"Hmmm . . ." Mr. Rappaport grinned. "On that question, I'll have to pass."

Dominique stopped and wagged her finger at him. "You're withholding valuable information!"

"You don't have to fall in love with Pierre du Lac. But would it be so awful to get to know each other? He seems like a nice young man. And while you're over there, you'll also get the chance to see your grandmother."

"That, I'm looking forward to!" Dominique said.

"So we have a deal? You'll suffer in Paris for your spring break?"

"Have I ever told you what an awesome dude you are?" she said, opening her door.

Mr. Rappaport stopped to consider the compliment. "An awesome dude? I couldn't be more thrilled. That and a dollar twenty-five will get me on the subway."

*The cop team is at it again,* Dominique thought as she closed her door behind her father. *But this time they'll never get me to cave in. This time I'm going to find something that "makes my heart sing."*

And then there was Paris.

She rushed to the phone and pressed the speed dial. With Kaitlin otherwise engaged—

so to speak—she'd have to make her trip as part of a duo instead of the old trio. "Sara, is your passport current?" she asked.

"Uh-huh," Sara answered. "What's up, Niki?"

"How'd you like to go to Paris for spring break?"

"Paris?" asked Sara. "You mean Paris, France?"

"Yes, I mean Paris, France, Europe. My father's treat."

"Paris! I can't believe it!" Sara screamed. "He's treating! You have the best father in the world. Paris in the springtime—what could be more perfect?"

"Sara, calm down! What do you say? Do you think you can talk your parents into letting you go?"

"They're putty in my hands," Sara answered. "As long as I get back here by the twentieth. For my recital at Juilliard."

"Would you kill me if I missed your recital? I want to spend some time with my grandmother in Ville de Fabian."

"Don't worry. My parents will be there embarrassing me with their video camera. I'll force you to watch the tape every day for the rest of your natural life," Sara teased. "Now, when do we leave?"

"Start packing, girl. We leave the day after tomorrow."

# CHAPTER FOUR

"April in Paris! I'm going to faint," Sara squealed, trailing behind Dominique as they rode the tunnel-like escalator at Charles de Gaulle airport.

"Not so loud," Dominique said over her shoulder. "We don't want to seem like a couple of clodettes!" She looked at the glass-enclosed structure surrounding them. More like an enormous spaceship than an international airport. "Believe me, this ultramodern architecture is nothing like the rest of the country. Most of it feels like you're going into the past."

Sara clutched her violin case to her chest, grinning. "But I *am* going to faint," she repeated, this time in a whisper. "I really am!"

"Fine, but just wait till I find Pierre so I don't have to carry you to the *voiture* all by myself."

Suddenly Sara stopped in her tracks. "Whoops! The air in the plane was so dry, I took out my contacts. Where's the ladies' room? Can't have France getting its first look at me in my glasses."

Dominique looked around. "Ah," she said, leading Sara to the rest rooms. She pointed to the sign on the door. "*Femmes*. Memorize that word, Sara."

"*Femmes*," Sara repeated with an exaggerated accent. "Showoffs! Why can't they say '-Ladies' like regular people?"

A few minutes later she emerged with a wide smile. "Ta-da! Look out, Paris, here we come!"

En route to the information booth Dominique spotted Pierre, his wave revealing pure delight. On the plane she'd wondered if she had built him up too much in her thoughts, visualizing him as better-looking than he really was. But now that she saw him, she realized that she'd been right on target. He was *gorgeous*!

*Shame on me*, she told herself, for being glad that he was so handsome. But what had Mama said about good looks being *à son avantage*, to one's advantage? *Well*, she thought, watching Pierre stride toward them, so tan in his tennis whites, *he certainly has that advantage down pat*.

"Dominique!" he called, flashing his dazzling smile.

She responded in kind. Then, suddenly, she felt self-conscious. All the daydreams she'd ever had about Pierre always stopped at this point: They met and then looked into each other's eyes. Then came the tasteful movie fade-out. What would the next picture on the screen be? What would it be like to explore new territory, to have a *dating* relationship, without both sets of parents on sentry duty? Slightly excited, slightly nervous, she toned her smile down just a notch.

"That's Pierre! My oh my!" Sara whispered as he approached. "That frog is one major prince!"

"Sara! The French do not appreciate being called frogs," Dominique hissed.

"I didn't mean it as a national slur," Sara hissed back. "I was referring to the fairy tale—"

"How good to see you, Dominique!" Pierre embraced her, kissing both cheeks in the French fashion.

Dominique made the introductions and Pierre took Sara's hand in both of his. "Meeting you, Sara, is a great pleasure. I am hoping you shall have an enjoyable stay in Paris."

Pierre's onslaught of charm turned Sara's face from pink to red to scarlet. *Merci,* " she said. "And excuse my poor French."

"If you will excuse my speaking of such poor English." Pierre beamed gallantly.

As Pierre looked for a porter to help with the luggage, Sara turned to Dominique. "That stud can speak to me of such poor English all he wants." She fanned herself briskly with the *In-flight* magazine she had taken as a souvenir.

Dominique shook her head at Sara and repressed a laugh. As Pierre led the girls toward the passenger pickup area, he said, "We will go now to the home of my parents, where you shall occupy the third floor. *Oui?*"

Dominique smiled and nodded while Sara replied with a vigorous *"Oui!"*

The Du Lacs' house, Dominique had explained, was in the grand Auteuil district, where Paris's most affluent and influential families and international ambassadors lived. Pierre's home, like the others around it, was concealed from the street traffic by a high wall of limestone and set behind an enchanting garden. From the balcony there was a breathtaking panorama of Paris.

The colossal art deco building had been divided into five lavishly decorated apartments, all for the use of the Du Lacs and their constant stream of friends and clients.

"It'll be hard, but I'll try to cope," Sara said, sighing dreamily, when Dominique had explained the mansion's layout on the plane.

At the passenger pickup, Pierre shielded his eyes from the sun and looked into the stream of moving cars. *"Voilà!* The BMW *rouge*—red—on the right. My friend Julian drove my car here from our game of tennis. He has spent many days working as a taxi driver. He can take the highway as if it is the Grand Prix."

When the car pulled to a stop at the curb, Julian hopped out to help with the luggage. While Pierre had the very lean physique of a runner, Julian's was broader. But as Dominique's artist's eye could not help but notice, the difference was accounted for by well-developed muscles.

"Dominique, Sara," Pierre said, "my good

friend Julian Adler. Julian, this is Dominique Rappaport, whom I have spoken much about. And I have the pleasure of also introducing Sara Melnick."

"*Comment ça va?*" Dominique said in her very best French.

A furrow appeared in the craggy brow above Julian's deep-set eyes, and Dominique wondered if perhaps her pronunciation had been off. "*Ça va bien, merci.* Fine, thank you," he said, surprising Dominique with his perfect English accent. He quickly turned his attention to Sara. "*Et tu*, Sara? How are you?"

"*Bien, merci,*" she answered, mimicking his French accent almost perfectly.

"A violinist?" Julian said, gesturing toward her case.

"*Oui,*" Sara answered, practically batting her eyelashes.

"*Elle est très douée,*" Dominique cut in. "She's quite gifted."

Pierre bowed toward Sara. "I am a lover of music. I hope we have the pleasure of hearing you play."

Sara shrugged shyly, blushing again.

"Shall I put your violin in the trunk? It will be safe there," Julian offered.

Dominique looked at the top of Julian's hands as they reached for the instrument. They were powerful-looking, but the fingers were long, with a nimble grace. Like the hands of a musician.

He put Sara's case with the rest of the luggage, then opened the front passenger door for Sara.

"Are you a music lover, too, Julian?" Dominique asked, to see if she had guessed right, if those really were a musician's hands. And to get another look into those dark, intriguing eyes.

But Pierre answered for Julian. "Unfortunately, Julian does not have the chance to listen to much music." He opened the back door for Dominique, then slid in beside her.

"With so many fun places for music in Paris, I'd think it would be impossible to avoid," Dominique said with a smile. Maybe they'd all go to Le Caveau de la Vaque in the Latin Quarter one night. She had read about it in *Elle*. A trendy club where you could dance to everything from old ballads to rock and roll.

But before she could get the words out, Julian said harshly, "Music clubs are very possible to avoid when you're busting your butt at work."

His words felt like a slap to Dominique. What had she done to bring this on?

*"Busting your butt,"* Pierre repeated laughingly, obviously oblivious of the tension between Julian and Dominique. "Julian speaks a more perfect English than me, *non*? He has learned well from the American tourists in his taxi."

But Dominique was still bristling from Julian's cutting tone. Nobody talked to

Dominique Rappaport like that.

"Driving a taxi. How fascinating," she said with a yawn. Sara shot Dominique a look. Dominique had never been a snob like some of the rich kids at Allwyn Prep. But she sounded like one now. When somebody got on Dominique's bad side, her temper went on automatic pilot.

"I have driven a taxi and I have worked in construction. Anything that paid me well," Julian responded coolly as he started the car.

"Really?" Sara chimed with awkward intensity, wishing they could rewind the trip to the part right before Dominique asked if Julian was a music lover.

Before Dominique had a chance to toss off another smart remark, Pierre said, "My sister, Lizette, was sorry she could not meet your plane, Dominique. But she had a hair appointment this morning—to get ready for the opening tonight."

Dominique's frown softened into a smile. "I can't wait to see her!" she said eagerly. Lizette was the same age as Dominique. It had been as much of a shock to see the changes in her last winter as it had been to see those in Pierre. The skinny, giggling little girl she had known throughout childhood had turned into a long-legged coquette. None of the young ski instructors on the slopes that winter had missed a turn at being the object of Lizette's fleeting but intense infatuation.

"Lizette and I had such a great time together

as children," Dominique added, remembering the time they stole all the chocolate truffles at the Hanukkah party. She also remembered how worried she'd been about Lizette the last time they'd met. Flirting with ski instructors in and of itself wasn't bad, but there was something about the single-mindedness with which Lizette had sought their attentions that Dominique had found troubling.

Dominique's musings were interrupted by Sara's gasp. "Is that the Arc de Triomphe? We're really in Paris! The city of a million dreams . . ."

"And a million crazy drivers," Julian said as a Citroën cut in front of him as he approached the bridge crossing the Seine. Dominique looked up, scanning the silhouette of the majestic Grand Palais, taking in the *bateaux-mouches*—tourist boats—cruising on the river. And then she caught sight of Julian in the rearview mirror. His dark eyes held her gaze.

It took a moment for Dominique to realize that Pierre had spoken to her. And was waiting for an answer.

Flustered, Dominique said, "I'm sorry. What did you say?" She turned her full attention to Pierre. Charming, attentive Pierre.

Pierre smiled. "When someone is as lovely as you, I forgive anything. I was saying that Lizette should be back at the house by the time we arrive."

"I can't wait to see her! You'll love Lizette to

pieces, Sara," Dominique said. "She's outrageous!" She just hoped she wasn't quite as outrageous as she'd been in Gstaad.

"Dominique Rappaport," Lizette greeted her at the door. "More beautiful than ever, *non*?"

"*Non!*" Dominique returned Lizette's embrace. "I'm so happy to see you, Lizette," she said warmly, then added, "Enough small talk. Where have you stashed the truffles?"

Dominique introduced Sara to Lizette amid their laughs, and then Odette du Lac, Lizette and Pierre's mother, came down the grand staircase to greet them.

At the sight of Odette, Dominique was reminded of her own mother and felt a sudden rush of affection. Odette and Amanda had been friends since they were teenagers. Both were petite, elegant Frenchwomen. They dressed almost exclusively in Chanel, and even though they lived thousands of miles apart, when they got together once a year they'd discover they had identical haircuts. But while her mother's hair was auburn, Odette's was dark brown. Now Odette's hair was quite short, like the runway models', and there were some very light, flattering silver streaks.

*Time to turn on the personality,* Dominique thought as she sailed into Odette's waiting arms.

"Dominique!"

"Odette!" she exclaimed. "You look beautiful. And I love your hair. Mama is probably having hers cut this instant, and I just might follow suit."

"Do not dare to change that magnificent hair, *chérie*! Do not even say such a horrible thing!" Odette held Dominique at arm's length, then drew her affectionately to her side.

Dominique introduced her to Sara.

"*Bienvenue!* Welcome, Sara," Odette said warmly, kissing her on both cheeks. "I hope you will have a very pleasant stay in our home. And, *s'il vous plaît*, you must let me know if we can make anything more comfortable for you." She led the girls through the marble corridor.

"*Merci*, madame." Sara smiled. "It's so nice of you to have me."

Dominique watched Sara's eyes light in wonder as she looked through the velvet-draped passage at the gold-leaf ceiling of the sitting room. Louis XIV chairs were boldly covered in mauve leather. Purple tapestries hung from the walls.

"No one but Odette du Lac could get away with such radical chic," *Elegance* magazine had written of the showplace. And the same article had quoted Amanda Rappaport as saying: "Who but the genius Odette du Lac would have the daring to try?"

After a light lunch of sumptuous cold salmon, crusty bread, and assorted cheeses, Odette showed them through the rest of the house. Her own separate flat, two stories up, was done in a blend of rich tropical designs and sprawling Turkish couches with clawed feet.

When the tour had wound up in the third-floor apartment that was to be the, girls', Odette clapped her hands together and said, "Now, *mes chéries*, I must get back to the gallery to put the finishing touches on the show for the opening tonight. And, I'm sorry to say, Armand and I must leave for Brussels in two days' time. There is an important exhibition there that we cannot miss."

Dominique thought how familiar this all was, running off to this show and that, always tending to the business of art. As if she could read Dominique's thoughts, Odette continued, "But we will have Shabbat with you. And Mme. Renault, our dear housekeeper, will look after you. And Pierre and Lizette can always reach us if you need anything. You will not hesitate, *oui?*"

*Well,* thought Dominique, *it looks as if Pierre and I really will have a chance to get to know each other!*

Odette turned to Pierre. "I know you would like to remain with our guests," she said with a smile in Dominique's direction, "but it is three o'clock and we have much to take care of for the opening."

"I will meet you there very soon, Mama," Pierre answered.

Odette said her farewells and while Lizette took Sara on a tour of the gardens, Pierre put his arm around Dominique's waist and led her into the sitting room.

"Dominique," he said when they were alone, "you cannot know how much I have looked forward to seeing you again since the Alps this winter. Before that, if I ever thought of you, it was always as the nine-year-old brat, hiding my bar mitzvah presents with Lizette." He took her hand. "And then, *voilà*! A stunning young woman took the place of that child!"

Dominique liked the way he held her hand and looked into her eyes as if she were more important than anything or anyone else in the world.

"I've been looking forward to getting to know you better, too, Pierre," Dominique said, feeling her cheeks grow pink in the intense light of his gaze.

"Tonight, as you know, there will be an opening at the gallery. Michel Steinier is exhibiting with us."

"Steinier," Dominique said with genuine pleasure. She knew his work well. Although her own art was representational—she drew pictures that looked like what she was drawing—abstract art was her favorite. And though Steinier had become the new darling of the New York art scene, a status of which Dominique was usually skeptical, his paintings had an excitement that she couldn't deny. "I can't wait to see his latest work."

"Then we shall have a wonderful evening.

After the opening, we will go to Le Pirate with some friends." Then he paused and looked into her eyes. "I want to make this trip a memorable one for you. A time when we will find ourselves"—he paused, brushing her hair from her face—"very well acquainted."

*He certainly has that famous French charm,* Dominique thought. If any other guy had tried that line, she probably would have laughed in his face. *But he'd be sexy reading the yellow pages. And his touch on my cheek was* très interessant*!*

Lizette and Sara, obviously getting along famously, came into the sitting room. "You can see the Eiffel Tower from here," Sara exclaimed, rushing to the French doors.

"So you think you will be comfortable at the flat, Sara?" Pierre asked graciously.

"Trust me. I'll find a way." Sara grinned.

"Then I am going to leave you until tonight." He brushed Dominique's cheek with a light kiss that made her whole body tingle.

Even with jet lag nipping at their eyelids, Sara and Dominique were too excited to relax with all of Paris sparkling outside their window. When Lizette went to her dressmaker to have her dress shortened for the party, they decided to explore the colorful and crowded shops along the Champs-Elysées.

A dapper little elderly gentleman stopped Dominique in her tracks as they came out of the flower market laden with spring daisies. He tipped his beret with a grand flourish and clapped his hands. *"Magnifique, mademoiselle! Ooh-la-la, très magnifique!"*

After a dramatic sigh, he threw his hands up in the air and turned to Sara with a big smile. *"Très chic!"* he exclaimed, tipping his hat again before moving off.

"Good old Dominique Rappaport. Driving guys crazy in Paris too," Sara said.

"That was no guy." Dominique laughed. "That was a two-thousand-year-old elf!"

"All the same, I'll trade you five *chics* for one *magnifique* any day."

"You've got it. I've heard the 'm' word one too many times from my mother to appreciate it!"

"And I noticed Odette lavishing the English version on you, as well. All the same, Dominique, I'm not buying this 'beauty is a curse' routine."

"I know, I know. It's just that sometimes I want to be noticed for something rather than my face. You know, like my rapier wit and quick intelligence."

Sara gave her a skeptical look, then relented. "I'm sorry to joke about it, Niki. I know it's a thing with you. But you should really just enjoy your good looks. 'Gather ye rosebuds,' and all that. And speaking of gathering rosebuds . . ."

"Yes?" Dominique asked, her attention caught momentarily by a window display in a trendy boutique.

"Was Lizette the one you were so worried about? Your friend who was throwing herself at everything in ski pants on your vacation?"

Dominique groaned. She couldn't believe she'd told Sara! When she'd expressed her concern about Lizette to her friend, she'd had no idea that they would ever meet. "Please don't say anything to anyone. I'd hate for her to think I was gossiping about her. Even if it was at our lunch table a zillion miles away."

"Mum's the word. But I feel sorry for her, don't you?"

Dominique nodded. "I do. And I wonder why she does it—"

"Well, according to Mrs. Myerson in sex ed, Lizette's type of behavior is a combination of hormones and low self-esteem."

"According to Mrs. Myerson in sex ed, *every problem known to man* is a combination of hormones and low self-esteem."

"Poor Lizette." Sara sighed dramatically. "Low self-esteem. And maybe she just has too many hormones. That could happen, don't you—"

"Shut up, Sara." Dominique groaned. "Just quit while you're ahead."

"Know what I want to do now?" Sara said, as she sipped the last of her lemonade at a café in St. Germain.

"Visit the Louvre?" Dominique asked hopefully.

"No, that's what *you* want to do now. Come on." Sara checked her Paris map. "Today the Quartier Latin, tomorrow the Louvre!"

The girls headed toward the Luxembourg Gardens, strolling along the Seine, where they smiled at the endless stream of lovers kissing as they stopped at the rail and kissing as they walked along.

"Paris is for lovers!" Sara sighed, and Dominique remembered again the feel of Pierre's hand on her cheek and his feather-light kiss. She wondered, for the millionth time that afternoon, what Paris would hold for her and Pierre.

They walked through the Luxembourg Gardens, filled with French nannies pushing huge baby carriages. Everywhere were the little green chairs that made Dominique feel as if she were on a movie set of a Parisian park.

From there they toured the Panthéon, the eighteenth-century "Temple of Fame," and were thrilled by the fantastic murals of the life of St. Genevieve. Inside they read the plaques at the tombs of Voltaire and other famous Frenchmen. Dominique felt overwhelmed by the sense of history here.

"There's one of Emile Zola," Dominique said.

*"J'accuse!"* Sara pointed a finger at Dominique, making her jump.

Then Dominique laughed. "That's right! He defended Dreyfus against charges of being a traitor, right?"

"Right. And he accused the people of trumping up the charges, because they hated Dreyfus because he was Jewish."

Dominique nodded. It was amazing how history class suddenly seemed relevant!

They walked on the tomb of Jean Moulin, who led the Resistance during the Second World War. World War II wasn't that long ago, but in New York it seemed as distant as the French Revolution. Though Americans had died fighting in that war, U.S. cities had never been ravaged by bombs, by Nazi occupation. Here, Dominique was acutely aware of a sense of the past, of a world full of things that no history text had ever been able to teach her.

At four thirty in the afternoon, exhausted from the effort of trying to nap, Dominique rolled out of bed and tiptoed across the floor. As quietly as possible, in order not to disturb Sara in the bed near the door, she reached for her small bag on the top shelf of the closet.

"Damn," Dominique whispered as the case on the shelf below came crashing down. She turned to apologize for waking Sara, but her friend still slumbered peacefully.

Dominique had felt a stab of envy when they came back from their walk and Sara practiced her violin. As her bow played over the strings, it was clear that Sara—free and funny Sara—had found what made her heart sing.

Dominique grabbed her purple silk kimono from the closet, wrapped it around herself, and padded barefoot into the sitting room. The antique clock on the wall ticked loudly. An annoying reminder that time was moving on and that if she didn't hear a few choruses from her heart pretty soon, she'd wind up in Dial-a-Smile gallery mode for the rest of her life.

Dominique went out to the balcony and surveyed the wonder of Paris spread out before her. The mellow April sun warmed her shoulders and cast a soft light over the entire city. *If I don't find it here, I'll never find it,* she thought. And again, as she had when she and Sara were walking along the Seine, she found herself thinking of Pierre. *I wonder if he'll play a part in whatever it is. . . .*

Back inside, she picked up her sketch pad. Too restless to do anything more than play, she let her charcoal pencil follow its own will. Sara with her violin, a look of pure joy in her face. Lizette as a laughing child. Pierre, so dashing and sophisticated.

Then, suddenly, Julian Adler found his way onto the page of her book. Julian, with that unruly head of thick dark hair. And those deeply set eyes. She stared at the page. What had possessed her to draw him? Yes, he had a riveting pair of eyes in a very interesting face, but he was so volatile. There was almost something dangerous about him.

Her drawing was interrupted by a knock on the half-opened door. Flustered by the intrusion, as she turned, she dropped her sketch pad on the Oriental carpet.

Julian! What timing. It would be *très* embarrassing if he caught her sketching *him*.

"I came to pick up some journals I left here yesterday," he said matter-of-factly.

He knelt to retrieve her pad. Acting on instinct, Dominique bent for it, too, hoping to close the book before he got a look inside. But her movement slowed as she looked at his hands. She was surprised by an odd desire to touch those tanned, tapered fingers.

Then she remembered the pad and hastily pulled it away from him.

"*Pardon,* mademoiselle!" His voice was heavy with sarcasm. "Wouldn't want to contaminate your property with my working-class hands."

What was it with this guy? As Sara would say, he had a chip on his shoulder the size of Montana. Sitting up straight after his reproof, Dominique realized that the top of her kimono had fallen open a bit when she bent. She quickly pulled it closed, then tightened her sash.

This activity brought an amused look from Julian—as if to say she had nothing to worry about, that the sight of her, even in a skimpy kimono, was nothing special.

As he poked through the bookshelf, it was Dominique's turn to feel amused. Finally she'd met a guy who wasn't drooling all over her, and he turned out to be Monsieur Gauche.

"They're not here. I need to look on the

73

shelf behind you. Could you get up a moment?"

No "Please." No *"Excusez-moi." You'd think he'd have picked up a pointer or two on common courtesy from Pierre.*

Well, whatever his problem was, she wasn't about to make it hers. Dominique rose from her chair, all sweetness and light. "Tell me the names of your publications, and I'll be happy to help you find them. I drive myself crazy when I can't remember where I've left something." She put her sketch pad down on an end table. He was standing close to her as he rifled through the bookshelf, and she could feel the warmth of his breath on her neck. A shiver went across her shoulders. *What's this about?* Did the fact that he didn't fawn all over her make him interesting somehow? No. She was too smart to fall for that.

"You needn't bother." He continued to pore through the books.

"Well, then, if you'll excuse me . . ." Dominique said amiably. Then, to Dominique's surprise, his eyes flickered for a moment as they lit upon his find. Dominique turned to see what "publications" he'd been talking about. *The New England Journal of Medicine?* Maybe he wanted to read up on evolution! Well, he could do it without the benefit of her company.

"Have a nice day, Julian," Dominique said, sashaying out the door. Halfway down the hall she realized she'd left her sketch pad.

She turned around and Julian's arm stuck

out into the hall, waving the black book at her. "Wouldn't want you to drive yourself crazy being so forgetful," he said with a grin.

Red-faced, she took the sketch pad from his hands and padded down the hall, hoping—*praying!*—he hadn't looked inside.

# CHAPTER FIVE

"Dominique, wake up," Sara said insistently. "We've got to get moving. We have zee big gallery party, *chérie.*"

"What time is it?" Dominique murmured.

"It's seven o'clock, Paris time."

"Fifteen more minutes." Dominique opened one eye and closed it quickly. Even the soft dusky glow streaming through the window felt harsh on her sleepy eyes.

Sara grabbed a lace doily from under one of the rose-filled vases and put it on her head. "I am now going to say zee prayer for zee jet lag.

*"Baruch ahtaw—"* she began to chant.

"Cut it out, Sara. You want us to get struck by lightning?" Dominique pulled the rose satin sheet over her head.

"If God had wanted you to stay asleep, he wouldn't have created me. Come on, get up. Lizette called from her friend's place to say that Julian is picking us up at seven forty-five and she'll meet us at the gallery."

Dominique stretched lazily. "Okay, okay."

Sara pulled two outfits from the closet. "What do you think? The blue lace or the green?"

"The blue lace. It's supposed to be a really dressy affair," Dominique answered.

Sara held the cobalt-blue stretch-lace dress against her to check the effect in the mirror. "I'm so excited. I went through the paper while you were out and the Du Lacs' party is even mentioned in the society column. All these *celebrities* are going. And the Earl of something, and Prince somebody or other."

Dominique yawned. "The Earl of *Something*, you say? He's pretty hot. But not in the same class as Prince Somebody or Other!"

"Easy for you to joke about it. Your parents are always throwing bashes like this. But what if I do something dumb? What if I call somebody 'Your Honor' who's supposed to be 'Your Majesty'?"

"I'll pray for you as they haul you off to the Bastille."

"As long as they mention my name in the society columns." Sara began fussing with her hair. "Up or down, Niki?"

"Up, definitely up."

"Will you help me put it into a twist?" Sara asked.

"Sure. Soon as I'm done with my shower." Dominique pulled a simple but elegant black dress from the closet and put it on the bed.

"That's what you're going to wear?" Sara asked.

Dominique looked worried. "Is it too plain?"

"It's too *exquisite,* if you want my opinion. If I were you, I'd be sick of having every guy in the room groveling at my feet," Sara said in a weary tone. "I'd don a potato sack and pull a bag over my head to give the rest of us a chance."

"*Salut,* Mme. Renault," Julian said as the housekeeper opened the door.

"*Ah, bien,* Julian," she answered. "Pierre called to say you would be here. *Un moment.*"

Julian looked around the lavish foyer while he waited. Again he was hit by a culture shock that left him dazed each time he entered the Du Lac mansion.

At the sports ground in the Bois de Vincennes where he and Pierre had met, all that counted was that they were well matched for a good competitive game of tennis. But their lives were so different off the courts, they might as well have been from different planets.

He wondered if he had made the right choice to come here tonight. But when Pierre had called him, he was so tired of his medical books and felt so trapped in his sixth-floor *chambre de bonne*—the former maid's quarters he rented, which could have fit easily in one of the Du Lacs' smaller closets—he had accepted the invitation.

But he never felt easy in the midst of their

elite clique of jet-set friends. The men used charm as a weapon to make their conquests. And the women! Debutantes, starlets, and models, all pretty to be sure, but their heads seemed full of the cotton candy sold in the amusement park of the Jardin d'Acclimatation.

Julian wore his one good suit so rarely that on a night like this, he felt as if he were in costume. And if he ever made an awkward movement in this foyer, he'd be sure to knock over a million-dollar Ming vase. *I could spend the rest of my life digging ditches and still not be able to pay for that kind of blunder!* he thought wryly.

Usually he avoided Pierre and Lizette's invitations in favor of trying to hustle up some extra money to supplement first his medical scholarship, then his meager intern's wages. Whatever else he could salvage went to his mother in the country. Poor Mama! As a young widow with a son to raise, she had never had an easy time of it.

The way her eyes lit up when she unwrapped the occasional something extra—like the Hanukkah present of her favorite lilac scent from the Saphora parfumerie—was worth anything. Of course, the presents would never repay her for the worries he'd caused her when he was a troubled adolescent, sneaking out of school to hang out on the streets of Paris with his pack of young upstarts.

What fools they were—thinking their petty thievery at the stalls off the Champs-Elysées made them big shots. All their swaggering was a poor cover for the emptiness they had felt inside.

"*Bonsoir*, Julian," Sara said, interrupting his musings.

"*Bonsoir*, Sara," he said, taking in the diminutive girl in her flashy blue dress. She was obviously very excited about her first night out on the town in Paris. "You look very beautiful tonight."

"Oh! Thank you! *Merci!*" she sputtered with an ingenuousness that Julian found charming.

Dominique came through the velvet curtains and nodded to him. "Thanks for coming to take us for the party."

"*De rien*, you're welcome," he answered stiffly. Quickly, he turned for the door. What was it about this redhead that affected him so? She was quite an eyeful in that stunning black dress; she obviously knew that her natural good looks didn't need any embellishment. But physical beauty was not an asset he valued much. He knew far too well how deceptive looks could be. This young American woman had something else, a *joie de vivre*—a joy of life—that was risky for him to spend any time dwelling on.

*Forget it, Julian*, he warned himself. He knew that, more than his fatigue and his cramped room, it was Dominique's presence at the party that had impelled him to forgo his books tonight. "She belongs to Pierre's glittery world." And *joie de vivre* or no, he had no time for useless detours into fantasy.

"There's no parking anywhere near the gallery," Julian explained as they drove along the quay bordering the Seine. "I'll drop you there and find a place for the car in an unrestricted area."

"*C'est loin?*" Sara asked, obviously delighted at the chance to use one of the French guidebook phrases she'd driven Dominique crazy with on the plane.

"Well, it's a bit of a walk, but it's not bad," Julian answered.

"Don't drop us off!" Dominique insisted. "I don't want to see Paris by car. I want to feel it under my feet."

"Whatever," Julian replied indifferently.

Dominique was too exhilarated by the moonlit dancing on the Seine and the carefree music of the party boats to let Julian's wooden manner affect her. *A new Dominique is debuting in Paris tonight,* she told herself as she stepped out of the car. One who would be ruled only by what was inside her. Mama and her wagging manicured finger and all the pressure of school in the fall were an ocean away, and she was going to enjoy herself. *After all,* she thought, *you're only eighteen in Paris once!*

"That monument wasn't here the last time I was," Dominique said, gesturing up at the huge obelisk looming before them as they turned onto the rue des Tournelles.

"The Colonne de Juillet, the July Column,"

Julian said. "It was only built a few years ago. Part of the Revolution bicentennial."

"Revolution," Sara said. "Oh, right. I keep forgetting you guys had one, too. What's that?" She pointed to the glass structure on the south side of the square.

"The new opera house," Julian said.

*This guy has about as much charm as the Missing Link,* Dominique thought in spite of her resolution to enjoy herself. *Or one of the stony gargoyle beasts on the Notre Dame bell tower!* Still, something drew her to him. Was it those dark eyes? she asked herself, wondering what went on behind them. They had an amused glint at one moment, then clouded over with a remote, almost angry look in the next. Whatever it was, she had to admit that tonight, in his evening attire, he almost passed for something a bit higher on the evolutionary ladder.

"Those buildings look like they're about a zillion years old!" Sara exclaimed as they crossed to the place des Vosges.

"They seem to have a golden glow," Dominique said, intrigued by the quiet dignity of the structures surrounding them. "This is the old section of Paris, isn't it, Julian?"

Julian nodded stiffly as the three of them walked on among the clusters of people out for a stroll through the Marais on the warm spring night.

Dominique groaned. "Come on, Julian. You can do better than that, can't you?"

He sighed. "When Paris was being rebuilt in the last century, they pretty much ignored this section. So it stayed just as it's been since the 1700s," he said quickly, eager to get the job of tour guide to rich Americans over with.

"That was a *little* better, Julian," Dominique said playfully.

"It pleases me no end that you think so," Julian replied, shooting Dominique a look of—what? she wondered. Irritation?

"You know what your trouble is, Julian?" she said, folding her arms.

Julian looked to the sky, avoiding her gaze. "No," he said. "But I have a feeling you're going to tell me what my trouble is."

"You need to loosen up! You wouldn't want us to go home and tell everyone that the rumors about the French being impolite are true?"

"A frightening prospect," Julian muttered sarcastically.

"Take a deep breath," she said, while Sara looked on with the "uh-oh" look she had when Dominique got in a frisky mood. "That's Parisian air filling up your lungs."

"Full of exhaust fumes from the endless traffic," Julian said in a testy voice.

"Full of fragrance and wonder from the masses of outdoor flower stalls!" Dominique said doggedly, thinking she had caught him repressing a smile. *Aha! Progress.*

As they turned onto rue Elzevir, Dominique's artistic eye was suddenly drawn to a small stone building set far back from the street. It looked oddly out of place after the elegant pink-toned residences in the place des Vosges.

"Is that a famous building?" Dominique peered through the porte cochere, the passageway, through which she could see a well-tended courtyard. The warm light of a candle radiated through a stained-glass window, making a pretty pattern on the gravel path.

Julian seemed startled by Dominique's question. When he spoke Dominique was surprised by a different, almost reverential tone in his voice. "You won't find it in a guidebook or on a tour, if that's what you mean," he answered. "But it has a critical place in the unwritten history of France."

A light went on at the side of the building, spreading over a patch of well-kept garden. There was a haunting stillness to the place that pulled at Dominique. "It looks enchanted," she said. "Can we go in?"

"If you'd like," he said quietly.

Dominique noticed a strange softness in his eyes. Clearly this place held some wonder for him, too.

"What is this building, anyway?" Sara asked, smoothing her dress. She was obviously anxious to get to the opening.

"An old church," Julian answered.

"We've seen dozens of churches today, Niki!"

"I want to see this one," Dominique said intently.

They walked along the winding path toward a pair of large stone benches. Dominique looked up at the building, studying its crumbling facade. She was sorry to see that some of the lovely stained-glass windows on the second floor had been replaced by ordinary panes.

"We'll be here forever, won't we?" Sara groaned. "You've got that peculiar look in your eye that comes when you want to be alone with your sketch pad. On one of your secret adventures."

"Ah, yes!" Julian smiled. "She is very secretive with her sketch pad."

Dominique was glad it was dark, so he couldn't see her flush at the reminder of their earlier encounter over that sketch pad.

By the lamplight she could make out a vegetable garden at the end of the path. As Julian knelt to yank at some weeds near a small bed of fragile green sprouts, Dominique noticed that his manner was proprietary.

"Tomato plants?" she asked.

Julian nodded.

"Someone lives here?" asked Sara.

Julian stood with the weeds in his hand and dropped them in a rusty old bucket at the side of the stairs. "No. But someone comes here regularly. Come on!" he called to the girls. "I'll introduce you to Rabbi Levi."

Before either Sara or Dominique could reply, Julian had hopped up the steps and rapped on the windowpane.

After a moment the door opened and a man in his sixties with bifocals perched on the end of his nose smiled out at them. He came outside and embraced Julian with obvious affection. "Ah! Julian."

The two exchanged some words in French; then Julian introduced the older man as Rabbi Levi.

The rabbi adjusted his glasses and squinted at Dominique's face. "We have met before, mademoiselle?"

"No, Rabbi, we haven't," she replied.

"You are quite sure?" he asked, looking very puzzled.

Dominique shook her head. "I'm certain that we haven't."

"Forgive me studying you so. But the red hair . . . and those green eyes . . ." Rabbi Levi ran his hand through his thinning gray hair. "Someone I knew had a face so much like yours. A wonderful face. But I cannot remember who it is that you remind me of. When you pass a certain age, some things you lose." He tapped his temple. "And sometimes things mix together in here."

As he led them through the small room—an ancient kitchen, bare except for a rusty sink and small enamel table—Rabbi Levi gestured toward a thermos. "I have brought some *potage*—a nice light soup—tonight. Will you children share it? Forgive my pride, but I make a good soup. Eh, Julian?"

"A very good soup." Julian smiled. "But we cannot stay long, Rabbi."

The easy relationship between Julian and the rabbi bewildered Dominique. Julian didn't seem the type to be hanging around synagogues, buddy-buddy with rabbis.

But this wasn't a synagogue. It was a church. What was a rabbi doing here, anyway?

Julian interrupted her musings. "Would you like me to show you girls around?" he asked.

"*Oui!* You must show them around," said Rabbi Levi. "You have seen our little garden? A reminder of days gone by," he said as they walked through the dingy room. He turned back to the girls. "You will kindly forgive the mess. We are trying to restore the place. But it goes more slowly than we would wish."

"Please!" Sara said as they trailed behind Rabbi Levi through the arched hallway. The old wooden floors creaked beneath them. "My room at home is in worse shape than this!"

Rabbi Levi pressed light switches as they entered a large room, half of which had been freshly painted. Some of the overhead bulbs flickered in their sockets. "Like many things in this old building, the wiring needs attention."

"I'll take a day later in the week to give you some help," Julian said.

"Not you, my dear young man," Rabbi Levi insisted. "You have such a full schedule. I appreciate all the help you've given. But your work is so very important."

Dominique didn't see why construction work was so important that Julian couldn't take a day off to help the rabbi. But her mind was spinning with many things she didn't understand, the most confusing of which was this different Julian. "Humble" and "gracious" were not two adjectives she would have picked to describe him before they walked through these doors; but inside, he was both.

The room was empty but for a paint bucket, a ladder, and a large scroll that hung on one wall. It was yellowing at the edges, like parchment.

"Now that really looks old," Sara said. "Looks like the Declaration of Independence or something."

"Not quite that old," Rabbi Levi said. "But it is important. Read the names."

Sara moved closer. "'Aaron . . . Abramovitz . . . Adler . . .'" she read. "'Adler, Jean'! Any relation, Julian?"

A soft, solemn *oui* escaped Julian's lips.

"What does it say?" Sara asked.

Dominique scanned the heading. "Heroes of Solidarité. That was the Resistance movement in World War Two, wasn't it?"

Rabbi Levi and Julian nodded. "How are you related?" she asked Julian.

"I'm his grandson," Julian said, a tone of pride in his voice. Then he looked toward Rabbi Levi and added, "At least, I am *trying* to be his grandson."

The rabbi patted Julian on the back. "He would be proud, Julian." Rabbi Levi looked around the room. "But this room has many memories for us, *non?*"

"*Oui*, Rabbi." Julian smiled.

"Are you going to explain or am I going to die of curiosity?" Sara folded her arms abruptly, in mock exasperation.

"This is where Rabbi Levi prepared me for my bar mitzvah."

"You prepared for a bar mitzvah in a *church?*" Dominique looked from the rabbi to Julian. "I'm confused. Did I miss something?"

Rabbi Levi laughed. "Tell them, Julian, so they are not confused."

Julian turned to Dominique and Sara. "When I was twelve, I was a budding delinquent. Hanging around with a gang of Paris street kids. Skipping out of school. Fighting with other gangs all the time. I was not very sociable."

*You? Not sociable?* Dominique felt like saying. But she settled on exchanging amused looks with Sara.

Julian turned to the rabbi. "They have a hard time understanding that I was not always a perfect gentleman, Rabbi."

After getting a big hoot from the rabbi and a cough from Dominique, Julian continued. "My father died when I was four, and my mother had to work much of the time. When I was small, Grandpère Jean took care of me."

"Jean Adler." The rabbi sighed. "A wonderful man. I miss him every day."

"*Moi aussi,*" Julian said, his voice thick with emotion. "I miss him, as well. He was like the whole world to me."

Dominique was taken by the vulnerable and boyish look on Julian's face as he talked about his grandfather.

"When he died I was very sad and very angry. So I took my anger to the streets. And the truth is, a few times I got myself into a little trouble."

Rabbi Levi turned to heaven and groaned. "A *little* trouble? A *few* times? When was this boy *not* in trouble?"

"So," Julian said sheepishly, "Rabbi Levi took pity on my wild little bunch—"

"'Took pity,' he says!" Rabbi Levi exploded. "I didn't want to lose any more beautiful windows to their *meshugge* games. This place has a precious history. The catacombs—the underground maze of tunnels built in Roman times—are linked to a stairway under this basement. The passages are closed off now, but once they led to the headquarters of the Resistance."

"It sounds like something out of a movie!" Sara said.

"A movie we were glad to see finally end." Rabbi Levi took off his bifocals and rubbed his weary-looking eyes. Then he smiled. "Years later, when I was a young rabbi, the good priest here was kind enough to provide me with a place for my small congregation to *daven*—to pray—together and thank God for better times."

"And it was here that Rabbi Levi took our gangs when the police were threatening to lock us up," Julian said, his eyes alive with respect and gratitude. "He begged enough rackets and balls to teach us soccer and tennis. The Jewish boys, he prepared for bar mitzvah. And for the Catholic boys, he oversaw their catechism."

"Catechism? From a rabbi?" Sara said, dumbfounded.

"During the war, an abbey in the south hid me and many other Jewish children from the Nazis. It is because of that abbey and Jean Adler, who rescued me and took me there, that I am alive," Rabbi Levi said solemnly. "Two years I stayed, until being placed in a home by a wonderful woman who found families for Jewish orphans. But who could forget how those priests risked their lives to hide us? Or the many things I learned about their faith. Who knew such experiences would prepare me to help their own boys? They were living saints whose compassion made miracles."

"Rabbi Levi worked miracles, too," Julian said.

Rabbi Levi waved his hand, as if the praise were excessive. "I was the one who was lucky. I had the lesson of seeing my investments pay off." Rabbi Levi nudged Julian's arm. "From a little hoodlum came a farmer."

"My grandfather worked on a farm when he was young," Julian said. "He would have laughed at my dozen beans. My three green tomatoes."

Rabbi Levi spoke again. "It was a good occupation for me. To try to make them into honorable young men, into *menshen*. Such a small part of what I owed, will always owe, to Jean Adler."

"How did Jean Adler rescue you, Rabbi Levi?" Dominique pressed.

"During the Nazi occupation, they packed the Jews of Paris into buses. We didn't know it at the time, but the bus trip was the first leg of a journey to the death camps. They put the parents in the buses in the morning. And they took the children in the evening. I can still remember my mother's face when I saw it for the last time. Trying not to cry as they pushed her up the steps. They had shot a little boy who couldn't stop crying when they pulled him from his mother's arms that morning." Rabbi Levi's voice was quivering.

"I can't imagine anything so awful," Dominique said, her voice choked. Her heart pounded with an ache she'd never known before.

"Jean Adler—the Guardian of the Night, he was called in the Resistance—had gotten word of the Nazi plans. Not soon enough to save the parents, for which he always blamed himself, though he was not at fault. While they filled the bus with crying children—myself among them—Jean managed to puncture the petrol tank. The leak was slow enough so that the driver didn't notice he was losing fuel until it was too late.

"As the bus finally stopped along a dark country road, Jean and a band of Maquis—Resistance fighters from the mountains—ambushed the driver and the Nazi escort vehicles. From there they took us to the abbey."

Suddenly the clock chimed out the half hour, startling them all. "Eight thirty," Rabbi Levi announced. "I have talked too much, *oui?*"

"Not at all," Dominique protested earnestly. "I wish we could hear more. My family doesn't like to talk about those times."

It was amazing to Dominique that she could be so many miles from home, in a foreign setting with two complete strangers, and feel so swathed in her own culture. To feel a profound connection to her Jewish heritage she'd never experienced before. She looked at Sara, and sensed from the solemn look in her friend's face that she was thinking the same thing.

"There are those who believe we should put such things behind us. Here in Paris, it is hard to forget."

"It's true," Sara said quietly. "We've seen memorials all over the city."

The rabbi wiped his bifocals with a tissue.

"Many sites of bombs—and the hallowed ground where ordinary people became champions, risking their lives to help their neighbors. In fact, tonight I am on my way to a meeting where we are planning memorial ceremonies to honor Resistance heroes all over France." He smiled at the girls and took each of them by the hand. "Your visit has made me so happy."

Dominique found it hard to say good-bye to Rabbi Levi. There was something awe-inspiring about this man, who had lived through such horrible things yet still had such a loving presence. The compassion she saw in his face, heard in his voice, made her want to know more about him. And she had a sense that his wisdom might go a long way in helping her sort through the dilemma of her future.

As they stood at the door, Dominique was aware that Julian's eyes were on her, studying her, boring into her soul. He was so enigmatic and complex. Like no guy she had ever met before—or, she knew, would ever meet again. She felt her face grow warm and quickly turned away.

# CHAPTER SIX

Photographers and fans swarmed in droves in front of the Du Lac gallery. Slews of familiar faces—from government dignitaries to celebrities from all spheres of the media—made their way toward the entrance. Some posed for the cameras or signed autographs, and some tried to maneuver their way inside before the flash of the cameras could catch them.

Sara stared incredulously at the happy pandemonium. "With all the limos and flashing lights, and those kids screaming their heads off, it's like the Academy Awards!"

"The *paparazzi*!" Dominique explained as they tried to figure out where to cross the street without getting swallowed up by the crush. "They follow the society set in Europe as fiercely as they do the Hollywood stars. And the fans always seem to have a radar that lets them know where the celebs are going to be."

"Wait a second." Sara grabbed Dominique's arm. "I want to know what they're screaming about." She strained to hear what the crowds of girls jumping up and down in front of a stretch limo at the sidewalk were screaming. Then she broke out into a huge grin. "They're yelling 'Garr.' I don't believe this! I have died and gone to heaven! Garr Haywood's inside that car! The lead singer of Dr. Hyde."

Dominique craned her neck toward the scene. "You're right!"

"And look over at the gallery window, Nik. See that woman in the red velvet dress who's signing autographs? That's Alisha Saunders. She's on six magazine covers this month!"

As Dominique looked around, she felt caught up in the exhilaration. Some of the people she recognized from her parents' parties across the "pond," as the jet set called the Atlantic. But some were people whose photographs she had seen in magazines. And none of her parents' parties had anywhere near the pizzazz that this one had. It was teeming with all the gleeful energy of New Year's Eve.

"This is going to be a major blowout!" Dominique said eagerly.

"I feel like I'm walking onto the set of a movie starring everybody who's anybody." Sara zeroed in on Garr Haywood again. "I've got to see how he looks up close." She turned to Dominique. "How do I look?" Sara asked.

"Ravishing is too mild a word," Dominique answered with a grin. "You look like a star, Sara."

"Then let's party on, girl!" Sara laughed, charging toward the door.

Dominique tried to follow her, but a barrage of flashing lights exploded in her face. Her vision was temporarily blurred by the glare. She tried to move forward, but the photographers blocked her path. Then she realized what was going on. They were taking pictures of her.

Pretending not to understand French, she ignored their questions. "What's the name of your modeling agency?" "Weren't you on the cover of *Cosmopolitan* in January?"

But when one of them became more aggressive and grabbed her arm, Julian—who had been beside them the whole time—stepped in front of her and forced the man back. Dominique breathed a sigh of relief. Julian's authoritative manner and obvious athletic ability were just what she needed to get past this swarm. "Are you her agent? Is she a model or an actress?" the photographer asked.

Julian turned to Dominique. His generous mouth turned up in a roguish grin.

"This, my friend, is the reigning Miss America," he announced, bowing in her direction.

"Miss America!" An electric buzz went through the crowd.

"Not funny, Julian!" Dominique scowled. It had been bad enough to have them all gawking at her before he opened his mouth. Now they doubled their efforts to get to her. Whatever magic spell Rabbi Levi had used to turn Julian into a sensitive, engaging human being had obviously expired.

Fully enjoying his own joke, but now trying to evade the intensified onslaught, Julian grabbed her arm. *"Pardon. Pardon,"* he repeated as he propelled them toward the door. "Pierre would never forgive me if I delivered his American beauty with a hair out of place."

The moment they reached the entrance Dominique yanked her arm from his grip. "In the States we have a saying: 'Just say no to drugs.' In your case, I would add, 'Just say no to comedy.' It's not your strong suit, Julian."

Turning toward the gallery Dominique felt a strong sense of déjà vu, as if she were at a Rappaport opening. The brightly lit room was packed with wall-to-wall art devotees and "wannabes"—the hangers-on of the rich and famous. All seemed to be sipping white wine. The crowd was lively with the amiable chatter, punctuated by outbursts of excessive laughter, that buzzed through her parents' openings.

She wondered if anybody had even viewed the new Steinier works yet. Ever since that first time, when she had been so transported by May Lee's wedding picture, she'd always looked forward to having her own private show when the new works had just come out of their crates. To be alone in the quiet room with all the paintings lined up around her was a divine privilege. To get the chance to tune in to the artist's impulse, to form her own impressions before the work could be reduced to party chitchat: That was the chief advantage of her parents' business.

Suddenly Sara was at her side, her brown eyes brimming with excitement. "Garr's here with Molly Binkus." Molly Binkus, a gorgeous blonde, did "Fashion Flops" for Channel 3. Sara gushed on: "He's not very tall in person. He'd look fine with me, but Molly is about five inches taller than he is, and"—Sara stopped for a quick breath, then raced on with her monologue—"she's supposed to be the emcee of the—"

"There you are!" Pierre said, making a bee-line toward Dominique from across the floor. "I have been looking for you." He nodded to Sara graciously and reached for Dominique's hand. "And, Julian, *mon ami,*" he said, clapping his friend on the shoulder, "accept my thanks for bringing the girls with you tonight."

"A privilege, Pierre," Julian replied cavalierly, "to escort such distinguished visitors."

Dominique regarded him with narrowed eyes. He had an uncanny knack for testing her temper.

"Mama and Papa are waiting to see you," Pierre said to Dominique and Sara.

Julian bowed deeply and turned to go look at the art.

"Such a gentleman!" Sara sighed.

*Not the word I would have chosen!* Dominique said to herself as Pierre steered them toward his waiting parents.

"Darling, it makes me so happy to see you again," Odette exclaimed. "I only wish your mama and papa could be here as well."

Dominique returned Odette's embrace. Odette's graceful gestures, her commanding presence, were so like Amanda Rappaport that Dominique was once again struck by a sudden rush of affection for her own mother. The two women even wore similar but unique Jean La-Feuille custom-designed perfume.

Odette turned to summon her husband. "Armand, come! It is our Dominique and her friend Sara."

Armand du Lac, a tall, refined gentleman—looking quite like a bookish professor, but with a far more generous clothing budget—excused himself from a little clique of elderly women dressed in the hats and veils of another era. When he reached Dominique, he pressed his lips to her forehead. "How good it is to see you, darling! And this must be Sara. Are you having a nice time?"

Dominique and Sara smiled. "We're having a wonderful time. *Merci*," said Sara.

Pierre took hold of Dominique's hand. "I will try to make sure she does not have a moment to complain about."

Odette looped her arm through her husband's and hung on him a moment, enjoying the sight of Pierre holding Dominique's hand. "Charming, *non*, Armand?"

As Armand nodded enthusiastic agreement, Dominique felt the color rise in her cheeks.

Odette put her arm around Dominique and

looked from her to Sara. "Have you children been able to get a bit of rest since your flight?"

They nodded.

"I am feeling such *tristesse*—such unhappiness—that we must be off for Belgium on Monday! I so much wish we had time to show you Paris in the proper fashion. But I would rather have a short time with you than no time at all." She touched her hand to Dominique's affectionately. "I am crazy for this child, Sara," Odette said. "Her mama, she is my best friend in the world. We make sure not too much time goes between our visits. It has been such a treat to watch our children grow up together. Ah, how I wish you could have seen Dominique and Lizette together when they were small. Such a pair of imps. And inseparable. We called them Daisy and Maisy."

Dominique laughed, remembering. "That's right. When we were out in the country we made up our own rodeo near the stables. 'On the Trail with Daisy and Maisy,' we called it!"

"And Pierre thought he was much too—what is the word?—*mature* to pay attention to you." Odette laughed.

Dominique smiled, remembering all the times when their families were together—how frustrated she would be that Pierre hardly seemed to notice her, no matter how she tried. Once, when she and Lizette were about eight, they had covered their faces with lipstick and eye shadow.

She couldn't wait to show Pierre, positive that he would ask her to be his wife on the spot. The outlandish makeup did get a big reaction from twelve-year-old Pierre, though not the one she had hoped for. She had wanted to hide in her room for the rest of the trip after he burst out laughing at the sight. Asking if *le cirque*—the circus—was in town!

"He certainly seems to be paying attention now, *oui*?" Armand said with a wink.

"Please!" Pierre said. "You will embarrass this poor girl and she will hate me forever."

"Hate you, Pierre? Impossible!" Dominique responded with a smile.

Dominique heard Sara cough slightly.

*Okay,* Dominique thought, *so I'm lapsing into Dial-a-Smile mode again and Sara is onto me.* Still, it did seem impossible to imagine that this well-bred charmer would ever do anything to incur any negative emotion at all. And—who knew?—he might inspire some very *positive* emotions.

Armand turned to his wife. "Odette, I must steal you away for a moment. It is important that you greet the new curator and assistant curator of the Kyoto Museum."

Odette looked toward the door to see the dignified, newly arrived guests survey the crowd, then bow toward her husband. She turned and took Dominique's face in her hands. "I will be back in a few moments, *ma chérie,*" she said. "I want so much to hear what you have to say about the new Steinier work. You always have such intelligent judgment!"

"Would you do me the favor, Pierre, of checking on the wine delivery?" Armand asked as he guided his wife in the direction of the guests. "I phoned for three more cases to be here an hour ago. This turnout is much larger than I expected, and we do not want anyone to leave thirsty."

"*Oui*, Papa," Pierre said. Then he turned to look into Dominique's eyes. "*Je reviens,*" he said softly as he walked away.

"I think I'm getting the hang of French," Sara said proudly. "He just said the name of your perfume, right?"

Dominique shook her head and laughed. "Actually, he just said that he'd return."

Sara sighed romantically. "Still has that major charm thing happening, doesn't he?"

Dominique folded her arms and nodded, watching Pierre as he headed for the office. He really did have such an air of assurance, and he always knew exactly what to say.

"Seems to have a big case of zee hots for you, Nik. Are you catching any sparks?"

"I'm certainly open to the possibility," Dominique said. "And I am attracted to him. But I have to say I'm a little overwhelmed. I still can't get used to the fact that my child-hood crush is interested in me."

"And his parents are going all out with that old-fashioned *shiddach*—matchmaking—spirit!"

"Dominique! Sara!" Lizette called, rushing toward them from the other side of the room.

"Oh my God!" Sara gasped as Lizette, wearing a revealing gauzy black dress, made her way through the crowd. "That's a slip she's got on! I can't believe she'd wear something like that with her parents in the same room! I have headbands made of more material!"

"Dominique! Sara! How beautiful you both look," Lizette enthused when she had reached them.

"You too," Dominique said, trying to look as if she weren't startled by Lizette's ultra-provocative look.

"Oh, this little nothing?" Lizette snapped her fingers.

"It certainly is . . ." Sara said and was about to leave it at that. But, feeling Dominique's glare, she quickly added, ". . . so interesting."

A tall, extremely thin young man in a white jacket and a red bow tie came by, and Lizette bent toward him and grabbed at his lapel. As Lizette kissed the fellow playfully, Sara murmured, "Sure hope she recovers from this bashful stage."

"Quiet, Sara," Dominique hissed. Seeing Lizette in action made Dominique feel sorry for her. She wondered if she was the only one who thought there was something a bit pathetic about Lizette's obvious attention-grabbing demeanor.

"Isn't that Bradford Banes, over there? The

one standing in front of the big watercolor? It looks like he's trying to grow a beard."

"Yes, it is," Lizette said, turning back to them. "The beard is for his new *King Lear* movie. He was knighted by the queen last year. Now he is called Sir Bradford. Would you like to meet him?"

"Yes!" Sara cried, agog at the prospect. "But what do I say? Am I supposed to curtsy? I mean just to be on the safe side, I should probably curtsy at everyone, right?"

"Sara, you are so funny! You do not have to curtsy."

"Why did you have to tell her that, Lizette? This girl has been dying to curtsy since we left New York."

"The truth is that many of these people don't have real titles," Lizette said with a devilish grin. "Some do have real titles. But, alas, they have nothing else." She turned toward the rear of the gallery. "Near the bar. See the fellow with the silly bow tie?"

The girls glanced at the man Lizette described.

"The Marquis de Chardon," Lizette murmured.

"A marquis! A royal? This is my big chance! Can't you see the caption under my yearbook picture: 'Sara Melnick, the Countess of Third Avenue.'"

"Sorry to bring you down, Sara. But that marquis is a royal pain!" Dominique laughed. "I remember him from my parents' parties." The playful mood she always felt when she and Lizette were children was rising up inside. "When I give the signal, let's all wave and smile."

At the count of three the girls waved gaily, and the marquis looked thrilled by the attention.

"His title is real," Lizette explained. "But he doesn't have two francs to rub together. Poor fellow! He crashes into all these affairs and stuffs himself with buffet food."

"Much as I hate to gossip," Sara said, still smiling over at the marquis, "why doesn't he get a job?"

"Because, silly child," Dominique said with a put-on haughty air, "that would be beneath him. Occasionally he gets a fee for introducing a client to a gallery. But *real* work is out of the question."

"The one in the red ascot across from us. Famous?" Sara asked, standing on tiptoe to get a better look.

"Famous for being a kiss-up who trails after celebrities. You know what they say about him?" Dominique said.

"What?" Sara asked.

Dominique winked at Lizette. "He would go to the opening of an envelope," they sang in unison.

"Tell you what, Sara," Lizette said. "If you do not fall in love with a real prince by the end of the evening, then I shall introduce you to the poor fellow over there. For three bottles of champagne, he will be very happy to sell to you his title."

"You're on," said Sara.

"Oh, and later, Dominique," Lizette said, raising an eyebrow, "I have a secret to tell you."

As Lizette turned to embrace an odd-looking man wearing a Sherlock Holmes cape, Sara whispered, "I hope her wonderful secret is that she's wearing a chastity belt. Though I somehow doubt it."

Dominique gave her a pained look. Sara shrugged her shoulders and mouthed, "Sorry," as Odette returned and pulled her away.

"Come, Dominique," Odette said, reaching out for her hand through the crowd. "Time to view the new collection."

Odette led Dominique into the second exhibition room up the small flight of steps at the back of the gallery. Pierre waved over the top of the crowd and indicated that he would meet her upstairs.

In the comparative quiet of the second-floor gallery, Dominique stood back and looked at the first painting, an oil titled *Womankind*. It depicted a woman in different phases of life. Each phase overlapped the other, so subtly that looking at the work was like looking at a dream in progress.

The next was a series of swirls that looked like the eye of a hurricane. It was done in yellow watercolor, which became gradually deeper at the outer edges.

"What do you think, Dominique?" Odette asked, folding her arms in front of her as they looked at the pictures.

"That one I love," she said, pointing to *Womankind*. "It's really spectacular. The title is sort of hokey. But the work is the best Steinier I've ever seen."

"And the yellow?" Pierre had just joined them. "What do you think?"

Dominique made a face. "Ordinary. He's done much better things than that."

Suddenly an attractive man of about thirty with dark curly hair and wearing a charcoal blazer appeared at Dominique's side. "An interesting critique, with which I happen to agree."

Odette held out both hands. "Michel! Dominique, this is Michel Steinier."

Dominique, mortified, bit her lip and said, "'Open mouth, insert foot.' That's my motto."

The artist burst into good-natured laughter. "And who is this charming creature? The new editor of *Art Journal*? She certainly has great instincts. And expresses them so very well."

"Dominique is the daughter of Amanda and Leon Rappaport in New York."

"Of course. I have been to the Rappaports' gallery," Michel said, his eyes fixed on Dominique. "I heard that they had very fine art. But I did not know they created it as well."

Eager to get off the subject of herself, Dominique quickly said, "Congratulations on your show. I really admire your work."

"And I, Mademoiselle Rappaport, am an admirer of you."

Pierre glowed with pride at the impression Dominique had made. He put his arm around her. "I am sorry for you, Michel. But I have claimed her first."

"Well, treat her well, Pierre. Otherwise there will be a million men happy to steal her from you. Including me," the artist said.

"*Magnifique*, is she not?" Odette smiled. "Her mother is a friend of my youth."

Dominique, oblivious to Odette's familiar choice of an adjective, looked up at the way Pierre was smiling at her. Wouldn't it be funny if, in *spite* of their mothers' plotting, they actually did hit it off? Certainly Pierre had the advantage of starring in all her childhood daydreams. She tried to figure out how she was feeling, but this switch from the old nonrelationship was still too new to get a handle on.

"Your youth was not so long ago, Odette," Steinier said, putting his arm around Odette.

What a shame, thought Dominique, that a brilliant artist like Steinier had to spend an evening kissing up. It seemed to Dominique that all this chitchat had nothing at all to do with the frame of mind needed to stir the creative impulse.

But she knew—or imagined, anyway—that it was difficult for artists to have the peace of mind needed to create if they always had to worry about money.

Even if Steinier was just kissing up to her

because of her famous parents, his compliment to her critical ability set her mind in motion. People—wise and eminent people—in the art scene always praised her for it. Maybe she should take a split college major. For the first time it seemed that the art administration track her parents were pushing her toward might make some sense. Maybe she would be able to find ways for gifted artists like Steinier to spend more time with their canvases and less time ingratiating themselves with the likes of the Du Lacs and Rappaports. Something to think about.

Odette turned to introduce a young couple, Lord and Lady Peabody, to Steinier.

Lord Peabody extended his hand. "Ah, yes, Steinier. So this is the fellow they're calling the new Picasso."

"Come along, Dominique," Pierre whispered. "We should say hello to the Sheffields."

"The Sheffields of West Palm?" Dominique said, mimicking the society columns.

"West Palm, Rome, and Lucerne!" Pierre said, leading her down the stairs. "Filthy rich, but no taste. A tedious couple who are sure to relive every moment of their boring day from the time they brushed their teeth this morning. Still, with a gentle shove, we may persuade them toward a little refinement, and maybe a Steinier, *oui?*"

As Dominique and Pierre spoke to the Sheffields—discussing the weather in Cannes, the crowds in Rome, and a new restaurant in Montparnasse—she began to feel acutely bored. The evening was like a page straight from her parents' book. The clock was ticking quickly into her own future. And this was the future her parents wanted her to have. Help!

*Stop it,* she told herself. *Relax! You're here to have a good time. You're in Paris. You're on the arm of an extremely handsome French guy. Get with the program, girl!* And then her New York reality intruded again. Her parents' friends the Bonets were over by a cluster of smaller canvases. *Time to play Dial-a-Smile again.*

"Pierre, I promised my parents I'd say hello to the Bonets. Would you mind?"

"Of course not."

"Mme. Bonet!" Dominique crossed the floor with her hand in Pierre's. "How well you look!"

*Yes,* she thought halfway into the conversation, *I am good at this. And Pierre and I do make quite a team. Both of us really know how to work the room, as they say. A strong common link, this history of ours. No doubt about it. We've learned from the pros—our parents—how to make clients feel comfortable. And I can't deny that there is some satisfaction, a kind of high, in doing it so well.*

Then she spotted Julian standing near the bar. He held up a glass to toast her. "Miss America!" he mouthed.

His amused look felt like a slap in the face. As if those probing dark eyes had exposed some truth she would rather avoid. But that was nonsense. Wasn't it?

To her relief, Sara was suddenly beside her.

"Don't look now, Nik. But see that guy standing near the painting in the far left corner?"

Dominique glanced toward the area discreetly. "Tall, with sandy hair?"

"He asked me how long I'll be in Paris."

"Sara," Dominique said, laughing, "he looks like a nice guy, but—"

"Nice *guy*?" Sara said, raising her eyebrows. "That's no *guy*. That's the Comte Victor de Dragoni. He's a count. A real one, Lizette said. He's twenty-one but he's been a count all his life. I wonder if they put his title on his bassinet in the hospital—" Sara rambled on breathlessly.

"Comte de Dragoni?" Dominique turned her head quickly to get another look.

Sara's eyes flashed panic. "What's the matter?"

"'Dragoni' is Italian"—Dominique paused dramatically—"for 'Dracula.'"

Sara began to laugh. "You really had me scared for a minute. I thought you were going to tell me he was *married* or something!"

Dominique gestured to the silk scarf around Sara's shoulders. "No, he's absolutely available, I hear. But I think you'd better move that scarf a little higher so it covers that delicious-looking neck of yours!"

114

# CHAPTER SEVEN

Le Pirate was the trendiest nightspot in Paris, the current playground of the rich European set. Huge Japanese goldfish swam in enormous glass enclosures that zigzagged in semicircles throughout the club. The design gave the impression that the patrons were dancing in a bowl while the fish looked on as spectators.

And the decor of the club was that of an ocean floor, with authentic-looking remnants of sunken galleons, coral reefs, pirate-hatted skeletons with patches over their eye sockets, and treasure boxes dripping silver coins and jewels.

Champagne glasses diligently refilled to the brim bobbed among the elite but boisterous clusters of young people on the dance floor. All gyrated to the pounding rhythm of the hot new Bengal Lancers group.

About half the place was taken up with friends of Pierre's who'd been at the gallery. As Dominique surveyed the room, she felt wowed by the spectacle but impatient with some of the company. Pierre's friends seemed so slick—smooth-talking, shallow guys who bounced from romance to romance.

As they were leaving the gallery, one of them, Marcus, a blond movie-star type, had even asked her to ditch Pierre and spend the rest of the evening with him. When she turned him down and said, "I thought you and Pierre were friends," he just laughed. "One night alone with you would be worth a lifetime of friendship with Pierre."

From his expression, Dominique could tell he thought she should be flattered by his come-on. Where did these guys get such dumb ideas *and* dumb lines?

"How do you like it, Dominique?" Pierre asked, leaning across their table to shout above the noise.

Not wanting to offend Pierre, who was so obviously proud of his exclusive nightspot, Dominique decided to accentuate the positive, as her mother would say. "I've never seen anything like this before. That 'people bowl' is a great effect," Dominique said. "And the line outside was amazingly long. Le Pirate must be very popular."

"*Oui.* The hottest place in town," Pierre said. "They are quite fussy about who they admit," he continued in French. "Only the very best people are allowed inside." He blew a kiss to a pretty young woman on a nearby couch made to look like an opened treasure chest. "I am well known here. That is why I was able to take our whole party past the line. Most of those people will never get in."

Pierre signaled the waiter for another drink—his fifth—and Dominique felt a bit worried. He seemed to be downing them like water. And with each drink, he acted more and more foolish.

As Sara danced by with her count, Dominique waved, envious of her friend's lightheartedness. All of her efforts to relax and enjoy herself weren't coming to very much. And the best part of the evening was supposed to be happening now. So why did her mind keep wanting to return to the ten-minute visit with Rabbi Levi?

"I felt so bad for that guy who was angry because the doorman let us in first," Dominique replied, trying to engage herself in the conversation. "He said he'd been standing there for hours."

Pierre threw back his head and laughed. "Poor fellow in his polyester ensemble! They can't open this place to the likes of him!"

Pierre's boastfulness and his manner of putting everyone down were grating on Dominique's nerves. She hadn't known he had such a side. But it had to be the result of all that liquor he kept downing.

"Let me order you a drink, *chérie*. Something stronger than Evian," Pierre said, signaling for the waiter again. "You don't look like you're having a good time."

Dominique shook her head. "I really don't want a drink, Pierre." She wished he would forget the next one himself, but it wasn't her place to play nursemaid. Maybe a gentle reminder of the Shabbat service in the morning might make him decide to slow down a little.

"Sara and I are going with your parents to synagogue tomorrow. Will you be there?"

"*Oui!* But I have a little secret I will share with you. When I go to synagogue, I bring these." He pulled a pair of sunglasses from his pocket. "That way, I can sleep during the whole dull ceremony. Everyone knows they must pray very softly if they are near to me or I shall begin to snore." Pierre laughed as if that were the funniest thing he'd ever heard.

To Dominique his manner seemed more arrogant than humorous. And did the fact that he brought sunglasses to synagogue mean he was always hung over, or always tired?

When he got no reaction from Dominique, Pierre asked, "You do not like my joke?"

"Was it a joke?" Dominique sat back along the crimson leather bench and studied Pierre.

Pierre looked surprised. "Now do not tell me that a vibrant creature such as yourself actually enjoys to go to the synagogue? It is the most boring hour of the week."

"Sometimes I do enjoy it. But I don't understand why you go if you don't like it. Why not just stay home and sleep in your bed?"

"I go from habit. I go because it is expected

of me. *Cela m'est égal*—it doesn't matter to me—and it pleases my parents. That is good to do, *non*? To please one's parents."

*Sure. Like they'd be really pleased if they saw how much liquor you were sloshing down tonight,* thought Dominique.

Pierre sighed. "You are in much too serious a mood for a night in Paris. Come. Dance with me."

He was right. She was too serious, and it was starting to ruin her evening. What business was it of hers if Pierre had a few too many drinks tonight? It had been a long day for them all. Now it was time to party.

The Bengals had relinquished the floor to a man at the piano. He was singing soft ballads, and the mood had changed from wild to amorous. And that was the direction Pierre seemed to want to take things as he pulled her close.

"It's been a marvelous night," Pierre said.

"It was wonderful!" Dominique concurred. "I'm sure the exhibit will be a great success." She looked up at Pierre innocently, knowing full well he wasn't talking about how well the Du Lac gallery would do with the works of Michel Steinier.

"Yes, yes, the show." He waved his hand. "The show is over now, and what I'm talking about is you. You are sensational, Dominique. Absolutely everyone is wondering about this beautiful girl I am with."

It was one thing to be thinking about Pierre when she was in New York, quite another to have him press her so close she could feel the heat of his body. "You are very special to me, Dominique," he whispered.

"What is it that you like about me?" Dominique asked, trying to sort out her feelings.

Pierre laughed softly. "Here am I, with a longing to kiss you. And you are giving to me what you Americans call the third degree. From anyone else, such directness would spoil my mood." He flashed his white teeth. "If I thought of you at all in the past, a little tomboy came to mind. And then at the chalet this winter—*voilà!*—I am seeing a film star."

"So it's my looks you find appealing?" Dominique asked, looking up at him.

"I would have to be a blind man not to notice," Pierre said. An honest enough answer, Dominique thought. She couldn't fault him there. But why, she wondered, did she have to fault him at all? *Maybe, Dominique, because in your girlish dreams, he did not have zee bleary eyes and zee snobby manner!* But in girlish dreams everyone was perfect—and in real life people were not supposed to be perfect, she told herself.

"*Oui,* you and I are good together, Dominique." He stood back and gazed at her with appreciation. "Even if you insist to drive me crazy with your third degree. We are of the same fine cloth and breeding. I felt that when we were 'working the crowd,' as you say in English, we were doing a pas de deux—a dance we have been practicing for our whole lives."

True, she had had that feeling too. And even if that Julian character had blown the moment for her with his smart look, it was interesting that Pierre had been thinking the same thing. *Did* they share some special fate?

"I can see from the look that is clouding over your beautiful face that that mind of yours is too busy. Here! I kiss it *bonne nuit*! Good night to you, busy little mind." He touched his lips to her temples. "And now you let your heart take over."

Dominique smiled, feeling as if the old, charming Pierre was back. *Okay*, she said to herself, *give it a rest and enjoy the moment. Take a lesson from Sara. She looks like she's on another planet, in the arms of her "titled personage."*

*Pierre really is such a smooth dancer. And if I close my eyes it's like being in the middle of one of those corny old movies. He's Fred Astaire and I'm Ginger Rogers—*

The crash of glasses followed by loud laughter intruded into the romantic mood.

"My sister cannot hold her champagne too well," Pierre said, groaning, as they spotted Lizette in the center of the commotion. She was trying to climb on top of the table, hollering something about doing her nightclub act.

"I'd better take her to the powder room," Dominique said.

Once in the ladies' room, Dominique tried to get the giddy Lizette to sit on the chaise

121

lounge. Lizette resisted, then flopped down in a giggling fit.

"*Merci*," Dominique told the matron, who handed her a cold cloth. She held it to Lizette's forehead.

"Oh, Dominique," Lizette said dreamily, "I am so happy that you are here. This is the best night of my life."

"That's terrific," Dominique said, wondering if her friend would even remember this "best night of her life" tomorrow.

"And my secret! I tell you my secret, Dominique! I am in love, Dominique! For the first time in my life!"

"Wonderful. I'm very happy for you. I hope he's a great guy. One who deserves someone wonderful like you."

Suddenly Lizette became serious. "Do you really think I am wonderful, Dominique?"

Dominique looked at her friend, and though she felt sad that Lizette was so blitzed at the moment, she knew what a vulnerable and sweet soul her friend really was.

"Of course I do, Lizzie. You're the best."

"Even if I am such a bad girl who is full of champagne tonight, you *still* will be my friend?"

"I'm always going to be your friend. We're Daisy and Maisy of the Rodeo. Friends forever."

"Well, you know that sometimes people say that I am too free with my affections . . ." Lizette began.

*Maybe, as a friend, I should tell her that I've*

*heard the rumors. . . . No, that wouldn't be good. But maybe there's a way I could suggest she get some help. Maybe if Lizette came to New York and stayed with us for a while and could get a new start . . .* But as Lizette began to ramble, Dominique realized she was in no condition for a serious talk.

"I have always wished I could be like you, Dominique." Tears filled Lizette's eyes. "I admire you so. You are so intelligent, so beautiful."

Lizette rose, but her legs were too unsteady to hold her. "Whoops!" She guffawed and the tears trickling down her cheeks turned to tears of laughter. She struggled to sit up. Then, with Dominique's support, she rose to her feet. "*L'amour! L'amour!* Love has done this to me."

Dominique stood and straightened her skirt. "I can't wait to meet the lucky guy," she said. *Who knows?* she thought. *Maybe if he's really great, he could make a difference in her life. Get the poor girl onto a track where she could feel more valuable. Then perhaps she wouldn't feel the need to go into her trampy act the minute a guy walked through the door.*

"But you've met him already." Lizette looked at herself in the mirror. She took a tissue and dabbed at the mascara splotches on her face.

"Was he at the gallery tonight?"

Lizette nodded.

"Don't keep me in suspense, Maisy. Who's the lucky guy?"

Lizette turned her beaming face from the mirror to Dominique. "It's Julian, Dominique. Julian Adler!"

*Julian Adler?* Dominique felt as if she had been doused with a bucket of ice water. "Julian Adler?" Dominique said, trying to keep her voice even.

Whatever else might be wrong with Julian, he certainly didn't seem frivolous enough for someone like Lizette to appeal to him. Nor was he reeking with charitable intentions. *He must be even more of a creep than I thought,* Dominique said to herself, *to take advantage of a defenseless girl like Lizette!*

"Are you okay, Dominique?"

Dominique nodded. "It's a little warm in here." If there was any way on earth she could protect Lizette from Julian, she'd better come up with it fast.

Lizette turned back to the mirror and fussed with her hair. Her countenance was joy itself. It didn't seem like a great time to plant the thought that Julian might not be the most suitable love object for Lizette. Or for anyone else, for that matter.

"Are you not happy for me?" Lizette asked.

"I am happy, Lizette, that *you're* happy," Dominique answered slowly. Tactfully.

"You are hesitating, Dominique." Lizette faced her directly. "*Pourquoi?* Tell me why."

"It's just—it's only—" Dominique stammered, wishing she could look anywhere else but into those liquid brown eyes, trusting as a puppy's. "I wonder how your family will react. I mean, he is really not of the same fine cloth." She cringed at how easy Pierre's haughty phrase tripped so easily from her tongue. "I don't mean to be negative, but why go looking for problems? Not that there's anything wrong with construction work and driving taxis. But my mother would—"

"Dominique, you are so funny!" Lizette laughed. "Julian is just working at such kinds of jobs because they pay him well. While he is on break from his medical training. He is a very smart young man. And they gave him such a fine scholarship, but there is not much money for living decently on an intern's wages."

So the medical journal on the sitting room shelf was Julian's after all! Now it made sense to Dominique that Rabbi Levi said his work was important. This did shed a new light on Julian. But imagine the shock for some poor patient expecting a kind bedside manner from the young doctor!

"And do you want to hear the best part? He is working as a plastic surgeon."

A plastic surgeon! Of course. That completes the puzzle. Someone like him wouldn't be in medicine to help heal the sick. He meant to get rich giving face-lifts to rich women like her mother's friends. Nothing that required any real compassion.

"If this is what you want, Lizette," Dominique said, "then I'm glad." What good would it do to voice her disapproval of Julian? That would only put a wedge between Dominique and Lizette.

Lizette hugged Dominique and opened the door to the powder room. Dominique watched as she ran toward Julian. His detached attitude annoyed Dominique. The way he stood there with his hands in his pockets, barely even glancing at Lizette. Poor thing, she thought, to be so desperate for a guy she refused to look at the warning signals.

"There you are, Dominique," Pierre said, pulling her onto the dance floor.

Dominique closed her eyes and leaned against Pierre's shoulder.

"Ah, *très bien*," Pierre murmured. "Much better. Now that I have you in my arms, I have a big wish, Dominique. . . ."

"What beeg wish?" Dominique said, playfully mocking his accent.

"*Pardon,* Pierre," someone said. Dominique looked over to see Julian beside them.

Though he spoke to Pierre, Julian kept his eyes fixed on Dominique. She hated the mocking glint in his eye. "Lizette has had too much champagne. I think I'd better take her home."

"Oh, *merci,* Julian," Pierre replied. He closed his eyes again and pressed his face against Dominique's.

*Maybe,* Dominique thought, *I should say something to Pierre about Lizette and Julian.*

*And then again, maybe I should mind my own business.*

She pressed her head into Pierre's shoulder, as if that might expel her preoccupation with Julian and Lizette. "You were saying something, Pierre?"

"I was saying how very much I want to kiss you," he answered. He searched her eyes hopefully.

Dominique was aware that Julian had turned to look at them. What nerve he had to be gazing at her and Pierre as if he were some kind of judge! And all the while he was leading Lizette to fall in love with him and behaving so coldly.

But Pierre, he certainly knew how to treat a woman with affection. *If Julian really wants to have something to watch,* she thought, *then here goes.* "Then why don't you kiss me, Pierre?" Dominique said.

"*Oui.* Why don't I?" Pierre murmured as he pressed his lips to hers.

"Stop, Pierre. Stop it right now!" Dominique said, trying to wrench free from Pierre's powerful grip in the Du Lacs' corridor. *Damn!* she thought. *This is all Julian's fault. If he hadn't given me that evil eye, I'd never have gotten into this mess.*

As soon as Dominique broke loose, Pierre moved as quickly as a jungle cat to block her escape. "You do not mean that, *chérie!*" he said with a drunken grin. "Just one hour ago, you made it clear to me you shared my desire."

"It was a kiss, Pierre," Dominique snapped. "Just a kiss."

"Ah, but it was a kiss that promised something more, Dominique." The blurry look in Pierre's eyes was gone. Now he looked challenged in a way that made Dominique wonder just how aggressive he would get.

"Look, Pierre, we've both had a very long day," she said, beginning to feel genuine alarm. *Maybe,* she thought, *if I try to sound reasonable, I can turn this thing around. Maybe—if I don't make him feel this is a contest—he'll feel he can back down without losing face.* "Why don't we talk about this tomorrow? Get to know each other a little more."

"We have known each other all our lives, Dominique."

"Not in this way, we haven't." Dominique moved to duck out of the fence Pierre had made with his arms against the wall.

But he caught her and held her. "Now is a very good time to continue what we began last winter."

*But you weren't acting like a drunken fool last winter,* she wanted to say.

"Let go of me, Pierre. Let go of me this minute!"

Instead, Pierre pressed her into the corner. "Ah, yes, Dominique. You are very strong. But I am the stronger one, *oui?*" He grabbed her hands and held her pinned against the wall while he planted a drunken kiss on her neck. "I know very well that you are enjoying this," he said, laughing.

For all his attempts at seeming playful, there was no mistaking the tenacity of his will. "Let go of me. Now!" she said angrily.

"So you are playing games with me, *chérie?* One moment you act the flirt, and the next you pretend innocence?"

"Cut this out, Pierre. I can't stand feeling so tense and trapped." She snapped her arms from his grip and folded them in front of her, regarding him with a mixture of fear and rage.

"Then relax and enjoy," Pierre said, pulling her head back and pressing his mouth against hers.

She pulled her mouth away and yelled, "Get away from me! Get away from me right now!"

"Not so loud, Dominique. Do you want to wake the household so they can see our little love game?" he said, trying to kiss her again.

"This is not a little love game, Pierre. This is you being an obnoxious boor," Dominique said between clenched teeth. "And if you don't get away from me this second, I'll scream so loud they'll hear me in New York!"

He put his arms around her and pulled her toward him again. "Did you know that when you are angry, your face becomes as red as your hair and that—"

Suddenly, to Dominique's immense relief,

she heard a door at the end of the hall open. They turned to see Mme. Renault, the housekeeper, padding toward them.

Pierre grunted, but let go of Dominique instantly and began smoothing his hair. "You are not asleep yet, Mme. Renault?" he said, unable to look her in the face.

She shook her head. "Neither are you, children. I am sure you must be very tired."

Shaking, very close to tears, Dominique looked gratefully at the old woman. "Actually, I *am* tired. Very tired, madame," Dominique said.

"*Très bien!*" she chirped, looping her arm through Dominique's and marching the trembling young woman toward the kitchen. "We will relax ourselves with a cup of chocolate and then we go right to bed! *Bonsoir*, Pierre."

# CHAPTER EIGHT

"*Comment ça va?* How are you, my darling? You sound a bit under the weather. Is there anything I can do for you, *ma petite?*"

Hearing her grandmother's voice on the telephone made Dominique feel like crying. As if the warmth she felt could dissolve all the creeped-out residue of her ugly run-in with Pierre the night before.

"Nothing's wrong, Grandmère. Just a little jet lag, I think," Dominique said, hoping to sound more lighthearted than she felt. She opened the French doors to look out at Paris, coming to life slowly on this Saturday.

"Are you sure that is all? Because if anyone is making you unhappy, you know that I will make short work of him!"

Dominique laughed. Her grandmother was full of fun, but her protective spirit toward her granddaughter was so ardent, Dominique suspected she *would* totally pulverize anyone who messed with her.

"What is that music I am hearing, my angel?

It sounds as if you are speaking to me from the inside of a concert hall!" Grandmère Mimi said.

"That's my friend Sara, practicing her violin," Dominique replied. She pulled back the velvet drapes and closed the sliding door of the sitting room to mute the sound. "She's very talented." Dominique flopped down on the immense Turkish divan and curled her legs under her. "But I'm not a big fan of the violin at this time of the morning."

"Between you and me—I am not either!" Her grandmother laughed. "Oh, I cannot wait to see you, *ma petite mignonne,* my little darling."

"I can't wait to se you either, Grandmère!"

"What time will you be arriving in Ville de Fabian?"

"The car service said it's less than a two-hour drive from Paris, so I should be getting there about noon on Tuesday. Can I bring you something from Paris, Grandmère?"

"Just you, my sweet!"

As they said their good-byes, Dominique felt a burst of excitement at the thought of seeing her grandmother.

Then, as she headed for the shower, she was again reminded of the incident with Pierre. *Maybe I'll be lucky and he'll be too hung over to get to the service—even with his stupid sunglasses!*

"Smile!" Sara whispered to Dominique outside the synagogue after services. "Here comes your future husband, right behind the in-laws!"

Late last night, after the Comte de Dragoni had taken Sara back to the Du Lac mansion, Dominique had filled Sara in on her tussle with Pierre. But, wanting to put the whole ordeal far behind her as quickly as possible, she hadn't gone into specifics about just how aggressive he had been.

"Cool it, Sara. One word about last night and we'll be saying kaddish"—the prayer for the dead—"over your corpse tonight," Dominique muttered. Though the sight of Pierre behind them made her feel like hissing, she did her best to Dial-a-Smile for Odette and Armand.

"There you are! Darling Dominique and lovely Sara," Odette called, waving her cream-colored kid glove toward them.

"*Shabbat shalom!*" Armand du Lac greeted the girls with the traditional sabbath greeting as he followed his wife through the massive carved-oak door of the synagogue.

"*Shabbat shalom!*" Dominique and Sara responded.

A self-conscious-looking Pierre was bringing up the rear at a sluggish pace.

"Pierre, I have asked you before. Remove your sunglasses when we go to shul," his father told him in an annoyed voice.

"*Oui*, Papa," Pierre replied, folding his glasses and looking sheepishly in Dominique's direction.

"Your eyes are so red!" Odette exclaimed. "Poor boy, he works so hard, he does not get enough sleep."

Sara and Dominique looked sideways at each other.

Odette shrugged. "But at least he is here. It seems, though, that Lizette overslept and has missed services once again."

"*Elle se croit tout permise*—she thinks she can do whatever she likes." Armand sighed, shaking his head.

Dominique couldn't help smiling to herself. Though Odette and her mother were similar in so many ways, parenting was not one of them. Both Pierre and Lizette had been raised pretty much by governesses; in her own mother's judgment, this was Odette's only imperfection.

Odette, exchanging smiles and greetings with the crowd of congregants milling along the sidewalk, looped her arm through Dominique's and led their group into the shade of a chestnut tree near the curb. "Tell me, Dominique, is Pierre taking good care of you?"

Sara began to cough.

"*Oui,*" answered Dominique, avoiding looking over at Pierre. It wasn't necessary to make Odette or Armand aware of the upsetting situation, but there was no way she wanted Pierre to think she had accepted his offensive behavior.

Odette took Dominique's face in her hands

and kissed both her cheeks. "*Mon petit chou*— my little sweetheart—has grown into such a lovely young woman." She turned to Sara. "I am so afraid, Sara, you will say to all the people in New York that the friend of Dominique's mama is a *femme folle*—a crazy woman—if I am so sentimental with this girl, but she is very precious to me. *Oui*, Armand?" Odette said, looking back over her shoulder at her husband.

"It's as if Dominique were one of our own," Armand said with a gentle smile. "And it is terrible that we have not more time to spend together today. The car is picking us up any minute for the airport. Will you girls still be here when we return on Tuesday?"

Dominique knew the sentiments were heartfelt. And no matter how miffed she was at Pierre, the rest of the Du Lac family would always be special to her. "Actually, we won't, Armand," Dominique answered. "Sara has to get back to New York and I'm off to visit Grandmère Mimi."

"Ah, *oui*, Mimi! Such a fascinating woman," Armand said, shaking his head.

Odette sighed. "Her life is something straight from the cinema."

"I can't wait to see her. But, Odette, maybe you'll tell me. What is so fascinating about her?"

"Ah, it is such a long story, darling. And so sad that she and your mama have not always had such smooth sailing," Odette said in a melancholy voice.

Dominique bit her lip. It bothered her so much that Grandmère and Mama weren't on better terms. But whatever had happened between them, it was clear from the admonishing look he shot Odette that Armand didn't feel they should discuss the sensitive topic.

"Enough! That's an old story, Mimi and Amanda." Armand put an arm around Dominique's shoulder. "But I know a visit from her *petite fille*—her granddaughter—will be so good for Mimi."

"Yes, it will. And I am so happy for her," Odette said, throwing her hands in the air. "But I am sorry for me that I will not have more time with you."

"It's too bad this visit was so spur-of-the-moment. Next time we'll give advance warning and make sure to lock up your calendar for days," Dominique said, hugging Odette.

Armand waved to the limousine pulling to a stop in front of them. "Ten on the dot. He is right on time," he said. He kissed Dominique on both cheeks and gave Sara a kiss on her hand.

"Thank you so much for letting me stay. Thanks for everything. *Merci*," Sara said, blushing.

"*Pas du tout*—not at all. It was a pleasure for us," he answered earnestly. He turned to shake his son's hand.

"We will hear from you soon, *oui*, Dominique?" Odette kissed the girls and Pierre. "You have our number if you need us in Belgium, children."

"They're really great people. And Odette reminds me so much of your mother," Sara said as they waved the car away.

"Yes," Dominique said softly.

Pierre, silent till now, suddenly perked up. "They really are alike, are they not?"

Dominique gave a brusque yes, without looking at him. She was not about to let him think he could just pick up where they'd left off, as if last night's conflict had never happened.

"*Salut!*" a female voice called. They turned to see Lizette, decked out in a red silk mini-dress and matching floppy hat, come hurrying toward them. "I have slept too late again and missed the service! Mama and Papa, they have gone to the airport?"

Sara nodded. "We tried to wake you before we left, Lizette, but you were too out of it to even answer."

Lizette threw her hands up in the air. "*Paresse!* Laziness! That is my tragic flaw!" Then she looked from face to face, puzzled at the laughter her lament had caused.

"Oh, Maisy," Dominique said, shaking her head. "You are one of a kind."

"Sara," Lizette began, "I must tell you that after you left this morning, Victor called and—"

As Sara and Lizette began to chatter, Pierre cleared his throat and turned to Dominique.

"*Pardon,*" he said in a subdued voice. "Let's stroll around the garden, Dominique, so I may speak to you a moment."

137

Dominique took a long breath. *Well, the least I can do is let him admit he behaved like an ass.*

Pierre pushed open the iron gate of the stone synagogue to the area that bordered the garden. Little boys with yarmulkes pinned to their hair whooped as they raced by. Young girls in bright, frilly dresses and patent-leather shoes stood in a circle, playing a clapping game, chanting a French children's rhyme.

"*Il fait beau*—it's a beautiful morning," Pierre began amiably.

Dominique rolled her eyes. "The *weather*? I can't believe you're discussing the weather, Pierre!"

Pierre cleared his throat. "I was a bad boy last night," he said with a naughty-child smile.

His attempt to make a joke out of his vulgar behavior infuriated Dominique. "*Il n'y a pas de quoi rire!*" she said. "It's not something to laugh about."

"*Ah, les règles du jeu*—the rules of the game—may be a little different in New York, *oui*? It is best if I wait until we have had three dates before I make the move, eh?" he began, still trying to make light of the situation.

"Damn it, Pierre," Dominique said, shaking her head as she began to walk away.

"Don't blame *me*, Dominique," he said insistently, as he caught up with her. "At Le Pirate you yourself said I should kiss you—"

"Oh, but I do blame you!" Dominique said angrily. Last night, while she was too upset to sleep, she had gone out to the balcony, playing the events over in her head. Maybe it was dumb of her to kiss Pierre as a reaction to Julian's belittling look. But nothing gave Pierre the right to ignore her when she told him to let go. "Don't you get it? *No* means *no!* No matter what you *thought* at the club, I couldn't have been clearer afterward."

As she began to walk away again, Pierre put his arm on her shoulder. "Don't!" she said sharply.

He removed it quickly, as if burned by the glare in her eye. "Dominique. I know you are right. It was that I had too much of the drinking last night. It was a day filled with much pressure and I did not have much to eat—"

Dominique rolled her eyes. She wasn't about to listen to his excuses.

"Allow me to finish, Dominique, please," Pierre said, his voice quiet. "I do not say these things as an excuse for my ungentlemanly conduct. But I do want you to understand. And I do want to tell to you that I have much regret over the whole messy business."

*At least he finally admits he was wrong!* Dominique thought. She didn't feel she had whatever it took to forgive him—at least, not now. But it was a step in the right direction that he was willing to acknowledge his responsibility.

"I know I am not really that way," Pierre said, looking genuinely sorry. "Because it was awkward for me, I make the joke. For that too, I am feeling sorry."

"Okay, Pierre," Dominique said, not wanting to talk about it anymore. "There's a lot I want to do today." The museums—the galleries—the sights of Paris were waiting for her, and she was anxious to get going.

"I'm asking for one more chance to prove to you what I am really like. It rests with you, Dominique, to give me that chance."

Accepting his apology was one thing. Making plans to spend time alone with him again was something else altogether, something she wasn't ready to do. "Not now, Pierre," Dominique said, striding through the gate toward Sara and Lizette.

"What's up?" Sara said, searching Dominique's face for clues to her tête-à-tête with Pierre.

"I'll tell you later," Dominique said under her breath. "What did the count have to say?"

Sara's cheeks dimpled in a smile at the sound of the title. "He's invited us all to his country estate tomorrow. Swimming pool, tennis courts—the whole nine yards."

Lizette turned to Dominique. "Pierre and I have been before to the Dragonis' chateau. *Fantastique!* And he has the best stables. The Daisy and Maisy Rodeo shall ride again—*oui*, Dominique?"

Lizette and Sara began to chatter about what to wear, and Pierre, who had sheepishly followed Dominique out of the garden, looked at her tentatively. "I would be most happy if you allow me to escort you."

140

"No, thank you, Pierre," she said, and turned to follow Lizette and Sara, leaving Pierre standing on the sidewalk, looking bewildered.

"That giant glass pyramid really blew me away," Sara told Dominique as they sat at their table in the La Palette café after their visit to the Louvre. "I wasn't expecting anything so modern."

"I'm not crazy about that addition," Dominique said. "It's just so New Age. More like some kind of laboratory than a museum. It does help the lighting, though," she said, a wistful smile turning up the corners of her mouth. "But I really like the old section better—with all those seventeenth-century sculptures, and the Corinthian columns."

Sara shook her head in wonder. "You have such strong instincts about design, I think you'd make a great architect."

Dominique took a sip of lemonade and thought for a moment. "That's something I hadn't considered. It'd be absolutely fantastic to work with someone like Pei."

"Like who?"

"I. M. Pei. He's the Chinese-American who's made so many changes in the field. Even if I don't give his work a total stamp of approval, he's still a genius." As the waiter passed them, Dominique signaled for the bill. *"L'addition, s'il vous plaît."*

Sara swished her spoon around in her melting *glacé*. "Can't we stay here for a while? This is kind of like a museum in progress."

Dominique looked from the tables packed with students from the Ecole Nationale des Beaux-Arts who kept the café buzzing and rolled her eyes at the embarrassingly bad painting on the wall.

"A fabulous hangout, but zee art leaves something to be desired, *n'est-ce pas*? And we are not leaving Paris without seeing Degas's dancers! Seurat's dots."

"When I'm getting zee Melnick blisters, I have a hard time caring about Seurat's dots. It's twelve thirty, Nik. We've been walking around since services were over two and half hours ago." Sara rested her pixie face on her hands.

"*Merci*, mademoiselle," the waiter said as he tore the check from his pad and placed it on the tiny table.

As Dominique searched through her wallet, she said, "What did you think of your first service at a French synagogue?"

"Certainly was French," Sara said, sliding her shoes back on under the table. "Lucky they had the Hebrew text. At least I knew we were doing the Shabbat ceremony. But the rabbi's French speech—totally Greek to me."

"Sara, you are so funny!" Dominique said in an imitation of Lizette, as she rose to her feet. "Actually, Rabbi Tolan said that it wasn't enough to be angry that tyranny still exists in the world. That we have to act. That being Jew-

142

ish means to share the suffering of all people. It reminded me of that part of the Passover Haggadah—where it says, 'Let the suffering of others be our suffering.' "

Sara handed her portion of the check to Dominique. "I must have forgotten that part."

"*You* forgot?"

"What's so extraordinary about that?" Sara asked as they wove their way through the animated clusters of young people toward the exit.

"I'll never forget your bas mitzvah speech. How everyone was so blown away by your commitment."

"We were thirteen years old, Nik! I can't believe you still remember that."

"Well, I was impressed. At thirteen, all I cared about was your party afterward. Then you shook the temple with your speech. Even my mother, the rock, wept her eyelashes off."

"Know what I remember about being kids?" Sara said as the two friends turned off the busy gallery-packed rue de la Seine onto the peaceful rue Jacob. "How everyone made such a fuss over you. The way Rabbi Altman's wife and her cronies would cluck what a beautiful little girl, what a *shayneh maydeleh*, you were."

Dominique shuddered. "I felt like a windup toy, having to smile as they patted me on the head."

"Maybe you hated it, Nik," Sara said, "but I was jealous as anything. We all knew that they'd pick you to play Queen Esther at Purim. Not only beautiful, but what a role! So while you were King Ahasuerus's wife, saving the Jews from the evil Haman's murder plot, who was I? Old Queen Vashti, whose husband dumped her for Esther. So my way of getting pats on the head had to be different. If being 'the beauty' was taken by you, I'd be 'the scholar.'"

"You couldn't have faked that bas mitzvah speech. That couldn't have been all an act."

"It wasn't *all* an act, Dominique. The more I studied, the more I got into it. But after a while, all my passion got directed toward Kenny Goldblatt."

"Kenny Goldblatt? Esther's wise uncle Mordecai, right?"

"The hottest Mordecai in the entire Judeo-Christian world." They came to a stop before a quaint little house and read the plaque. "Stendhal, the guy who wrote *The Red and the Black*, lived right here!" Sara said, pointing eagerly to the sign.

"That was no *guy*," Dominique said, glad Sara seemed as thrilled as she was to be in the midst of such history. "That was a ten-point question on our senior English exam!"

They both began to laugh. Then Sara glanced at her watch. "I've got to get back to the flat. Victor and I are going to Versailles for the afternoon and to the opera tonight. And I've got to get another half-hour violin practice in before we leave."

"But I thought you were going to the Musée

d'Orsay with me," Dominique said, her voice a mix of surprise and disappointment.

"But I don't know when I'll get to Paris or Victor will get to New York, and we want to spend a lot of time together," Sara said.

"You just met the guy," Dominique said. "And you're making him the whole focus of this trip." Her piqued tone startled them both.

Sara's brow wrinkled as she eyed Dominique. "You know, Nik, it sounds like you're jealous or something."

"Jealous? Absolutely not!" Dominique exclaimed hotly, folding her arms in front of her.

"Are you *sure?*" Sara probed. "I mean, this whole trip was supposed to be about you and Pierre. And instead of being the prince of your childhood dreams, he goes into a major masher act and moves in on you like a creepy pig last night. That's got to be a bummer. Especially when I'm going out with Victor and Lizette dropped her bombshell about being in love with Julian. I mean, everybody seems to be pairing off, and you aren't the slightest bit envious?"

*Julian and Lizette!* She didn't even want to be reminded of that lopsided relationship. "It's just that—it's just—" Dominique threw her hands in the air. "So maybe I *am* jealous."

"I can't believe it. Dominique Rappaport is jealous of me, little Sara Melnick!"

"Cut it out. You'll make me sorry I ever said anything."

Sara clapped her hands gleefully. "This is so great! You don't have to buy me a present for the next ten birthdays."

"Sara, shut up."

Sara looked down at the ground, shaking her head. "I am so impressed that you admitted it. I feel like kissing you."

"Don't even *think* about it," Dominique muttered. "Or you'll wind up in tomorrow's headlines. 'Promising Young American Musician Found in Front of Stendhal's House with Violin in Her Mouth.'"

# CHAPTER NINE

Dominique went back to the Du Lacs' with Sara and changed from the sedate taupe linen she'd worn to go to synagogue and into jeans and a T-shirt. Then she grabbed her sketch pad and took off for the former railway station that had been converted into the Musée d'Orsay. A happy thrill went through her as she circled the famous sculpture of the Four Quarters of the World—the huge guardians, larger than the earth sphere they kept aloft, but straining under its weight.

After glancing up at the huge domed ceiling, with its ornate clock at the entrance, reminiscent of the museum's railway days, Dominique rode the escalator to the upper level. For a while she stood gazing solemnly at the collection of Van Gogh self-portraits. Each at a different, yet always melancholy, stage of his life. Beside her a young English couple, holding each other around the waist and appearing to be as in love as newlyweds, kept talking about how awful it was that the artist had worked his whole life without recognition. "Such a pity!" the pretty young woman said to Dominique as they walked off. Dominique nodded in agreement. Poor Van Gogh! So heartbreaking that he suffered rejection and struggled in isolation his whole life. That he never lived to know how revered his work would become.

Dominique walked on to the west wing of the museum, where the Toulouse-Lautrec series was on exhibit. Another artist who suffered great difficulties—she had read that his legs were crippled in a childhood accident. *But,* she thought to herself, *his work is proof that his heart could sing!*

After paying her respects to the sweeping landscapes of Pissarro and the ballet series of Degas, Dominique left the museum and took a walk along the waterfront on the quai Malaquais, alone among the tourists and Parisians who ambled on the well-kept green around her. Yet Dominique felt oddly connected to the intent young artists who stood sketching along the bridges in scruffy sub-grunge-look clothes—and felt warmed inside by a silent prayer for them all.

At one time she'd thought it would be wonderful to study art in Paris. But, as much as she loved looking at art, making art, she knew that she didn't aspire toward making a name for herself. Her own art was a way of rousing an inner awareness that let her know that—no matter how jumbled life sometimes felt—there was something magical about being alive. Though she could get engrossed with her sketching to the point of obsession, she'd never yearned to make it her life's work.

After wandering for a while in a happy, trancelike state, Dominique realized she was not far from the old church where Julian had taken her and Sara to meet Rabbi Levi. *Perfect!* she thought as she made her way through the still little courtyard. *Just the person I want to see!*

"Ah, it is Dominique, *oui!*" the rabbi said as he opened the door, his wrinkled countenance brightening with a broad smile. "How nice it is to see you again." He pressed his glasses back onto his nose. "Still, it puzzles me . . . who is it that you look like? Anyway," he said, leading Dominique into the kitchen. "Can I give you some tea? I have some challah and jam."

"I would love some, Rabbi Levi."

Sitting at the small wooden table as Rabbi Levi set the plates, Dominique was glad she had found her way there again. The rabbi's soothing presence made her feel as comfortable as if she were with someone from her family.

He offered Dominique a plate of challah and jam, then watched as she pulled a piece from the soft, yellow, braided bread and spooned on a bit of the raspberry spread.

She took a bite. *Mmmm!* Sweeter than the Sabbath challah she ate in New York. And, as it was after two and she had been too enchanted by her meanderings to take the time for lunch, it was extra scrumptious. "Delicious," she pronounced to the rabbi, who was watching her expectantly.

"My wife will be proud to hear you liked it."

"She sounds like my aunts in New York. They all take such pride in their cooking." Dominique laughed.

"*Oui*. It is a mitzvah"—a good work—"to eat a tasty meal and thank God for it. In the past, if a Jewish family was lucky enough to escape a pogrom—the wholesale slaughter of their village—the next challenge was to be able to eat. To move up from surviving to enjoying food, that was a sign of prosperity. A way to say, 'See? We have overcome our hard times!' Of course, we can carry this too far now." He patted his belly and smiled. "I would do better to take a smaller piece of challah. Maybe tomorrow. For now, *bon appétit* and *B'tayavon*!"

The combination of French and Hebrew entreaties to enjoy her food brought a grin to Dominique's face.

"I am so pleased that you came to visit me once more when there are so many other things to do in Paris."

Dominique took a sip of the hot, sweet tea and put her cup back into the plain glass saucer. "Well, talking to you yesterday was one of the most fascinating parts of my trip."

"You poor child." The rabbi laughed. "If this is a high point, I am feeling sorry for you!"

Dominique laughed. Then she took a deep breath. "But I'm really not kidding, Rabbi," she said earnestly. "Something about being here yesterday, hearing you talk about the war, got all these feelings mixing around inside me. My family at home, they hate to talk about it. The Holocaust is a major taboo subject. But I feel like I want to know—like I've *got* to know more about it."

Rabbi Levi sat back in his chair. "I can't say I blame your family. Who wants to recall such terror—a time when to be born a Jew was to be marked for death?" he said quietly.

Dominique shook her head sadly. "I can't even imagine anything like it."

Rabbi Levi looked up at the stained-glass windows for a moment. When he spoke again, it was almost in a whisper.

"Even when it was happening all over Europe, it was still unimaginable. That millions should be put to death because they were Jewish."

Rabbi Levi bowed his head and ran a hand through his thinning gray-brown hair. "Yet even in such monstrous years, there were miracles. There were some who escaped death, because there were people who could not allow murderers to reign unchallenged. So many gentiles who could have looked the other way could not be so heartless—even at the expense of their own lives." The rabbi went to the old sink and refilled the teapot, then lit the stove.

"I told you how the priests kept me and many other Jewish children at their seminary? Father Edouard—he got us false Christian birth certificates and took us to church so the Nazis would not be suspicious. But he made sure we celebrated Shabbat in secret, so that we wouldn't lose the roots the Nazi beasts were trying to destroy.

"My wife was not so lucky as I. When she was a child, she was in the work camp of Birkenau. Malnutrition and disease were widespread in the filthy, inhuman conditions. If you showed signs of weakness or illness, you were put to death.

"My wife was getting so weak that everyone was ready to say kaddish for her. And then, a Polish Catholic woman, Karolina—a political prisoner who worked as a cook—took pity on her. She sneaked bread and scraps to my poor wife. A torn blanket and a pair of socks to keep her from dying of pneumonia or the gas chamber. Because of Karolina, my wife survived. The following week, the camp was liberated."

Tears filled Dominique's eyes, and she looked up to see the rabbi brushing away his own.

"In Israel we have now a memorial day to thank those wonderful people who saved Jewish lives. Yad Vashem, it is called. My wife and I went to Jerusalem on Yad Vashem last year where trees are planted on this special day. Each one bears the name of a gentile who saved one of us. We planted a tree in Karolina's name and in the name of Father Edouard. And that is why I am working to make a memorial of this place. For our beloved gentile heroes as well as for the Jews who were part of the Resistance."

Dominique looked down at her plate for a long time, too touched by what she had just heard to speak. When she found her voice, she said, "I really wish I could do something to help, Rabbi Levi. Maybe—maybe I could help with the painting."

Moved by Dominique's sincerity, the rabbi looked at her with a warm smile. "Tell me, Dominique, do you enjoy painting walls? This is something you have done before, *non?*"

"Not really," she said. "But I want to do *something.*"

The rabbi nodded. "Your heart is compassionate, Dominique. A quality rare and wonderful. Scholars of every faith"—Rabbi Levi rolled his eyes—"Jewish ones included, have spent lifetimes debating theory. Even within one religion people become divided by opinion. But the years of my life have taught me something. To be able to go inside *au fond du coeur*—in one's heart of hearts—and choose compassion, that is what it is to be formed in the image of God. Not the color of your skin or the services you attend. For me that is what you Americans call 'the line at the bottom,' *oui?*"

"The bottom line," Dominique said.

"*Oui!* The bottom line that separates us from the beasts." The rabbi clapped his hands. "So did you think, mademoiselle, you could visit a rabbi and avoid a sermon?"

Dominique laughed. "I'm not complaining!" She looked down at the challah crumbs in her plate.

"More?" the rabbi asked, offering her the challah dish.

"Not more to eat," Dominique said, biting her lip. "But more talk would be good."

The rabbi raised his eyebrows. "I am at your disposal. Does something trouble you, Dominique?"

"After talking about such serious things, my life doesn't seem so important, but—"

"*Pardon*—forgive me if I stop you," the rabbi said. "Your life is very important. There is something special for you to do. Or else you would not have been born."

"Do you really believe that?" Dominique asked, excited by his words.

"*Absolument!*" He slapped the table.

Dominique lifted her teacup and swirled the now cool liquid around. "My parents—they want me to learn to take over their business. I really don't want to." She shook her head emphatically. "I made this deal with my father that if I couldn't figure out what I wanted to do during this Paris trip, I'd go along with their plan. But I know there's something I want to do—something that would help people. I feel so tangled up inside because I can't figure out what it is."

"When we are young, we are impatient with the time it takes to discover. An egg cannot force itself to be a chicken overnight, *eh*? Do you know the word *bashert*?"

"Destiny?" Dominique asked. "What's meant to happen?"

"*You* were meant to happen, Dominique. Or you wouldn't exist. You have choices, *oui*? But

154

someday you will learn that your *bashert* is also looking for you. Something suited to your natural abilities. Though your offer to help me with this painting was very nice, I am thinking you have a different *mitzvah*, a different good work, to perform."

Dominique sighed. "I wish I had some clues as to what it was. My dad says I should look for 'what makes my heart sing.'"

"A very smart man."

"Actually, he didn't say it. His *bubbe* Sadie did."

"A smart *bubbe* Sadie, then. Still, a smart papa for remembering. And for passing it along."

Dominique laughed.

"I would like to say one more thing. What makes your heart sing will also make God and the world sing."

"Tell that to my mother," Dominique said, rolling her eyes.

Rabbi Levi reached for the challah plate. "My last piece." Dominique grinned. The man took such delight in life. From sharing bread, to helping wayward teenagers, to making silly jokes. In his presence, it was hard not to feel that things would work out.

"I had some time—" a voice called from the doorway.

Dominique looked up to see it was Julian. They stared at each other in wordless surprise.

Rabbi Levi greeted his visitor with a bear hug.

"Two young volunteers, but I cannot accept either offer. I must prepare for a ceremony this week. We are honoring Resistance heroes in the countryside."

Dominique's face flushed in the heat of Julian's puzzled stare. She rose. "Rabbi Levi won't accept my help and—and I was just leaving."

"I enjoyed so much our talk," Rabbi Levi said. "Now where are you off to?"

"I don't feel like fighting the crowds at the museums any more today, so I was thinking of going by the Galerie Cinque."

"On quai Voltaire. They're having a poster exhibit, *non*? They have some fine Toulouse-Lautrec and some of Ibels and Chéret, too, I think," Julian said.

He looked at her with such intensity that Dominique averted her gaze. "I didn't know you were such an art lover."

"It was forced on me. My grandfather would carry me to museums when I was small. I'll find you a cab," he offered.

"Thanks. But I planned to walk there," Dominique said. He was being so sweet again. But of course, they were in the enchanted presence of Rabbi Levi.

"I think you should have a walk there yourself, Julian," the rabbi put in. "It would be good for you to have a change. To see something other than a medical book or a construction site, *non*?"

The thought of strolling around Paris with this Julian was appealing. But what if the minute they left the church, he switched into his Missing

Link mode? She tried to read his expression as he looked from her to Rabbi Levi. He appeared to be struggling with the prospect himself.

Then they both began to babble at the same time. "You probably have lots of other things to do," Dominique said, just as Julian said, "Of course, if you prefer to be alone—"

After they stopped laughing, Julian began again. "Would you mind some company?"

*What's the worst that could happen?* she thought. *If he goes into one of his evil moods, I'll give it right back to him.*

Besides, it was important to give Julian the benefit of the doubt, for Lizette's sake. And one thing about Julian—there was no need to play Dial-a-Smile with him. "That might be nice," Dominique replied.

They said their good-byes to Rabbi Levi and walked down the garden path. "Be careful, Dominique." Julian turned to help her over a loose step. *"C'est dangereux."*

*Yes,* Dominique thought, wondering why she felt a warm tingle flow through her as she looked again into the sparkling dark eyes. *C'est dangereux.*

"*La Trappistine!*" Dominique exclaimed as she walked across the highly polished wooden floor of Galerie Cinque. She gazed in delight at the picture of the aloof beauty holding a bouquet in one hand, while the other rested on a bowed glass bottle.

Julian studied the picture intently, than looked back at Dominique, comparing images. "There is something familiar to me about her. Where have I seen such red hair before?" he teased.

"Very funny," Dominique said, rolling her eyes. It was strangely satisfying to see him be so playful, without his usual edge. She craned to read the signature in the corner of the work. "Mucha," she said aloud. "Was he the one who did all the posters for the actress Sarah Bernhardt?"

Julian nodded. "That's what made him. The first one he did made everyone think—what do they say in Hollywood?—that he'd never work in this town again. But he did all of her show posters after that—*Hamlet, Médée . . .*"

"There's one of Sarah Bernhardt he did for *Gismonda*," Dominique said, delighting at the sight of the velvety rich texture of the blue, red, and gold of the strikingly beautiful poster. "Almost like mosaic."

"This was the start of art nouveau," Julian said. "Much of the technique came from Japanese color woodcuts. A lot of people looked down on illustration as being frivolous. But they were arrogant know-nothing jerks," he said bluntly.

"Don't sugarcoat it, Julian," Dominique said with a sardonic smile. "Tell it like it is!" It was kind of sweet, she thought, to see this athletic-looking guy all fired up on behalf of the art nouveau movement.

"Was I sounding too crabbby?" Julian said,

the twinkle back in his eye as he looked at Dominique.

"*Un peu,*" Dominique answered. "A little bit." She opened her arms in a wide gesture that contradicted her words.

"Sorry." Julian laughed. "It's just that commercial art gets criticized so much, and people forget that a lot of masterworks—even the Sistine Chapel—were commercial projects."

"I never thought of that," Dominique said. *So maybe the Rappaport gallery will have a place in history, after all,* she said to herself with a smile.

"Art nouveau was a revolutionary form. Van Gogh came right out and said how the artists of the movement inspired him. Edouard Manet, too. And Émile Zola was a great collector. They were open. And honest enough to appreciate the genius without checking to see if it was okay with some stodgy old gouty critic with poor digestion."

"Don't say another word. I don't want to forget that! A stodgy old gouty—" She broke off, the perplexed look on his face making her too giddy to finish. Who knew Julian could be so much fun?

Julian raised an eyebrow and said in mock impatience: "Would you like me to get you a pencil and paper, Dominique, so you can write it down?"

Dominique laughed so hard, she began to cough and Julian started to pat her on the back. A middle-aged couple walking around the gallery glanced at the scene, and exchanged annoyed looks.

"Whoops!" Dominique whispered into Julian's ear. "A couple of stodgy old gouty digesting critics!"

As they hurried out of the gallery, trying to feign a sense of decorum, Dominique and Julian exchanged wicked smiles.

All the day, as they toured the galleries of the Rive Gauche, she kept being surprised at how glad she was to be with him, how easy yet alive she felt in his presence.

"Not fair," Dominique groused as the guards in the Samuels gallery advised them that seven o'clock was closing time.

"Maybe we should protest," Julian said. "Chain ourselves to that bronze sculpture of Mercury and refuse to leave."

Dominique held her wrists up to Julian. He reached out and pretended to handcuff her. His touch was surprisingly gentle. As they left the gallery, Dominique found herself thinking how quickly and happily the day had slipped away in his presence. *What a shame he can't be like this all the time. But Julian's moods are none of my business.* He was Lizette's problem. And that was that.

# CHAPTER TEN

"This place looks like the flower market on the place de la Madeleine!" Sara gasped when she came out of the shower and saw all the roses Pierre had sent to Dominique. In each bouquet there was an apologetic note.

"I want things to be different between us, but I do not know how to go about it," one read. *"De plus en plus"*—more and more—"as I think about it, I feel worse and worse." Another: "I would not forgive myself if you left Paris with such bad feelings that I have caused."

"I think you ought to give him a second chance," Sara said, closing her eyes and smiling as she leaned over to enjoy the beautiful scent.

Dominique sat back on her bed and pulled her knees to her chest. It certainly seemed as if Pierre was trying his best to make up for the other night's drunken pass.

"He just seems so *humble* and sincere, Nik."

He had phoned from downstairs the night

before; he really did seem so troubled by what had happened and so earnest in his desire to be able to find a way to make it up to her.

"To err," he had said, "it is human—they tell us. To forgive, it is divine."

"It's behind us, Pierre," Dominique said into the phone.

"But what good is it, if you will not let me take you places?"

When she hesitated, Pierre said, "Do not answer me at this moment, Dominique. Spend a while in thinking. Tomorrow I shall call to ask if I can escort you to the château of the Comte de Dragoni. Until then I shall at least remain with my hopes!"

Back in New York Kaitlin and Sara were always saying that she had impossible standards when it came to guys, that no one could ever measure up to her ideal fantasy. *Ms. Critic,* she thought as she took one of the roses from the marble night table beside her and stared into the soft satiny layers of pink petals. People weren't just one way or another. That was her mother's way, to put labels on people, keep them in "good" or "bad" boxes and never give them a chance to be different.

Yesterday, for instance, Julian had turned out to be a really great guy. Maybe one very off night with Pierre—whom she had had on a bit of a pedestal since childhood—was not a very realistic way to form an opinion. To throw away their whole chance for something special because of one stupid offense. And it would be awful to leave Paris with such awkwardness between them. A party in the country, surrounded by lots of other people, would be a perfect way to smooth things over.

There was a knock on their door. "Mlle. Dominique, Pierre is on the telephone," Mme. Renault announced.

Sara picked up her violin and tucked it under her chin. "You have two choices. Either stay here and listen to me practice or take Pierre's call," she joked. Then she added in a more serious voice, "Aw, give the guy another chance, Nik."

"I'm not sure I should be taking dating tips from someone whose neck is covered with vampire bites!" Dominique said as she went to the phone.

The Dragoni estate was too splendid a setting for anything but feeling happy. A sprawling mansion set on a rolling hillside of lush greenery with the majestic purple mountains rising in the sky all around them. A whole day of partying. Tennis. Swimming. Riding! *What could be bad?*

"Dominique," Pierre said, as they headed toward the tennis court for a noon game. "Forgive?"

"Forgive," she said.

Pierre looked at her with a hopeful smile. *"Vraiment? Really?"*

*"Absolument!"* Dominique said, taking hold of the hand he extended her.

He threaded his fingers through hers and she smiled. It was nice to be with him when he was like this. Charming and sober!

"I'm glad I got to see these glorious hills this trip," she said.

"This quiet country is much too monotonous," Pierre replied. "As for me, I prefer the action of Cannes or Monte Carlo. I prefer the nightlife. This place is a bore."

Dominique squelched her annoyance at Pierre's snobby tone. *I'm here to have fun, not to pass judgment.*

"Tell you what," she said, skipping ahead on the gravel path toward the court. "Since you love to gamble, we'll bet a million francs on our tennis game. I'll try not to beat you *too* badly."

"Hah!" Pierre laughed. "You are joking, *chérie!*"

"Joking? Not a chance," Dominique called, running the rest of the way to the court. "You better have your checkbook with you, Pierre. I don't take American Express."

Pierre laughed, tossing the ball in the air. "It is not my habit to lose—especially to a girl."

"Now you're really in for it," Dominique called. She twirled the racket in her hand.

After a few volleys, Pierre was complimentary. "Your game has improved very much." But as the points began to pile up in Dominique's favor, a scowl replaced Pierre's smile. "This is boring," he muttered, tossing his racket on the ground. He wrapped his towel around his neck and started up the hill.

*He's not* really *going to go into a snit because I was winning?* Dominique thought. "I thought we were going riding!" she called. Maybe a ride would smooth things over.

"I am going to the château. You are coming?"

Annoyed at his testy attitude, Dominique stood her ground. "Are you upset because a girl isn't *supposed* to win?"

He refused to meet her gaze. "Ridiculous! My arm has been hurting and I do not feel like tennis or riding. I am feeling parched. I need a drink. Well?"

Dominique wondered if she should go back to the mansion with him. Then she decided a little time away was probably the best thing to help them both cool off.

"No, thanks. I think I'll take a walk." She wasn't going to let a tiff ruin this lovely day. There were wonderful landscapes to see along the river, and her sketch pad was in her tennis bag.

"Suit yourself," Pierre called, displeased with her choice. Near the edge of a wooded cliff, Dominique sat on the stump of a tree. When she opened her sketch pad, she saw a sketch of Julian she'd made after their day on the rive Gauche, and she smiled. Nice to know he wasn't such a bad guy after all. Then she turned toward the rolling hills and began to sketch.

\*　　\*　　\*

"Dominique!" Lizette waved from a chair beside the pool.

"Lizzie! Sara!" Dominique hurried down the hill, her sketch pad back in her pack. "What have you little angels been up to?"

Sara raised her iced-tea glass in Dominique's direction. "Gossip! Gossip! Gossip!" she said with a phony wink.

"Much as you hate it!" Dominique took a chair beside them.

Sara poked Lizette in the arm. "Tell her, Lizzie."

Lizette peered over the tops of her sunglasses and giggled. "You are so funny, Sara. You tell her."

Sara leaned forward. In a loud, dramatic whisper, she said, "Victor asked if he could visit me in New York this summer."

"My, my. You don't say!" Dominique folded her hands in front of her. It would be nice if she felt as good toward Pierre at the moment as Sara felt about Victor.

"And," Sara continued with a wink at Lizette, "Lizzie and Julian got pretty cozy after everyone was in bed last night."

Lizette added coyl,. *Je n'ai pas dormi toute la nuit!*" Batting her eyelashes: "I didn't sleep a wink!"

Dominique felt her heart stop for a moment. She was glad the sunglasses hid the shock in her eyes. Why was she so upset? she asked herself. Because they just seemed so very mismatched? But who was she to be deciding who was right for whom? *You're just jealous because Sara and Lizette are both having hot little romances. And you're trying not to bop Pierre with a tennis racket.*

"We were having a celebration. Julian just learned he was accepted into the finest intern program in a New York hospital. I can visit both of you in New York, *non?*" Lizette beamed.

Dominique took a long sip of Sara's tea, trying not to reveal the envy she felt. Why dump it on them? Was it their fault things weren't going as well for her? Maybe she should go back up to the château to see how Pierre was doing. Not let something as stupid as a tennis game mess things up again.

They heard noisy chatter as the people from the party were coming down the hill toward them. The same chic crowd that had been at Le Pirate. Laure, a young woman in a string bikini, waved a newspaper. She shouted something to Lizette in French.

"What's she saying?" Sara asked Dominique.

"She says there's something spicy in the 'Exposé' column."

*"Ooh-la-la!"* Laure whooped, tossing Lizette the paper.

Sara leaned forward to look over Lizette's shoulder. "A gossip sheet! Translate it for me, Lizette." Then Sara, looking shocked, sat back in her chair.

Lizette cursed in French. Then she glanced

miserably at Dominique. "Nasty snipes!" She began shredding the paper.

Laure grabbed it away. "I have not finished it yet!"

"May I see?" Dominique held out her hand to Laure. "It seems everybody else has."

Lizette shot Laure a look of rage. Clearly, she wanted to protect Dominique from whatever was in the paper.

But the paper was already in Dominique's hand.

She looked over the pictures with a shrug. Then she spotted the source of the excitement: a series of candid shots of Pierre. In passionate poses with a variety of young women.

"*Caught again!*" said one caption. "*And again! . . . and again!*" said the others. Underneath there was a blurb: "Does Marie know about Claude? Does Hélène know about Aimée?"

Suddenly Dominique realized that everyone was gawking, waiting for her reaction. She struggled to keep her face blank. Then, giving the paper to Laure, she dialed up her most radiant smile. "No wonder that poor boy has no energy for a decent game of tennis!"

Instantly, the mood changed. The crowd exploded into laughter. Sara and Lizette exchanged looks of relief.

"No doubt about it, Nik," Sara said with a grin, "you're the master."

"So it has been decreed, observant one!"

Dominique replied. Again she appreciated her gallery training, appreciated all the phony affairs at which she had learned not to let anything shake her cool.

Dominique stood and headed up the hill. "Truffles, anyone? I hear they've got a large stash at the château."

Blaring music engulfed them as the three girls neared the house. The earth around them pounded with the rhythm.

"Having fun, ladies?" Victor called from the patio.

"Poor Victor. You have been so busy hosting!" Sara said.

"How about a swim?" he asked.

"Love to," said Sara. She turned to the others.

"You go ahead," Dominique said. "I wasn't kidding about finding those truffles." She looked over at the long buffet table piled with exotic treats. "How about you, Lizzie?"

Lizette shook her head. "I am still so angry at those rag papers. They put pictures from many years together so it looks like they are recent. They always make a stupid joke of us!"

Dominique felt a dose of relief as Lizette's words sank in. They had put a bunch of *old* pictures together. She knew Pierre was a flirt, but he wasn't as bad as the gossip columns made him look. Why was she so quick to believe bad things about him—even when the evidence was from a shoddy tabloid?

"I'm sorry those dumb gossips are on your

case," she said sympathetically. "I guess you just have to learn to ignore them."

"I try, Dominique." Lizette's red bee-stung lips quivered.

Dominique wished there was some way she could cheer her up and put the hurtful business to rest. She clapped her hand. "How about going for a ride? 'Daisy and Maisy Hit the Trail'!"

"You will not be angry if I say no? I think I would like to find Julian."

"Of course not," Dominique said with a sigh. She hoped Julian would be able to cheer Lizette up.

Dominique took a plate from the buffet and took a bit of grilled tuna and endive salad. She carried it over to the deck to see if Pierre was dancing there with the others. It would be nice to give the day a fresh start. But she didn't see him.

She remembered Sara mentioning that Victor's parents were art collectors. Brightening, she put down her plate and went through the patio door to the study. *Beautiful!* Dominique thought as she looked around. The massive nineteenth-century oak furniture went so well with the bronze sculptures grouped around the room.

Chagall! Dominique smiled as she moved to the picture over the mantel. A study of his ceiling design for the opéra. Then a work beside the window caught her eye. A Jewish family gathered in prayer. A special occasion, probably Shabbat.

A male voice startled her. "Intriguing, isn't it?"

She turned to see Julian on an antique fan chair.

"Julian!" she said with a laugh. He looked so strangely modern in the quaint setting. Khaki pants and a pencil behind his ear. His medical book in his hand. "Lizette was looking for you out on the patio."

"Really?"

Dominique found him so uninterested in the message that she was sorry again for Lizette. She turned toward the picture.

He came toward her. "I see you like Morozowsky's work."

"It's a fine painting."

"Most of the Jewish art in France was destroyed in the occupation. Collectors like the Dragonis hid what they could. But it's sad so much was lost."

A wave of sorrow came over Dominique. But as tragic as those times were, whenever she learned something new she felt a deeper sense of her Jewish identity. Each discovery—painful as it was—fueled her with a tangible essence of dignity, with a reverence for life and her precious roots. And an even stronger yearning to do something good in the world—to help make life better for other people.

Dominique said softly, "You mentioned your grandfather was an artist. Was his work destroyed during the war?"

"In a way," Julian said quietly. "During the

war the Resistance became his whole life. Later on, whatever he did was for his private satisfaction. Or to amuse me."

"I'd like to see some of his work," Dominique said.

Julian's face softened into a smile. "Ah, *oui*! I remember you like to keep your sketches from the world, too."

Dominique laughed, feeling a strange flutter in her chest as she saw the light in Julian's eyes. "But . . ." Julian hesitated. "I will be a good sport, as you say in America, and let you see his work sometime."

Lizette's voice from the doorway cut into their talk. "There you are!" She moved toward Julian, gyrating her hips suggestively. "*Bonjour,* handsome! Welcome to the Folies-Bergères!"

Dominique took a deep breath and wondered if Lizette had had too much of the champagne that was flowing like water today. "Lizette, maybe you need some fresh air?" she asked.

"That is not all I need! *Oui,* Julian?" She winked at him.

Dominique felt the color rise in her cheeks. As she got a closer look, it was clear that Lizette was not drunk, just using the party mood as an excuse for some outrageous behavior.

"You know, Julian," Lizette said, putting her right leg seductively on the arm of the chair and swaying back and forth, "they have a Jacuzzi downstairs. It is very nice to go into the hot tub together. And it is very, very private. We shall have a very good time, *oui?* I do not think you have ever seen my tattoo in the daylight!" she said, bursting into hysterics.

There was no mistaking the intimacy of Lizette's words, Dominique thought, shocked and dismayed at her friend's display.

"Join us for a walk?" Julian said, turning to Dominique and looking embarrassed as Lizette draped herself around him.

"I'll pass," Dominique said.

She felt relieved as Julian led Lizette through the door. Good! The last thing she wanted was to witness their amorous antics. Poor Lizette! Throwing herself around like that. And Julian! How could he be so detached and indifferent while his girlfriend made such an obvious fool of herself?

"There's another Morozowsky in the room at the foot of the stairs," Julian called. "You'll really love it."

"And you, Julian," Lizette whooped, "will love what you see!"

*Ugh!* Dominique thought with a shiver. *But their weird little affair is none of my concern. At least Pierre—even with his moody moments—isn't detached and remote like Julian.* She'd hate to date anyone who treated her like Julian treated Lizette. So Pierre wasn't a dream prince. He was only human—which was more than Julian seemed sometimes.

# CHAPTER ELEVEN

Dominique strode toward the room at the end of the staircase. The door was slightly ajar. She pushed it—and as her eyes swept the room she felt her insides reel. Pierre and a young woman were dancing to some off-key music of their own. Pierre looked startled, then sheepish as his partner bristled. *"J'en ai marre!"* she muttered, storming away.

Pierre ignored her and winked at Dominique, trying to look like a little boy caught—again—in a bit of silly mischief.

"I'm pretty fed up, too," Dominique said, annoyed at Pierre, and at herself for being taken in by his apologetic act.

"Jealous, *chérie?* Ah, but the girl, she means nothing." He tried to snap his fingers, but was too drunk to pull it off.

"Jealous? No. Disappointed? Yes. But I'll get over it!"

Pierre ignored the brusqueness of her tone and grabbed her hand. "Such a naïve, sheltered little Jewish girl from America."

She fumed. "And *you're* a sophisticated Frenchman?"

He tried to cut her off with a kiss. But she turned, and his kiss landed on the door. It was such a ridiculous sight that Dominique laughed in spite of herself. Thinking her anger had passed, he moved in again. "You're drunk, Pierre," Dominique stated simply. A fact, like the height of the Eiffel Tower.

"I have had but a few drinks."

"However many it was, it was too many."

"You are saying I cannot hold my liquor?" He took her arm.

"Bingo!" said Dominique. "Now let go of me."

"You know what your trouble is, *chérie*?"

"At the moment, you're my trouble, Pierre."

"You need to have a drink. To loosen up."

*Pathetic!* Dominique thought as he staggered toward the bar.

"You do not understand. I am a Frenchman and—" He added a flourish, trying to look cool, and fell on a hassock.

When he began to make retching noises, Dominique grew alarmed. "I am fine," he insisted as she helped him to the bathroom. But as soon as they got inside, he began to throw up.

*"Je voudrais être mort!"* Pierre moaned.

*Wish you were dead?* Dominique thought as she steadied him. *But what would France do without such a champion to represent her?*

Thankfully, a valet had heard Pierre being sick and rushed into the room. "Do not worry," he told Dominique, "I'll take care of it."

*"Merci!"* Dominique said, unable to prop Pierre up any longer.

"I assure you, I did not mean to do it, " Pierre cried weakly.

Ignoring him, Dominique asked the valet, "Is he all right?"

"He'll live!" the man said, assuring Dominique that she could leave. Dejected, angry, and frustrated, she headed outside.

For a while she leaned against a giant willow, watching the people on the deck dance to the music echoing through the hills. Then Sara called out, inviting her to join them for coffee on the patio. But Dominique shook her head and took off down the hill. She needed to be alone—away from all the people and noise—to make sense of the jumble of emotions churning inside her.

This was turning into one of those muddled foreign movies—from Pierre acting like a jerk at tennis, to Lizette carrying on with Julian, to Pierre doing his playboy number in the room under the stairs. *I'm not about to hang around acting like a wronged woman,* Dominique thought. There had to be something she could do to change this down mood. Dominique Rappaport, strong, independent, lover of life and of art and of . . . and of . . . horseback riding! Yes! The stables. Where were they? Across from the vineyards. Near the waterfall. That's what Victor had told them that morning.

\*　　\*　　\*

Ambroise, the elderly stable hand, tried to talk Dominique out of riding alone. "A young man will be coming to take out a horse at four. Only a half hour from now. Why not wait?"

"I'll be fine," Dominique said, eager to be galloping through the emerald hills alone. No better way to shed this gloom.

As Ambroise saddled up the horse he said, "Valentin is a good fellow, but he can be spirited." He grinned at her. "Like the mademoiselle, eh? You must always show him who is the boss."

"*Merci,*" Dominique said, mounting the dappled horse and giving him a pat. Valentin raised his head and whinnied.

"*Bien! Bien!* I think he understands." Ambroise laughed, taking off his cap to scratch his gray head. "Still, it would be good to wait for the young man. These hills can be tricky."

Dominique tugged on the reins, turning the horse in the direction of the trail. "I'll be fine."

Cantering along, surrounded by moss-carpeted woods and bright patches of wildflowers, Dominique filled her lungs with country air. What did her yoga teacher at Allwyn used to say? Breathe in the good, breathe out the bad! But as she inhaled, she was overcome by a well of melancholy she was not prepared for.

"Well, well, Valentin. What have we here?" Dominique said with a sad smile. "If you can keep a secret, I'll make a startling confession.

178

This whole Pierre mess? I think it's hit me harder than I thought. Ever since I was little, Pierre has been there, playing peekaboo from some corner of my mind. When I'd dump some guy I was dating—like Josh 'Octopus Hands' Savitsky—I was never *really* bummed out. Because I always wanted to believe that someday Pierre and I would end up together. *Bashert,* as Rabbi Levi says.

"All that clucking our mothers have done over us? Whatever else I pretended, it was a kind of glue to keep the fantasy in place. Think I'm a dope, Valentin? Stamp once for yes, twice for no." Dominique tried to fight the sense of loss that was moving into the place where the romantic dream once lived.

For a moment the horse and rider stopped to survey the rushing river cascading over the rocks. Then they moved on. "I feel like a dope, even if you're too polite to answer. I mean, any illusions I had about Pierre were blown right out of the water when he got so damn pushy. But I made myself believe I was just being unforgiving. For future reference, Val, there's a difference between being obsessed with flaws and ignoring major problems. Blinders are for your species, old buddy, not mine."

And then, of course, there were Mama and Odette. Dominique had even gotten wind of their plan for an eventual partnership between the Paris and New York galleries. *Yikes.* Too heavy. Too complicated. Too unfair to have to deal with all at once. Dominique shuddered. She undid her barrette and let her hair swing loose. She bent to murmur into the horse's ear. "We'll be like Scarlett O'Hara and think about that stuff tomorrow. For now, let's have fun!"

Picking up speed, Dominique felt a thrill as they galloped beyond the plateaus cloaked in vineyards. The aroma of thyme and lavender growing wild along the path was delicious. A joyous sense of freedom flooded through her as the amber light of late afternoon danced over the ancient castles dotting the mountainside. For now, all that counted was the splendor around her, the wind, and the ground beneath Valentin's hooves. Nothing was going to bring her down!

After riding for an hour or two, Dominique realized that the sun was very low in the sky. Time to start back. She stopped at a huge outcropping of rock and looked around. In the fading light, she felt disoriented. Then she heard the sound of rushing water and headed toward it. Of course! She would follow along the water's edge back to the falls. From there she would be home free.

After following the river for a while, she came to a place where it branched. She pulled on the reins and looked around. Damn! Nothing was familiar. She should have paid more attention. She tried to stay hopeful, but anxiety was moving in as quickly as the darkness swallowing the land around them. "You'll get us back, right, Val? Stamp once for yes."

The wind rushing through the trees grew more fierce; Dominique wasn't sure whether she was imagining that roll of thunder. Should have listened to Ambroise and waited for the other rider. *This is what I get for being so stubborn!*

"Did I tell you, Valentin?" Dominique said as she guided him toward a fork where she thought she discerned fresh hoofprints. "Some people think I'm stubborn." Hoping the sound of her voice would reassure them both, she went on. "They say I'm like Grandmère Mimi. An outrageous character, they tell me."

As Valentin trotted up the winding path, Dominique felt the rain begin. "I've got to see my grandmother again," she said as earnestly as a prayer. "Last time I was too young to really get to know her."

A thunderbolt lit the mountains, rocking the earth as the skies opened up. Valentin reared and whinnied with fright, almost throwing Dominique from her saddle. All at once, the horse charged forward, ignoring the pressure of the reins.

"Valentin!" Dominique cried out. "Whoa! Valentin!"

But he was too out of control to obey her command, too terrified by nature's show of power. The reins went flying from Dominique's hands. She gripped his neck as tightly as she could.

As Valentin raced through the forest,

Dominique's face was scratched on a branch. She crouched lower against his neck to avoid the next obstacle in their path. Faster and faster Valentin sped, his hooves losing traction in the mud, his knees almost buckling as he ran. Every muscle ached from Dominique's effort to hold on. He reared again, and the abrupt movement almost jarred her loose. Through the din of the storm the rushing waterfall was getting nearer. If she lost her grip when he reared—as he seemed about to do again—Valentin might crush her. Or would he, in the next fraction of a second, head straight for the falls? Either way was certain death.

Behind her, she thought she heard the rumbling thunder. She clutched for the reins with one hand as the torrential downpour threatened to loosen her grip on Valentin's slippery neck. But this time it wasn't thunder.

"Hang on, Dominique. Just hang on!" Julian called out as his horse gained on Valentin. When he got close enough, he called to her, "Try to grab the reins!"

"It's no use!" Dominique cried. "I can't reach!"

In the next moment, Julian was beside her, clutching her tightly with one arm around her waist. A single second before Valentin reared, Julian had lifted her from his back. As the horse's front hooves hit the ground, the animal stumbled and toppled onto his side. His fall might well have killed

Dominique were she not safely in Julian's arms.

Julian clutched the trembling Dominique as they rode, trailing the spooked but unharmed Valentin. When they reached an ancient chapel near the clearing, he lifted her from his horse and carried her toward it. Once inside the partial shelter of the crumbling stone ruin, Julian kept her in his arms.

The gale whipped rent boughs in angry spasms on the floor of the decaying relic. Julian carried Dominique to a windowless corner beyond the wind's reach. As they searched each other's eyes and touched each other's faces, an electrified charge passed between them, so powerful it amazed them both. All at once they understood their profound connection. As he brought his lips to hers, flesh confirmed what spirit knew. They were helpless against an inner commandment they both heard.

They held on to each other as they slid to the primitive foundation. "Dominique," Julian murmured as he kissed her forehead, her eyelids and her soft sweet mouth. How useless it had been to think he could have countered this pull that transcended reason. One his soul told him they shared.

"It is okay to cry, Dominique," he whispered. "Nothing can hurt you. I've got you now."

*    *    *

Dominique was as touched by the love in Julian's face as she was by all she felt for him. *Home safe at last*, she thought as she leaned against his sturdy chest and gratefully surveyed what was left of the weathered gray sanctuary. Vines covered its surfaces, and weeds sprouted through the cracks in the floor. The severity of her near tragedy became overwhelming and the tears that had been pent up through the ordeal and all the distress of the day's trauma erupted at last.

"Julian!" she cried. "Thank God for you, Julian!"

"Thank God and Rabbi Levi!" he said. "To keep me off the streets in summer, he arranged a job as a stable hand on the other side of that forest." Julian looked down at her, stroking her hair. His dark eyes engulfed her with their marvelous warmth. "Do not tell Rabbi Levi, but I found some young hoodlums to pass my time with. When the owners were away, we sneaked off with the horses. We would play like cowboys in old American movies. I was crazy for them. Now I find I'm crazy for many wonders from America."

The gentle pressure of Julian's hand on her back felt as if it belonged there. She just felt so peaceful beside him. "You weren't so crazy about me when we met!"

"I admit I did not think much of you at first."

"Oh no?" she teased.

"I suspect you didn't like me very much either."

"I thought you were—ugh!" She groaned.

"How bad?"

"Not quite human!" She faced him to catch his expression.

"Did you think I was an ape?" Julian said, his eyebrows raised.

She held her hand out and flipped it from side to side. "Somewhere in the middle."

Julian's laughter was a delightful roar.

"But what did I do to make you hate me so quickly?"

He pulled her to him. "You were too splendid to be real."

"You didn't like my looks?" *That's a switch,* she thought.

"To look like you—one of Pierre's beautiful girls—and not be superficial? Impossible."

He took her chin in his hand and looked at her as if recording every inch of her face. She felt a longing to stay just as they were forever. A voice began to call to her from somewhere inside her head—something about Lizette. But the chatter was vetoed by the exquisite feeling of his mouth on hers.

It was a long time before the sounds of the rain had softened into a tapping on the foliage that rustled faintly around them. On the ground there was an artful display of swirling patterns, made by the full moon on the swaying trees outside. Then the crunch of twigs under a car's wheels startled Dominique and Julian in their sanctuary.

"They're up ahead," someone shouted. "I see a horse."

Dominique and Julian stood and moved toward the decomposing threshold to look out at the intruders.

"Dominique! Am I ever glad to see you, girl!" Sara shouted as Victor's Jeep screeched to a halt. "We were so worried!"

Lizette jumped from the Jeep and ran toward them. She hugged Dominique; then she wrapped her arms around Julian's neck. Dominique's heart sank. *Too late! It's too late for Julian and me. It's Julian and Lizette, and that's that.*

"Okay, Nik?" Sara took her arm. "You look so out of it."

"I'll be fine." Dominique shook her head as if waking from a dream. "I *am* fine," she told Sara, walking toward the Jeep. While Lizette clung to Julian, Dominique inhaled deeply and tried to smile at the others. Julian and Lizette. How could she have forgotten? Damn! Nothing like a little near-death experience to give a girl total amnesia.

# CHAPTER TWELVE

"Merci, Mme. Renault," Julian told the Du Lacs' housekeeper as he put down the phone. Why hadn't Dominique returned his calls? "Damn!" he muttered, banging his hand hard against his secondhand desk. Julian Adler was no schoolboy infatuated with some young beauty. His life was dedicated to a career in medicine, and he hadn't been interested in spending his energies on a woman—though there had been plenty of chances to do so— until Dominique. Something magical had beamed from those brilliant green eyes, confirming that this was no ordinary moment in either of their lives.

So why had she pulled back so abruptly? If he didn't have to drive to the country to pick up his grandfather's records for Rabbi Levi's Resistance memorial, he would go to the Du Lacs' and just wait for her. Make her tell him these feelings his whole being knew to be true were only a mirage.

\*     \*     \*

In the noon light streaming through the glamorous Deux Magots café, Dominique and Sara wrote some postcards home. "To Kait and Zach," Sara said, looking up. "'Bought a trendy Jourdan outfit that cost as much as a year at the conservatory.'" She stopped reading and asked, "How do you spell the name of the museum we went to this morning?"

"Marmottan. It's on the front of the card, genius," Dominique said as she tucked her cards and pen back into her bag.

"Right! I am *such* a genius!" She laughed and continued reading. "'As for the early Picasso work at the Musée de l'Art Moderne, my little brother does better collages! But Niki says, "Cubism was part of Pablo's artistic evolution." So la-di-da!'"

Sara leaned across their tiny round white table to peek at the golden fruit tarts topped with cream that the waiter was carrying to an Italian family near them. "And keep your bogus eclairs, Manhattan. Gay Paree has the stuff of dreams!"

Dominique smiled and peered through the café's glass front at the busy street. "Let's go over to the Delacroix Museum now."

"I know you told me this morning, but I forgot," Sara said, her brow wrinkling. "What's his claim to fame?"

"He was one of the Romantic school, but his range was amazing." Dominique's oval face beamed reverence. "He did that *Dante and Vir-*

*gil in Hell.* Nobody in his time—except maybe Géricault—used color so dramatically."

"You do know your stuff when it comes to art," Sara said.

Dominique shrugged. "Well, I do love it. Like you feel about your music." Though Dominique teased Sara about her commitment to practicing every day no matter what, she truly respected it and envied her friend's steadfast direction.

"Any closer to figuring things out, Nik?"

Dominique shook her head and sighed deeply.

"What are you going to do about school in the fall?" Sara asked with genuine concern. "Or should I shut up?"

"I will not panic," Dominique chanted, closing her eyes. As they paid the bill, she said, "Rabbi Levi says we all have a unique purpose or we wouldn't exist. That our destiny, our *bashert*, is looking for us as hard as we're looking for it."

"Coolest thing I've ever heard a rabbi say." Then Sara looked confused. "So we just hang out waiting for *bashert?*"

As they walked along the cobbled place St. Germain des Prés, Dominique shook her head. "No. He said we should try our best, but not to worry so much about how it's all going to turn out."

"I love it!" Sara smiled. "Now explain it to me again. What's the difference between Manet and Monet?"

"Manet has an *a*, Monet has an *o*," Dominique replied.

"Thanks for straightening it all out," Sara said archly.

"No problem," Dominique said with mock humility.

They stopped to see a tall mime performing in black clothes and white face near the Café de Floridor. He was pretending to ride the crowded Métro—the Paris subway—hanging on to an invisible strap and getting jostled by an invisible crush of bodies. Then Sara poked Dominique and nodded toward a couple locked in an embrace.

"Much as I hate to gossip," Sara whispered, "check out Fifi and Alphonse L'Amour!" These were the names they'd given the kissing lovers who adorned every block in Paris.

As the mime looked at the couple and feigned sobbing, Dominique had an uninvited reminder of how marvelous it had been to be so securely locked in Julian's arms. Well, whatever kind of warped game Julian Adler was playing, she wasn't going to fall for it. She had made that mistake already with Pierre—trying to ignore the obvious. But when it came to *amour*, Julian's character was even worse than Pierre's. Pierre was clearly a silly playboy. But Julian had the sport down to a science. First the brooding persona, then his pretense of such profound caring. All part of an Oscar-winner act to rack up points on his scorecard of romantic conquests. He even had one act for Lizette and another for her! How could he dare such a maneuver when he knew she and Lizette were friends? And how had he triggered such a powerful response in her that he almost got away with it? *I will not think about him a moment longer!* she commanded herself. *Let go, girl, and lighten up!*

Dominique averted her eyes. "Tell me when I can look."

"It's fine now. They've fallen into the Seine."

"That's a relief!" Dominique said as they walked on.

"Not to mention all they saved on a hotel bill!" Sara said impishly.

"Sara!" Dominique exclaimed in mock horror. "Hey! The Louvre is open late. We won't have to rush through it today!"

The Louvre Museum was home to the finest and most extensive art collection in all of Europe. A gorgeous palace that sprawled over three buildings, it had history dating back to the twelfth century. And it was the ultimate art lover's paradise.

"Sorry, Nik!" Sara wrinkled her nose apologetically. "Victor's taking me to Montmartre. Lizette said that Julian—"

As Sara chattered on, Dominique turned her head to see a new Fifi and Alphonse L'Amour arm in arm. The world was full of lovers. Fifi and Alphonse. Sara and Victor. Lizette and . . . Enough!

＊　　　＊　　　＊

The next morning Dominique flipped through her sketch pad before sticking it in her valise as she prepared to leave Paris to visit her grandmother. Strange that her drawing of Daumier's *Don Quixote,* which she'd seen on the rue de la Perle, the bust of Napoleon— even Van Gogh's self-portrait—all looked remarkably like Julian. Just as she was thinking about crumpling the bunch of them, she heard him greeting the housekeeper. Dominique tucked her pad into her bag and zipped it shut.

He entered the sitting room. "Dominique! There you are!" The glow in his eyes was so dangerously magnetic.

Dominique turned away and searched for anything she might not have packed. "Just getting set to leave," she said, trying to sound light.

"Without even saying good-bye?" In three steps he was at her side. He took hold of her arm. "What's wrong, Dominique?"

"Oh! I almost forgot my hairbrush," she said, ignoring him. He pulled her toward him. The feel of his mouth softly brushing hers was enough to send her reeling. As if a kiss could make the truth disappear in a swirl of delicious sensation. But the truth was that he was snaring Lizette with the same spell.

"Don't!" She hoped she sounded more definite than she felt.

Julian shook his head. "You are an absolute

puzzle. I tried so hard not to care about you. To believe you were one of those spoiled beauties of Pierre's set. But something kept drawing me to you. And that evening in the old chapel—"

"Yes, yes. At the old chapel"—Dominique's voice was rising with impatience and anger—"when I was scared out of my wits and my defenses were down and you handed me a phony pack of lies!"

"What are you saying?" Julian shouted. "What pack of lies? You shared my feelings, I know that!"

She was not going to listen to any more of his lines. Soon he'd be calling her unsophisticated just as Pierre had done. For these guys and their French male egos, sophistication meant jumping from one set of arms to another. Not for her. No way!

"Drop the act, okay? Go. I don't care if I never see you again." She turned so he couldn't see her tears. The apartment door opened, leting in the chatter of Lizette and Sara. Before they arrived in the sitting room, Dominique got out one final comment: "I just feel sorry for poor Lizette."

"What does she have to do with *us*?" Julian asked in a rage.

So he thought it was fine to be seeing Lizette and be moving in on her at the same time! "Lizette is your—"

Lizette broke in, smiling. "I heard my name, *non*?"

Dominique forced a smile. "I was saying that I'll miss you."

Lizette rushed to embrace her. "But I will visit New York. You will help me make sure Julian does not work too hard, *oui*?"

"I was just leaving," Julian said, storming from the room.

"Julian, wait!" Lizette cried, rushing after him.

Sara studied Dominique intently. "Are you okay?"

"Couldn't be better," Dominique answered, knowing that if she began to tell Sara everything that had happened she'd burst into uncontrollable tears. Instead she reached for her hairbrush and ran it through her heavy red tresses. "One, two, three . . ." she counted as she brushed. By the time she reached fifteen Julian Adler would be a fading memory, as far away as yesterday's dream.

# CHAPTER THIRTEEN

Ville de Fabian was less than two hours from Paris since they'd built the new highway. Dominique lay against the seat of the cab and sighed. Seeing Grandmère would be the best way to get out of this emotional whirlwind. Between Pierre and Julian, Paris seemed like a crash course in Foolish Romance 101. Well, this was one class she was not going to repeat.

Thank heaven she had left before Pierre could arrive with a fresh round of absurd apologies and expensive flowers. If her luck held, maybe she'd miss him when she returned for her luggage before going to the airport at the end of the week.

Sara was probably fast asleep on her New York–bound plane by now. She looked so tired when Dominique had dropped her at the airport this morning after her last night on the town with Victor. "Must be love!" Dominique had teased her. "That's the longest he's been out of that coffin in years."

She was glad she hadn't told Sara about her

and Julian. The only hitch was how Sara kept trying to give her "the latest dish," as she called the gossip, about Julian and Lizette. How Lizette said they would probably have a weekend in Deauville before Julian left for New York. Dominique rolled down the window and looked out at the rustic terrain. "Breathe in the good," she told herself. "Breathe out the bad. . . ."

"That's the house!" Dominique told the driver with a grin as he drove up the bumpy country road. Ville de Fabian at last!

Hard to believe that her own mother could ever have come from such modest surroundings, though it had been about three decades since she'd lived here. Dominique couldn't imagine Amanda Rappaport, Tiffany's finest jewels dangling from her neck, inside the small cottage.

Dominique bent to lift her bag, but the driver took it from her. "*Tiens,* I'll see to that," he told her.

Once they were up to the old wooden door, the driver thanked her for the bundle of francs, tipped his hat, and left.

Before Dominique had a chance to knock, the door flew open. A wrinkled woman squinted at her from behind thick glasses.

"Dominique?"

"*Oui,*" Dominique answered, with a tentative smile.

Her heart fell as the woman embraced her. Though Grandmère had been getting on, this woman had no hint of her radiant magic. Suddenly a spirited voice called from inside: "My Dominique!"

Dominique's heart soared, and she almost ran through the simple country room. Her own Grandmère Mimi was sitting next to the fireplace, vital and aglow. Mimi's arms stretched out to embrace her. "*Shayneh maydeleh!* Beautiful girl!"

"I've missed you so much, Grandmère Mimi!"

Joyful tears trickled down their cheeks, but they were nothing compared to the sobs of the woman near the door. "It is so very, very beautiful to see you together at last!" she wailed.

Mimi kissed Dominique on both cheeks. "I hate to let go of you, *ma petite fille,*" Mimi said. "But if you do not get Sophie a handkerchief, she will drown us both."

Dominique handed the woman a handkerchief from the small wooden table where her grandmother pointed. "Here, Sophie."

"*Merci, merci!*" She sobbed as she looked at them.

"Shall I get her something to drink, Grandmère?"

"If we give her a drink, she'll turn it into more tears. If we leave her alone, maybe she'll finish crying by Rosh Hashanah."

Dominique laughed. Mimi took Dominique's

197

hand and brought it to her cheek. "We are going to have such fun together!"

"She is the image of you at that age, Mimi," Sophie said, sniffling. "It is impossible how much she looks like you."

Mimi beamed. "My grandchild is a dozen times prettier."

Dominique started to protest, but Mimi waved her cane. "This is my house. And in my house, what I say goes."

"In your house," Sophie said, "the child will starve. It is lunchtime." She headed for the kitchen.

"I have known Sophie all my life and I love to tease her, but she does make the best chicken in France," Mimi said.

"This is the first time in all the years I have known your grandmother, Dominique, that she has complimented my cooking."

"Today's a holiday, Sophie. Today's the day Dominique came to Ville de Fabian. Now let me show you your room, angel."

Seeing that her grandmother had a hard time rising to her feet filled Dominique with worry. "Are you all right, Grandmère?"

"When it gets a little damp, this leg lets me know. Don't give it a second thought. Are you tired from the trip, darling?"

"Not even a bit," Dominique said. "I rested in the car on the way here so I wouldn't miss a moment with you."

As Mimi took Dominique to a cozy room at

the back of the cottage, Dominique tried to preserve every detail with her artist's eye. A soft, melancholy light streamed across the rich dark tones of the old furniture, as in a Rembrandt painting.

Next to Dominique's room was a smaller one with piled-up boxes. "I never can get around to fixing that mess," Mimi said.

"Because your *grandmère* is always too busy helping others," Sophie called, rattling the pots. "I wanted to fix it, but she says I will make it worse. As if that junk is worth anything!"

"Maybe I can help, Grandmère," Dominique said.

"I don't want you to bother."

"Do not bother, Dominique," Sophie called.

"But I want to!" Dominique insisted.

"Mind your own business, bossy Sopheleh!" Mimi laughed. "My Dominique shall do as she wishes!"

That afternoon, Dominique and Mimi walked through the town. The quaint houses with window boxes full of herbs and flowers seemed out of a storybook. Neighbors greeted them warmly and smiled at their reunion.

Later, when she was in bed and the breeze was softly blowing at her lace curtains, Dominique's brain whirled with the day's impressions. Remarkable to see how much she resembled Mimi in the old photographs. Black-and-white pictures of Mimi swinging a bat in a clownish, seductive pose made her laugh out loud. Clearly Mimi had been a spirited girl, and Dominique recognized that spirit in herself. Their bond was much more complex than their physical resemblance.

It seemed so odd that Amanda and Mimi were even in the same family. Mimi was casual and spontaneous, with little concern for external appearances. So alive with energy. Dominique could not deny that Amanda had energy. But that was the only quality her mother and grandmother had in common. Amanda was as upset by a chipped nail as she would have been by a chip in her Rosenthal china. As for "casual and spontaneous," Amanda couldn't make it across the room without her Filofax.

Dominique flicked on the lamp near the bed to look at the snapshots from Grandmère Mimi's chest. How awkward Amanda seemed as a child. So serious, her hands clenched tightly in front of her too-large jumper. And that little girl's eyes! As full of heartache as a lost puppy. Why was she so unhappy? And how could those same eyes now give off the force of two laser beams?

She lay down on the goose-down pillows and searched the fragile child's face for clues of the tough dynamo the art world knew as Amanda Rappaport. She couldn't find the slightest hint.

# CHAPTER FOURTEEN

Dominique's sleep was so satisfying that she tried to ignore the racket of the birds for as long as she could. When she opened her eyes, it took a moment to remember where she was. Cherry trees and hyacinths right outside her window! And her door was open just enough to make her mouth water with the aroma of warm crepes. The morning light beaming across the room smacked of Van Gogh's work in Arles. Ville de Fabian. *Yes!*

As she stretched, the picture of her mother as a child fell across her knees. She gazed at it again. Questions! So many questions!

Barefoot, she padded to the kitchen. No Grandmère Mimi. The table was set for one and there was a note against the mug:

> *Good morning, dear one—Hope you slept well. I'm at a meeting. Crepes in the pan. Berries in the bowl. Cream in the pitcher. Chocolate in the pot. Joy in my heart!*

At the bottom of the note, Grandmère had drawn a cartoon of Dominique waking.

The note delighted her as much as the skill of the picture surprised her. Immediately, so she would always have this memento, Dominique packed the note between the pages of a book in her bag. Then she quickly ate her savory breakfast, pulled on her cotton print sundress, and stepped outside into the day.

After the hectic streets of Paris, the relaxed pace of Ville de Fabian seemed as odd and wonderful as watching an old movie. Women with bundles in their hands, en route to or from shopping or laundry, stopped to talk by the marble cherubs and flower patches along the town square. Men in the fields went about their plowing, shaking their pipes amiably at passersby.

The sound of her name diverted her from her meandering. "Dominique!"

"Sophie!" Dominique returned her wave.

"I have just heard that they will finish the meeting soon. They are making plans to raise money so Mimi can convert her childhood home into an orphanage."

Sophie tore off the end of the fresh bread she had carried in her mesh bag from the market and offered it to Dominique. As good as the aroma of the warm, crusty loaf was, Dominique had to refuse after her crepes. And so, to Dominique's amusement, Sophie stuck the portion inside Dominique's pocket "for later."

The old woman chattered excitedly as they walked to the town hall, but she spoke so quickly that it took Dominique a moment to understand what she was saying: that Mimi was going to be honored in a ceremony for those who had fought the Nazis during World War II.

Dominique was incredulous. "Grandmère? In the Resistance?"

"*Oui, oui.*" Sophie nodded. "Mimi was a legend."

Dominique could hardly believe it. Rabbi Levi had told her about the heroes who had fought to thwart Nazi monstrosities. Julian's grandfather Jean Adler had been part of that secret alliance. But her grandmother had risked her life in the war as well! Why was this as taboo a subject as the rest of her family's history?

"But she kept refusing to accept the honor." Sophie took out a handkerchief to dab at her onslaught of tears. "Finally she agreed to a modest ceremony. Only if the money they saved went to the new orphanage and to the old people's home she founded."

They started across the creaking footbridge that led to the town hall, and Dominique gasped with surprise. Standing on the top step of the small white building was Rabbi Levi.

"I met that man in Paris!" Dominique said excitedly.

"In Paris, you say?" Sophie shaded her eyes

from the sun. "You know Rabbi Levi? He is our good friend!"

At the sound of his name, Rabbi Levi turned to face them. "*Salut,* Sophie," he called. Then he shielded his eyes from the sun and shook his head in amazement. "Dominique? Is that you?"

Dominique hurried toward him, her smile radiating happiness. "I never expected to see you here either."

"Sophie," Rabbi Levi said, taking the old woman's hand. "I'm glad to see you're looking so well. But"—he shook his head—"how is it that you know this lovely child?"

"This is Mimi's granddaughter, Rabbi Levi."

"Mimi's granddaughter! But of course!" Rabbi Levi studied Dominique's face. "All this time I have been trying to figure out who you recalled to my mind. It was Mimi!"

"You know my grandmother?" Dominique asked, incredulous.

"You come from the very best stock. Your grandmother has been a blessing to so many. Including me. It was she who found me a new family after the war. And many years later, she located my brother in Canada. Each of us thought the other had died in the camps." The rabbi looked to the sky and sighed. "With such a heritage, your life cannot help but be the same."

Again the rabbi's words sparked a yearning in Dominique, a yearning for a life that made a difference in the world. "I'm just beginning to find out what an incredible woman she was, Rabbi Levi. I don't know if I could ever live up to that."

The hall door opened and Mimi smiled from Dominique to Rabbi Levi. "You introduced them, Sopheleh?"

"We were already old friends," the rabbi said, smiling from Dominique to Sophie. "It was *bashert!*"

That night—the night before the ceremony for Mimi—the townspeople gathered in the Jewish chapel for a service for those who were lost in the Shoah—the worst catastrophe in Jewish history—which the rest of the world knew as the Holocaust.

Amazed at the huge turnout in the tiny chapel, Dominique looked at her grandmother. "Are all these people Jewish?"

"No, but when the Nazis were in power, many of them and their parents were part of the Resistance." Mimi's eyes grew misty. "If they were found helping Jewish people, they would be killed on the spot. Still, they did all they could to help. Tonight they wanted to come to this special service. To say that we are all part of the same human family."

As Rabbi Levi rose to the podium, a hush came over the crowd. "Our prayer book says, 'Who rise from prayer better persons, their prayers are answered.' As I look around this room, crowded with good people, I feel very humble and very proud.

"The Germans looted the town in that horrible time. They took what they thought were all the valuables. But they could not steal what was most valuable—the humanity of the people of Ville de Fabian.

"'*A bas les tyrans!*'—'Down with the tyrants!'—these people shouted inside their hearts. This rallying cry turned ordinary people into heroes and saints. Whatever theologians or philosophers or scientists argue, none can deny that we are offspring of the same creation—that we have evolved from and share the same creative energy. No one who lives is not fueled by it. Brutality against any one of us is brutality against all. . . ."

When the rabbi had finished the kaddish, the prayer for those who had died, the congregants linked arms. In the amber light of the candles, their voices lifted in the hymn "Rock of Ages" and then in the French national anthem and the folk songs of determination and hope that had emerged in the Resistance.

Dominique held on to Mimi and cried, her heart echoing the profound emotions of the people all around. Ordinary people, Rabbi Levi had said. Yet each pair of damp eyes shone with a light of goodness. Dominique felt alive with the joyful awareness that she was an "offspring of the same creation."

As she dried her eyes on one of the tissues Sophie had had the foresight to provide tonight, a lovely blond woman crossed the room to embrace Mimi. "I'm so happy to see you!"

Dominique was touched by the warmth between them.

"Régine, this is Dominique, my granddaughter."

Régine smiled. "Your mother and I went to school together!" So odd, Dominique thought, that her mother so rarely came back to this town. Her visits with Mimi usually took place in Paris. "I hope to see you again," Régine said. "I have to say good-bye now. My husband is meeting me at the entrance."

"Régine's family was Catholic," Mimi told Dominique as Régine walked away. "They hid two Jewish families in a hayloft. When the Nazis came, they pretended to be anti-Semitic and told lies about Jews being hidden over the hill. The Nazis thanked them and marched right into the arms of American soldiers!"

The more people they spoke to, the more Dominique was awestruck at the cleverness and daring of their schemes to hinder the Nazis. She felt privileged to be there to thank the small but blessed minority who couldn't ignore the plight of their Jewish neighbors.

"The Jardin family you just met," Mimi said to Dominique. "Maybe you read in your history book about the Huguenots?"

"I remember hearing the word in school. But I've forgotten what it means."

"After tonight," Mimi said, "you'll remember. They were Protestants when Protestantism

207

was forbidden in France. Thousands were slaughtered in 1572, on August 24—St. Bartholomew's Day. The Jardins are descended from Huguenots. Because of their tragic history, it was impossible for them to stand by while Jews suffered."

Then an old man, François, recalled how all the members of one Jewish family in the village were made to dig their own graves and lie down in them while the Nazis fired bullets into their hearts. Dominique was so overcome with grief, she wanted to run from the room. Instead, she grabbed her grandmother's arm. "If I'm having a hard time with this, Grandmère, it must be fifty times as hard for you to be reminded."

Mimi's gaze was so full of sorrow that Dominique could hardly bear it. Then a sublime glow replaced the pain. "We who survived must remember the suffering, my child, so we will always be alert to the sufferings of others."

*"May the problems of all who are downtrodden be our problem . . ."* The words of the Passover service played once more in Dominique's head.

*"Je suis fatiguée,* I am so tired suddenly." Mimi sighed. "And I've invited Rabbi Levi to the house for supper."

"Rabbi Levi and I are old friends," Dominique said, trying to hide her worry. "I'll be happy to entertain him. You should rest."

"Are you comfortable, Grandmère?" Dominique asked as she helped Mimi into bed.

"I just wish I hadn't agreed to that ceremony tomorrow. To spend time applauding ourselves when people are homeless!"

Dominique shook her head as she closed the door quietly behind her.

"How is she?" Rabbi Levi asked as Dominique entered the living room.

"She says she's just tired."

Sophie carried a tray of tea and cookies into the room, clucking her tongue. "She has been working night and day to raise money to make the old farmhouse into an orphanage."

The three sat quietly for a while. Then Dominique looked up. "Please tell me about my grandmother's life. My mother won't tell me anything."

Rabbi Levi put his teacup down and clapped the cookie crumbs from his hands. "Amanda. I knew her when she was a child." He smiled. "I was one of the orphans Mimi kept at her house until she found us homes after the war." He shook his head. "Where do we start, Sophie?"

Sophie looked at Dominique, then closed her eyes. "I can still see Mimi as a teenager. We were all friends in the village, but Mimi and Jean Adler were inseparable."

"Jean *Adler*!" The name hit Dominique like a bolt of lightning. She turned to the rabbi. "Julian's grandfather?"

Rabbi Levi nodded. "We spoke of Jean in Paris. I thought you knew about your grandparents. But of course, how could you?"

"They had their problems, though," Sophie said emphatically. "Mimi's family was rich and prominent socially. Her father was a very respected doctor, connected to the Rothschild Jewish Hospital in Paris."

"*His* parents were poor Russian immigrants," Rabbi Levi said.

"The Adlers escaped from their shtetl, their Jewish village, during the pogroms—those murdering rampages against the Jews. They roamed all over Europe to find a safe home," Sophie added.

"He had a job in a Paris clothing factory. But the owner was a German Jew who was taken away, then killed in the camps," the rabbi went on.

"Awful times," Sophie murmured. "Even when the Nazis took Paris, we still thought our part of the country would be safe."

"Poor old Adler was trying anything to keep his family alive. Dr. Landau had treated him for his ulcers in the hospital," Rabbi Levi said.

"If people who were struggling needed him, Dr. Landau wouldn't charge them a cent," said Sophie.

"My great-grandfather?" Dominique put down her teacup.

"He helped people—Jewish, gentile, it didn't matter—with whatever they needed. Jobs, food, money, whatever."

Sophie reached for her handkerchief. "But as much as they came from different worlds, Mimi and Jean were inseparable. . . ."

# CHAPTER FIFTEEN

## 1939. Ville de Fabian, France

Fifteen-year-old Mimi Landau sneaked into her father's car and hid under a blanket. It was warm and the blanket itched, but she knew the look on Jean's face would make up for it.

At last his footsteps crunched over the gravel drive toward the car, the soapy water sloshing in his bucket. She could hardly keep from laughing as he began to hum "La Vie en Rose."

"La de da de da . . ." His voice was becoming more bass daily. Then, like a cabaret singer he belted out, "La vie en *rose!*"

"If it ain't Maurice Chevalier!" Mimi sprang from her hiding place and did a perfect parody of the American star Mae West. "Why don'tcha come up and see me some time!" Young Sophie, Mimi's brother, Gérard, and the other children burst into laughter as the stunned Jean dropped his rag.

"Got you good!" Mimi stood on the running board, her green eyes watching Jean's face for a clue to his next move.

211

"Mimi!" Jean said with a big grin. "What a surprise!"

"Nothing like a sneak attack to get your blood pumping!"

"A sneak attack has advantages, if you're on the weak side."

As Jean moved along the car toward her, Mimi went in the other direction. "Sounds like a threat to me!"

"I never make idle threats," Jean answered coolly.

"Run, Mimi, run!" Sophie and the girls shouted as Jean grabbed his soapy rag and took off after her.

"Wait, Mimi. Your face is a dirty. I'll wash it for you."

The boys began cheering Jean on. "Get her!" they hollered.

The servants in the Landau house were watching the scene through the kitchen window. Mme. Landau left her embroidery to see what the racket was about. One glimpse of the show between Mimi and Jean sent her temperature boiling. "Marie," she said to the maid, "tell Mimi to come inside this minute."

"*Oui*, madame," Marie said, biting her lip. She knew that Mme. Landau hated it when Mimi and Jean spent so much time together.

That evening, no sooner had Dr. Landau's fingers touched the mezuzah—the tiny box containing biblical verses, placed at the doorway of Jewish homes as a reminder of God's presence—

than Mme. Landau started in on him. "Albert, I am very upset about Mimi and that Adler boy."

Mimi listened at her door as Mme. Landau blamed Jean for the incident, even for the dress Mimi tore in the brambles. "We should have spent the year in Paris. The children who go to the synagogue there come from wealthy, prominent families. Appropriate companions for our children."

"'When you pray, pray in the synagogue. . . . If you are unable to pray in the synagogue . . . meditate in your heart.'" Dr. Landau washed his hands at the sink. "That's in the *Midrash Tehillim.* It doesn't say a thing about praying with wealthy, prominent families."

Mimi repressed a laugh. Papa was the absolute best.

"Nothing good can come from Mimi running wild with the son of a—of a wandering Jew. Farmhand! Tailor! Whatever he is!"

"A tailor by profession, a farmhand out of need. Lucky he's a tailor. I'm sure he can fix Mimi's torn dress beautifully."

Mme. Landau knew his casual attitude would bring only problems. "Jean will not do any more chores for you, Albert!"

Dr. Landau took the Jewish newspaper from the table. "Young Jean has dignity, Claire. He offers help because it shames him that they can't pay the rent. It's his way of becoming a man. I'm not going to take that pride from him."

"*Oui,* he's becoming a man," Mme. Landau muttered. "And she's becoming a woman. That's just what I'm talking about."

Dr. Landau sat back on his chair and folded the paper on his knee. "Jean is a *mensh.* A decent and caring person."

Mme. Landau rolled her eyes. "There are plenty of young *menshen* at the Paris synagogue. Running around with someone of his class, the next thing you know she'll be dating goyim. That's all we need, children cozying up to people who hate us."

"Not all gentiles hate us." Dr. Landau sighed. "I know many wonderful gentiles. Both here and in Paris."

"And in their hearts, they hate each and every one of us!"

Dr. Landau waved his paper. "Your father's propaganda, Claire. There's good and bad in all people. I know some Jewish people I wouldn't want to have supper with."

Mme. Landau smiled, issuing what she thought was a winning point. "*C'est ça!* Right! That's how I feel about the Adlers!"

"The sad part is that *you're* the one missing out by not getting to know them." The doctor sighed again, opening his newspaper.

Mme. Landau examined her nails, thinking how ragged Mimi's looked after her escapade this afternoon. Next week she would bring her to the Paris salon. Let them make a fuss over her. Mimi really was so beautiful—and once she realized it, she'd think more of herself than to run around with that Adler boy.

"I'll need your guest list for Gérard's bar mitzvah. I want to order invitations printed this week," Mme. Landau said, dropping the subject for now.

Mimi closed the door. She had heard enough. Papa was not going to give in to Mama's nasty bigotry. She flopped down on her bed and picked up her Hebrew-school notebook. She turned to the page with the notes and pictures she and Jean had done.

"Great!" Jean had written under her sketch of the rabbi.

A compliment from him. Her sketches were playful, but Jean's work was so true to life it nearly jumped from the page.

"Let's be starving artists in Paris one day," Mimi had written on the top of one of the notebook pages. "How about it?"

His answer still tickled her. "Just name the day."

Jean! There was nobody in the world like him. And nobody, not even her mother, could keep them apart.

# CHAPTER SIXTEEN

"*Bonjour*, Mme. Rothschild," Mimi greeted the elegant woman as she entered the château for Gérard's bar mitzvah party.

"So good to see you, Mimi! My, how you've grown!"

*I must have,* thought Mimi. *This is the first time the whole crowd of them didn't nearly pinch my cheek right off my face.*

"Gérard made a wonderful bar mitzvah, Claire," Mme. Rothschild told Mme. Landau as they moved into the lavishly decorated dining room. She looked back over her shoulder at Mimi. "That girl of yours has grown into such a beauty. Remind me to introduce her to my nephew Arnaud when you come to Paris."

"That would be lovely," Mme. Landau answered. Her face was pink with delight at the success of the party. Every eminent Jewish family in Paris had come to attend the celebration at Ville de Fabian. The Landaus' social standing was assured.

She looked over at her daughter. A work of

217

art. The beautician had shaped the beautiful hair into a lovely bob that framed her delicate features perfectly. And the diamond pin at Mimi's collar was an exquisite complement to the sparkling green eyes and the blue Chanel suit. It had cost a fortune, but the money was well spent. To have the best, a girl needed to grow accustomed to the best.

Mme. Landau's thoughts were interrupted by Gérard and the boys' noisy play. "Gérard," Mme. Landau said. "You are a man today. Men are much more refined in their behavior."

Mimi felt that her mother's remark was meant to impress Mme. Rothschild.

"Don't be hard on him today," Mme. Rothschild said.

"Ah, yes," Mme. Landau agreed in her phony voice. "Maybe we should send them outside to play after the banquet.

"Say hello to the Balinget girls, Mimi," her mother called after her as she excused herself.

Mimi returned their fake smile. She had met them at a Hanukkah party when they were small. Prissy little phonies! Too mean to pay her the nuts they owed for winning the dreidel game.

"I'll be there in a minute," she called. "I have to ask Suzette to fill up the *nut* bowls." Quickly, before her mother could get her attention, she disappeared into the kitchen.

If only Jean could be here, she thought. Both she and Gérard were irked that her mother refused to invite Jean or Sophie or any of their neighborhood friends today. She had heard her parents have another argument over that matter. Her mother had gotten hysterical this time, so her father finally gave in.

What would Jean think if he saw her all dressed up with her Paris hairstyle? When she'd looked in the mirror she'd had an embarrassingly satisfied feeling, powerful and womanly. Maybe Jean would beg to do a serious portrait of her. Or say something like, "Darling, you are absolutely ravishing!" just the way Charles Boyer said it in that film last week. Or maybe he would be more like Humphrey Bogart—give her the "once-over" and say, "Wow. Get a load of you, toots. You really are some hot tomato." *Ravishing or hot tomato.* She picked up a coin and began flipping. *Ravishing or hot tomato . . .*

Suddenly Marie rushed into the room. "The Adlers' baby is coming and something is wrong!"

"Please tell them that Papa is on his way!"

Dr. Landau rushed for his medical bag as soon as Mimi relayed the message, but his wife stopped him. "Where are you dashing off to during your son's bar mitzvah celebration?"

"Mme. Adler is having trouble with her delivery." He turned to Mimi. "Get some fresh towels, Mimi, and some brandy."

When Mimi got back, her mother was raging. "They can't feed the mouths they've got, and they keep on having children!"

"I'm a doctor, Claire. Not a judge," Dr. Landau snapped.

"Shall I tell our guests that your own son's biggest day doesn't matter to you?" she screamed as he hurried down the path.

"Lives are in danger and you insist on talking nonsense!"

Mimi watched as her mother composed herself. "Mimi," she said, "make sure Marie has enough foie gras."

The moment her mother left, she was racing down the path after her father. Jean was waiting on a stool outside the cottage when Mimi got there. His little sister Anna was sucking her thumb, and his brother Edouard was fighting tears beside him. Jean looked up at Mimi and smiled weakly. She put her hand on his shoulder. It felt so strong, like the rest of him. But right now he looked like a frightened child. Maybe, if she concentrated, she could send him some of her strength.

Anna touched Mimi's hair. "Mimi so pretty." Then she put her thumb back in her mouth.

Jean looked at Mimi and smiled. The warmest light was in his eyes, as if to say "Yes. Yes, she is." It was so much better than "ravishing." And about fifty times better than "hot tomato."

If Dr. Landau hadn't been there to turn the baby, the newborn could have strangled on his own umbilical cord. But after an hour, the newest Adler and mother were doing fine.

"*Mazel tov*, M. Adler!" Dr. Landau raised his glass.

"Bless you, Dr. Landau." There were tears in his eyes.

"I would love to stay," Dr. Landau began, "but—"

"I know. *Mazel tov* on your son's bar mitzvah." M. Adler shook Dr. Landau's hand. "Go now and we'll see you at the *bris*."

Dr. Landau nodded. "For both of us, it's a big day."

Mimi and her father said good-bye to the Adlers.

When they were out of earshot, her father said, "I am so ashamed that they weren't invited to our house today."

Mimi turned to look back at Jean as he watched her walk away. He smiled, but his eyes looked sad, as if he were losing her. She shouldn't have worn her beautiful new dress to his house. Instead of pleasing him, it was just another painful reminder of the gap between his family's fortune and hers.

"It's nearly ten o'clock. I think we've worn the poor child out with our reminiscing," Rabbi Levi said.

"*Jamais!* Never!" exclaimed Dominique, leaning forward on her grandmother's sofa. She could hardly believe all the similarities between herself and her grandmother. How many times had she clashed with her mother over "appropriate companions"? And the fact that her grandmother had been in love with Jean Adler and she had been so close to falling for Julian was uncanny. That she and Julian had even *met* was incredible.

"Was my great-grandmother furious about Mimi's running off to the Adler cottage that day?" Dominique asked eagerly.

"Livid!" Sophie gasped. "She forbade Mimi to see him and told the Adlers to keep Jean away from her. Her excuse was that it was risky for children that age to be together so much. But she had a way of talking to them as if they were dirt." Sophie shook her head. "The Adlers knew very well what she meant. But Mimi would sneak off to see Jean—until her mother caught them kissing near the old mill house. After that, Mme. Landau thought she could keep them apart if she moved the family back to their Paris flat.

# CHAPTER SEVENTEEN

## 1941. Paris

After the Landaus left Ville de Fabian, Sophie became a secret envoy passing letters between Jean and Mimi. But Jean always expected that each one he received would be his last. After two years away, Mimi was seventeen, close to marriageable age. It was impossible, given the constant round of parties the Landaus attended, for someone as exceptional as Mimi to avoid attracting young men. Surely some lucky fellow who met her mother's rigid standards would make her forget him. And that would be best for her sake, he told himself sadly as he sat on the steps of the chapel to once again read her latest letter.

> *Dear Jean,*
>     *Why can't you understand, dear, sweet Jean, that I am always thinking of you? If you think you can get off the hook by saying that you would understand if things had changed between us—that it would be "for the best" if I fell in love with someone else—you're*

*mistaken! Get it through your head, I love you, and you can't get rid of me so easily.*

*Meanwhile, things in Paris continue to deteriorate. Our teacher told us that the Cesar Cinema is showing a film called* The Jewish Threat. *They say that the Talmud teaches us to hate Christians. How can they be allowed to tell such hateful lies? You told me once long ago that I was too sheltered to understand what persecution was really like. Let's hope I don't have an opportunity to understand it further.*

*The city is full of German soldiers. They have already taken French identity cards away from the Jews, and now they're firing them from any kind of government jobs and taking over Jewish businesses. They'll be taking a census soon to make sure Jewish families don't change residences. A doctor at the Rothschild Jewish Hospital told Papa that we'd better leave Paris before it's too late. Even the Rothschilds have left. Oh, Jean, the things they are talking about are too horrible for me to write.*

*But Ville de Fabian is still under the Vichy French government and things can't be as bad as they are in Paris under the Germans. We must wear yellow armbands now so they know which of us are Jewish. They shoot any Jews out past curfew. But the one good thing that might come out of this is that soon I may see you again in Ville de Fa-*

*bian . . . so out of something so horrible my
dream may come true!*

The next week seven synagogues were
bombed and Nazi soldiers began storming the
streets of Paris. Dr. Landau hired a car to take
his family back to Ville de Fabian, but he
stayed in the city to help care for the survivors
of the bomb blast.

As the car pulled into the drive at Ville de
Fabian, Mimi pretended, for her mother's
sake, that it was an ordinary day. As if Jean
Adler had never crossed her mind, though her
heart was already racing toward him. As they
entered the house, Mme. Landau announced
that they needed to have a talk, and Mimi was
sure the topic would be Jean. "Since you're
nearly seventeen, you may think you can do as
you please. But I am hoping that since you
have been exposed to finer things in Paris, you
will make wise choices." Mme. Landau reached
for her embroidery. "Have I been clear?"

Mimi smiled, knowing that if her expression
was just right, her mother would assume that
Mimi agreed with her. And she would never
have to utter a lying word. Then, when Sophie
called for Mimi to attend a welcome-home dinner at her parents' house, Mimi would rush off
to meet Jean as they had planned.

At five o'clock, Mimi caught sight of Sophie
on the path and ran to her. "Sopheleh, I've
missed you so!"

Crying, Sophie hugged her. "You look like a movie star, Mimi! So beautiful and grownup!"

When they were out of range of the château, they ran to the swing in the meadow to meet Jean. But as the chapel clock chimed seven, Sophie had to leave, and there was still no sign of him.

Panic took hold of Mimi. What if something was wrong? She remembered the old man who stood wailing outside the tobacco shop in Paris yesterday. "*De grâce!* For pity's sake! They are rounding up the foreign Jews to take them to Auschwitz. They will either work the poor souls to death in the factory, or gas them in the showers. Listen to me! Someone listen to me!"

"Crazy!" said the people who walked by. But what if he wasn't? What if they were rounding up immigrant Jews in Ville de Fabian—while they all thought the south was safe? *No!*

Mimi raced across the footbridge to the Adler cottage. When no one answered her knock, she said a prayer and touched her fingers to the *mezuzah* on their door. *Dear God, let them be safe.* . . . It was dark inside, but she ran to Jean's room to find something to comfort her frantic mind. In a box on top of his dresser were all of her letters—and a sketch he had made of her. She found a shirt on his doorknob and pressed it to her face, taking in his scent. She knew she couldn't stay any longer without arousing her mother's suspicions. "I love you," her heart called to Jean—wherever he had gone—as she held the shirt to her.

The wind was so fierce that night, Mimi almost missed the tapping at her window. She was wide awake in her bed, trying to push from her mind the terrifying vision of Jean being carried away by the Nazis. She prayed that he was safe and would come back to her. Then she heard him.

*Jean! He's here!*

She opened the sash, sat on the sill, swung her legs around, and fell into his arms.

"Oh, Mimi," Jean repeated as he kissed her hair.

Relief flooded her as they moved to the shed at the side of the house so her mother wouldn't hear them. "I've been praying all night. And now my prayer is answered."

Even in the moonlight she could see that he had grown more muscular, though he still had the look of an agile cat. How long she had waited to look into those wonderful eyes again! "I looked for you at your house tonight, but it was deserted."

The pain on his face made her want to cry. There was no trace of the boy who had chased her at the river. "We learned they plan to deliver foreign Jews like us to Auschwitz," Jean said.

*Then the man outside the tabac wasn't crazy,* Mimi thought in terror. *And nobody was listening to him.*

"I found a contact to make false passports to get them all to Spain. But we had to wait three hours before they were completed."

It was too much to take in. "Things cannot go on like this!"

"No. They'll be getting much worse." Jean's eyes flashed rage. "The Vichy government tried to placate the Nazis—and to pretend to us that they are making things better. But soon things will be as bad in the south as they are in Paris."

Mimi searched his eyes. "But you're staying?"

"I've joined Solidarité, Mimi. We can't sit back and watch while the government hands France over to the Nazis."

"But that's so dangerous, Jean!"

"Danger is now a fact of life." He leaned against the worktable in the shed. "But I just can't let fear chase me one more step."

Mimi shook her head in sorrow. "After all this time of being apart, I can't stand to think about you going into such danger."

Jean took her in his arms. "I'd give anything if we could find a world where all that mattered was how much I love you."

Through her tears, Mimi smiled and said, "Tell me about that world, Jean."

"We'd be able to go anyplace we like. We'd put our easels down in the middle of a street and traffic would stop until we got tired of painting." He kissed her forehead. "And we would have our chance at last to hold each other tight in the sunshine, like all those Paris lovers you wrote me about. At night we'd count the stars until we ran out of numbers."

"I want to go there, Jean," Mimi said wistfully, trying to get lost in the hope and laughter of his dream. To believe in something besides a world where each day brought more insane stories of Nazi atrocities that turned out to be true.

He held her hand to his face and kissed it. "If only I could, Mimi. But there isn't one safe square inch on earth now."

For a while they held on to each other in silence. Then Jean said, "I should go now. If your mother—"

"She won't be a problem. She sleeps till seven." Mimi clung to him. How could she let go after so long without him?

Jean smiled softly into her eyes. "Last time you said your mother was no problem, she popped up at a very awkward moment."

Mimi tried to stop her tears. "The day you were fishing." It was a scene she had replayed daily in Paris. She tapped her finger to her lip, hoping he couldn't see how her hand was trembling. "It isn't nice to keep a lady waiting."

At sunrise, Mimi opened her eyes and smiled across at Jean on the straw mat beside her. *Que deviendrons-nous? What will become of us?* she suddenly thought in fright. The world was exploding around them and all she was sure of was that she didn't want to live without Jean Adler. In that instant she vowed that nothing would separate them again.

Jean stretched and drew her to him, kissing her on the forehead. "A magic night."

"Let's get married, Jean." The words burst right out of her. "Your family is gone. Let me be your family now. If the whole world is up for grabs, then let's grab any happiness we can."

Jean's face was full of anguish. "But I want to marry you when I can give you a good life. Not one of setting traps day and night—"

"Now is the only time we've got," Mimi said steadily. "My parents gave me a diamond pin worth a fortune. You can sell it. It won't bring a fortune now, but it'll give us a start."

Jean looked into her eyes until he was sure that she was serious. "Tonight at my meeting in Paris, maybe someone knows—"

"Listen to me," Mimi said, knowing she'd never been more certain of anything in her life. "There's a jeweler near chemin de la Muette, right near our Paris flat. His name is Davis. He'll help you."

Jean stood and helped her up. "I'd better go now."

"Wait near my window for a minute. I'll hand you the pin." She wrapped her arms around his waist and pressed her face against his chest. "My husband."

Jean kissed the top of her head. "You are

such a stubborn, bossy Mimi. Always were. Maybe I should think this thing through a little more. What if you turn into a real harridan the minute we're married?"

Mimi laughed. "When you don't behave, I'll chase you with a rolling pin."

They started out of the shed. Then Jean turned to Mimi. "One more kiss to last until Friday, my sweet almost-bride."

# CHAPTER EIGHTEEN

Eric Wiener—code name Lion—the leader of Jean's Resistance group, greeted him in the rectory headquarters. "Am I glad to see you, Jean. We've got a problem at the Rothschild Jewish Hospital."

Though most Jewish organizations had been taken over, some still operated under Nazi jurisdiction and for Nazi profit. The Rothschild Jewish Hospital now ran on a skeleton staff. And though all Jews were restricted, respected doctors and eminent people like Dr. Landau were, for the moment, still being protected by the Vichy government.

"Mimi's father is a doctor at Rothschild!" Jean exclaimed.

"What's his name?"

"Dr. Albert Landau," Jean answered. He held his breath.

Eric shook his head. "A German officer was in an accident outside the hospital. Landau saved him. But the fellow was delirious and his superiors are afraid he divulged confidential information. An SS officer is en route to grill Dr. Landau now." Eric handed Jean a hospital uniform and an identification card. "We've got to get Dr. Landau out of there."

Jean took a breath. Eric was an expert at these operations, but what if Jean made some amateur blunder and brought harm to Mimi's father?

In less than ten minutes Eric and Jean were walking through the Rothschild Hospital, dressed for surgery. Eric had mapped out the scheme on the way. "From a scaffold outside, I'm going to enter the room where the SS officer is holding Dr. Landau. You must distract the guard in the hallway. André, a big guy with a patch on his eye, will help. He'll create a drunken scene across the hall. You will help to make a good show so the guard will leave his post. I'll get Landau to a laundry truck outside."

As Eric headed up the stairs, Jean's heart pounded furiously as he pretended to study a medical chart while two Nazi soldiers went by. Then he heard the ruckus. The hall guard looked toward André as he stumbled out of a room. "I want a drink! Somebody get me a drink!"

Jean rushed past the guard. "People are sick. Be quiet!"

André beat his chest. "I'm Tarzan, king of the apes!"

The guard laughed. "King of the fools is more like it!"

Jean tried to lead André back to the room, but he went limp and began to snore loudly. Then he laughed. "Fooled you!"

A crowd had gathered, but the guard was still at his post. Jean turned to him. "Could you give me a hand with him?"

"Probably the only way I'll get any peace." As he tried to help drag André, he grunted, "Heavy as an ox!" Just then there was a loud clattering outside the window.

"What's going on?" The guard reached for his gun.

Jean grabbed a bedpan lying on the floor. He hit the guard in the back of the neck. The guard turned and shot Jean in the shoulder. The pain was excruciating. André tried to tackle the guard, but the next bullet hit him in the chest. As the guard turned to Jean, Eric called from the window behind him. "Drop your gun or I'll shoot!" Eric had no gun. But the guard, unaware that he was bluffing, dropped his gun. Jean picked it up. His shoulder was on fire, but he quickly tied the guard with a sheet.

"You won't get very far," the guard said.

"You talk too much." Jean took a wad of gauze from the table and stuffed it into the guard's mouth, then stepped out onto the scaffold and jumped down to stacks of sheets on the truck.

"André—" Jean said as Eric pulled him into the vehicle.

"Add him to our kaddish prayer. The list is getting too long!" Eric shook his head as they raced through the streets in the battered truck, past the SS men who now prowled each block.

Jean turned as Dr. Landau leaned forward from the hiding place behind the seats and clasped Jean's shoulder. His face was bruised from the Nazi's fist. "You're hurt, Dr. Landau!"

"I'll be okay, but you're losing a lot of blood!" He tore a piece of his shirt and bandaged Jean's arm tightly.

"Diane will take care of it," Eric said of the woman back at their headquarters who, before the Nazi scourge, had been studying to be a doctor. She routinely took care of all the wounded Resistance fighters. "But you, Dr. Landau, are in danger here. We've arranged to transport your family to Canada."

*Mimi! Canada!* Jean thought. *I've lost her again!*

"Father Malot has already picked them up," Eric continued. "Your passports say you and your wife are Mary and Jules Scott."

"But the Nazis are bombing a synagogue tonight. I've got to make sure the people are out of there!" Dr. Landau cried.

"I'll do it. Give me the address," Jean said.

"Your shoulder!"

"Don't worry." Lives were at stake. His pain would wait.

\* \* \*

Wearing the jacket Dr. Landau had given him to conceal the wounded shoulder, Jean stayed close to the buildings along rue Rambuteau to support his body, weak from the loss of blood. The occupation was picking up momentum daily. The German and French police darted in and out of homes in the Jewish quarter, hunting for Jews who had evaded the census. Searching for Resistance headquarters and for informers and weak links in the Solidarité chain—*les derniers des hommes*, the most contemptible men, who would gladly turn in friends to get one more ration book for food, which was now so scarce.

He hobbled to the synagogue steps, where old men rocked and prayed for light in this darkness. After he had compelled them to leave, he thought he heard noise on the roof. Sometimes children played there. He struggled up the dark, winding stairs and pushed open the roof door in time to see a mangy cat dart to an adjacent roof. He started down again, but the pain slowed him and he could feel himself growing dizzy. As he staggered into the courtyard the building exploded in smoke and rubble all around him. He dragged himself through the flames that were scorching his senseless body, and fell unconscious on the abandoned street.

Dominique took a deep breath. "Was he dead?"

"No, thank God. Later that night a woman named Brigitte found him, his face charred and his blood nearly depleted. For months she nursed him, and came to love the wonderful soul inside the shell of his body, came to love this man whose scarred face was now so oddly distorted he couldn't bear to look in the mirror."

How could Brigitte love someone with this horrible mask? Jean wondered. And with the dream of Mimi gone, his gratitude for Brigitte's care turned to love. And finally, after she had spent months begging him to marry her, and he had constantly refused (how could she not grow to hate the face he found so revolting?), he accepted.

As soon as the rest of his body recovered Brigitte pleaded with him not to go back into Solidarité. But the scarred face gave Jean a strange sense of freedom—as if he were invisible. And an invisible man could be a daring one.

"Is it you, Jean?" Eric had said the day Jean found his way to the new headquarters. He had recognized the husky voice, but tried to conceal his anguish at Jean's appearance. "I'm so happy to see you alive. We all thought you died in the synagogue bombing."

Jean recounted the story of Brigitte's rescue. Then he said: "If the enemy thinks I'm dead, I may be useful." *And maybe,* Jean said to himself, *now I have one reason not to hate this face.*

That Jean Adler was alive would remain a secret. For all anyone knew, this strange man with the big hat and the scarf had no name. The man who risked his life to rescue Jews marked for death was known only as the Guardian of the Night.

"And what about Grandmère? Did she go to Canada?"

"She went as far as the depot with them. She said she was going to the ladies' room. But she slipped her brother a note and ran off. She couldn't leave without Jean." Sophie sniffled.

"Did she ever find him?" Dominique leaned forward.

"No. She scoured Paris for a woman he had spoken of who worked in the Resistance—code name, Sparrow. Diane from the hospital. Diane told her that Jean died in the explosion."

Dominique's hand flew to her mouth. "My poor *grandmère!*"

"Her parents had gone to Canada, and she believed the man she loved was dead. She'd never felt more alone in her life. She joined L'Organisation de la Jeunesse Juive, the Organization of Jewish Youth, which worked with Solidarité to foil the Nazi attacks. From here in Ville de Fabian, our Sopheleh worked with them, too," Rabbi Levi said with a nod.

Sophie waved her hand. "All I did was paperwork in the office. But Mimi's life was always in danger. She trained boys who came from North America to help. Before she took on the mission, one of them had been shot by a Nazi because he pulled out a pack of American cigarettes and gave himself away. The French-Canadians could speak the language well enough, but they needed to be drilled in customs and the lay of the land.

"Mimi was good at spying, because she could pass for a gentile. One of the many times she almost got killed, she was in the room of a Nazi officer. In the bar, she pretended she was going to show him a good time. But she had drugged his wine, and when he collapsed she searched for his company's attack plans. She stuck them in her bodice and went to the stairs. Three Nazis stopped her, but she flirted with them and promised to return the next night. Then she walked off like the Queen of Prussia."

"But what about Jean? Didn't she miss him terribly?"

"Terribly. Mimi thought she'd never find love again, but the heart is a resilient muscle. She met Henri through her work. They were a great spy team—and they fell in love."

"Henri. My grandfather," Dominique said. "Then what?"

"Two months after they were married an informer pointed Henri out to the Gestapo. He never lived to see his daughter."

"Mimi was heartbroken. Then in '42 the Vichy French Commissar, Xavier Vallat—anti-Semitic, but not a murderer—was replaced by Darquier de

Pellepoix, the Nazis' choice. He had no qualms about cooperating fully with the Final Solution—the extermination of all Jews. Things were worse than ever, and Mimi knew she had to continue in the Resistance."

"Wasn't she afraid for her child?"

"In those times, Dominique"—Sophie was weeping—"the Nazis were snatching Jewish babies from the arms of their mothers who were boarding the death trains, and shooting them on the spot. There were those who couldn't arrange to hide their children or give them away. Some of them decided it would be better to smother those children than watch them die by Nazi bullets.

"Mimi, a new mother, heard these tales and remembered what Jean had said about there not being one safe square inch in the world. About not letting fear chase him one more step. She determined to fight with all that was left of her to make the world better for her Amanda."

Dominique's eyes welled up with tears. She couldn't believe what her grandmother had had to live through, and all that she'd accomplished.

"We have a big day tomorrow," Rabbi Levi said, mussing Dominique's hair. "We shall honor Mimi, *oui*? Tonight, I think we'd better go to sleep."

But as she lay in bed, Dominique was wide awake. Her head was reeling at the thought of her mother, a tiny baby in the middle of the Holocaust. How had such things happened? How . . . how . . . how?

# CHAPTER NINETEEN

Rabbi Levi stood at the podium of the small chapel where he had stood the night before. He looked at the loving faces before him and his voice was choked with emotion. "Le Chambon, the small town just to our south, was founded by the Protestant Huguenots who fled to this cold, tough climate in the 1500s to escape being murdered for their beliefs. What grew from their struggles was a lasting humanity. Their pastor, André Trocme, lived by his code: 'It is evil to deliver a brother who has entrusted himself to us. That we would not consent to.'

"The people of Le Chambon held fast to that oath. They welcomed endangered Jewish strangers with open arms and hid them in their farmhouses, in their lofts, and in centuries-old hideouts in the hills. Many of us are alive today because of their heroism, and we know we bless them and those like them daily.

"And we bless one of the women who led the Jews to them. Who brought the Jewish children to the Cevenol school . . . who has made another Le Chambon of love here in Ville de Fabian: Mimi Cohn."

Dominique heard the stories people had come from all over the world to tell. A woman wept, full of gratitude that Mimi had reunited her with her family after the war. Thanking Mimi for his own life was the grandson of a man for whom Mimi had found a hiding place after his parents had been killed. As Dominique listened to each tribute, so full of gratitude and so deeply touching, tears of pride filled her own eyes.

After the ceremony was over, they enjoyed their coffee; people crowded around Mimi, who returned their embraces and exchanged blessings and *kvelled*—beamed proudly—at the pictures they had brought and listened to family anecdotes with rapt attention. And Dominique couldn't help but wonder why her mother had never told her anything about this. Why was it kept such a deep, dark secret?

While Grandmère was so engrossed by her "other family," as they called themselves, Dominique decided it was a good time to attack the piles of books and cartons in Mimi's spare room. Back at the house, as she surveyed her project, she was glad she had started now. It would take time to sort through all of these things, and she would be leaving in a few days.

A small carton with string tied around it

seemed like the best place to start. If she could put some order to that, she told herself with a laugh, she might build up the nerve to tackle the huge crate beside it. Dust flew everywhere as she moved the carton closer to her and looked over its contents. A toy car, a storybook, a large envelope stuffed with papers. Dominique pulled out the paper and laughed. Children's drawings: Trees, houses, animals of unknown species grinned back at her.

There was a stick figure of a smiling woman with long squiggles and circles of red hair. Beside her was a small girl. Even in the crude drawing, the girl's eyes seemed to be so sad. One hand was reaching toward the smiling tall woman. Dominique studied the child's scrawled letters at the bottom. A sudden shock came over her as she realized what she held. The child had tried to write her own name, "A M A" followed by a backward "D." Amanda, her mother, had made this picture!

The discovery made Dominique light-headed, and at the same time frantic to find more clues. She didn't need to be a therapist to figure out that her mother had been a very sad little girl. But how could she have been so sad with wonderful Mimi, the woman the whole world loved, for her very own mother?

Farther down she found a sketch, obviously of Mimi and probably done by Jean. Dominique kept it aside rather than return it to the envelope. Exceptional work. Then she spotted some old school notebooks and flipped through. A diary! Obviously her mother's, left behind with the rest of her in Ville de Fabian. Dominique was so taken with her find that she jumped at the noise from the doorway.

"*Pardon,* Dominique," Rabbi Levi said. "I will leave for Paris soon and wanted to say good-bye." He sneezed. "I'm allergic to dust. But you are having the fine time, *oui?*"

"*Oui!* I've found my mother's diary. And a picture Jean made of Grandmère." She held it up. "He really had talent."

Rabbi Levi nodded. "But that sketch was done by Amanda."

"My *mother?*" Dominique was incredulous. "I never knew she cared about art as anything other than high-priced merchandise."

"There is much you do not know about your mother." Rabbi Levi sneezed again. "If you give me some tea away from all this dust, I will tell you what I know of her from my early days as part of Mimi's 'other family.'"

Dominique took her new discoveries and followed the rabbi out of the room. All the way back to the close of 1944 . . .

The American army had liberated Paris and ended the Nazi tyranny in Europe. French citizens were decorating their Christmas trees with tinfoil ribbons, remnants of the material that flew from American planes to thwart German radio-detection equipment. And now that the war was over, the groups that had survived by secrecy came together openly with their new mission: to help France get back to the business of living.

The Landaus' old house, taken over as a Nazi headquarters during the war, had been left in such a state of disrepair that Mimi moved into the deserted Adler cottage and made it her home and office. There was a shortage of the barest essentials—food, clothing, soap. From the cottage, with her baby in her lap, Mimi wrote letters to recruit volunteers.

But the most pressing problems—far more pressing than material matters, Mimi realized—were the needs of the children whose families had been torn apart. "We have each other, Amanda," she told her daughter. "But these children have nobody." She worked tirelessly to reunite families and to find good homes for orphans. Her cottage became a way station for all of them.

The only time Mimi slowed her pace was in April, when news of Franklin Roosevelt's death came over the radio. She heard that vendors at the Paris flower stalls on the place de la Madeleine gave flowers to American soldiers in his memory.

Mimi read the Roosevelt editorial from *Le Monde* to her staff: "'Let us weep for this man and hope that his wise and generous conception of the human communities remains like a light to brighten the path for all men of goodwill.'" She put the words on the wall of her house and read them every day.

Her accomplishments were so many that before several years had passed she had become a legend. So much so, that talk of her achievements reached all the way to Paris. To Eric Wiener, Jean's comrade from the Resistance, who now worked with Jean in a group called Those of the Liberation.

Eric Wiener and Jean Adler watched their children delight in the Punch and Judy puppet show, which had just resumed in the Champ de Mars. The once commonplace park entertainment was a spectacular sight after the long nightmare of war.

As Jean pulled his scarf up on his face, Eric said, "The woman they spoke of in the café today, she's Landau's daughter."

Jean felt weak. Mimi! But she had gone to Canada the day they rescued Dr. Landau. The day of the synagogue bombing.

"They say she's in Ville de Fabian. Your old town, *non*? Maybe you should pay her a visit?"

Jean shook his head.

"But why?" Eric began. "I'm sure she'd be glad to see you."

Then he regretted pushing. Usually it was hard to guess Jean's feelings from looking at him, since his face had been so badly burned. But at this moment, Eric sensed it was contorted with pain.

*Once he had such a handsome face,* Eric thought sadly. And now, because of the scars, Jean wouldn't leave the house without his sunglasses and that big hat pulled down over his forehead. Even in the sizzling summer heat, he wore his collar up or a scarf that covered the bottom half of his face.

As they walked home from the park with Jean's son and daughter and Eric's twin boys, Jean kept feeling that his knees would buckle under him. His life was so many light-years away from Ville de Fabian, and it was a good life. He had thought of Mimi over the years, hoping that she had found happiness too—in Canada. He had begun to make inquiries to see if he could find out where she was so he could return the diamond pin she had given him to sell so long ago. But she was in France! How could he get it back to her without seeing her? More to the point, without her seeing *him?* The thought of those green eyes filling with pity at the horrible sight of him was too much to bear. Maybe he could send it to her. But then she might come looking for him and . . . No, that wouldn't work.

# CHAPTER TWENTY

### 1949. VILLE DE FABIAN

Five-year-old Amanda watched with big, sad eyes as her mother hugged little Louis. "Tuesday you'll have a lovely home, *tateleh*, little one. But Amanda and I will miss you so much."

*I won't miss you one bit, Louis,* Amanda thought angrily. She wished she could pull him right off her mother's lap. But why bother? Tomorrow some new child would be getting fussed over in the same spot. Some newcomer would be stealing Mama's lap and all the hugs and kisses she never got anymore.

"You're such a big girl now," her mama had said one day when Amanda tried to crawl up on her lap. She had said it in a voice that meant Amanda should be proud of herself. But Amanda felt bad because she wasn't proud, she was angry.

Maybe tomorrow Mimi would run off again to Le Pecq to help the "poor children." And leave her with Aunt Sophie or whichever neighbor had room for her. Even Aunt Sophie hardly paid attention to her anymore. Everyone told Amanda she was so lucky to have a home and a mama like Mimi. But she didn't feel very lucky.

Mama didn't even seem to notice her, except to tell Aunt Sophie that she was a very special child, that she was hardly a bother. How she could sit for hours quietly looking at a book.

Why couldn't Mama tell that she wasn't really reading, that she was only thinking of one thing as she stared at the pages: the moment when Mama would say, "My very special big girl."

But now Amanda hated being a special big girl. She wished and wished she could be a bother, like all those other children. "Louis loves you, Amanda. See how he smiles at you?"

"Well, I don't love him," little Amanda snapped angrily.

"Amanda!" Mimi said in a scolding voice. "We have to help this poor baby. He doesn't even have a mama."

*He does too!* Amanda thought, storming from the room. *He has my mama. Everyone has my mama except me! If they make a fuss, they get kisses. If I make a fuss, I get scolding looks.*

She ran toward the meadow, to her special spot under the chestnut tree. Maybe she would find another present there. Once she'd found a package right on top of the swing. On the front was a drawing of a girl who looked like her, with long, dark braids. That was how she knew the present was for her—the wonderful

Peter Rabbit coloring book and the crayons that had hardly been used.

When she showed the new book to Mama, Mama had asked where she got it. But before Amanda could answer, a man had come with a bag of clothes for the poor children. He stayed forever, talking with Mama about how wonderful it was that the Americans helped so much with coal and cotton and wheat. He said that soon the French would be able to get milk and cheese without ration books.

And Mama said, "Isn't that exciting, Amanda?" Mama cared more about stupid ration books than Amanda's new Peter Rabbit book. "France was feeling unhappy for so long, but now it's getting happy again," her mother said with a smile.

*I wish I was happy,* Amanda thought. *I wish I was as happy as Mama says France is.*

Now, as Amanda rushed down the hill toward her tree, she thought she saw someone walking away. She watched from the footbridge until the man had hurried past the tree on the other side of the road. Then she spotted the package on the swing and ran toward it. Quickly, before someone else could come along and try to steal it.

This time the picture on the package was of Amanda in the blue jumper she had worn last week. This picture had a smiling face with a tooth missing. It made her laugh. There were pencils in the package, and a game of connect-the-dots. And even a pad to draw pictures on. She hugged the pad to her.

As Jean watched from behind the tree, he warmed at the smile on the little girl's face. Then he turned back toward the road, lifting his collar and adjusting his scarf. He headed for the car he had borrowed from Eric.

This was the second time since he'd learned of her whereabouts that he had come to Ville de Fabian intending to see Mimi and give her the diamond pin. Both times he'd lost his nerve at the thought of her pitying the sight of him.

Even worse, there would be pain in dragging up the past. He could sell the pin and send her the money, but he couldn't get much for it now. And she was sure to put it toward her charity. That was important, yes. But her daughter should benefit from it.

On his first visit, he had gotten as far as asking one of the youngsters if he knew Mimi and Amanda. The boy had pointed Amanda out to him. She was sitting on the footbridge, kicking her skinny legs back and forth over the little brook. The little girl looked like Mimi at that age, but so sad. Even when a girl called her to play, she sat there and continued to kick.

His daughter, Margot, was about the same age. But even in her worst moods, she was full of life. Sometimes he accused Brigitte of spoiling the girl with too much attention. But Brigitte just laughed and accused him of doing the same thing.

Margot's eyes lit with such love at the sight of his face, the face he was still afraid to show the world—how could he not spoil her? And, after the bad times they'd all had, it was hard not to want to see children enjoy life again.

That last time in Ville de Fabian he'd watched Amanda until she left the footbridge and headed for the chestnut tree with the tire swing. After a few halfhearted swings, she slipped onto the soft grass and leaned against the tree. For a few minutes she'd sucked her thumb; then her eyes closed and her thumb dropped from her mouth.

When he had walked back to the car on that first visit, he saw the Peter Rabbit book and crayons he had picked up for Margot lying on the front seat. He would leave them for Mimi's child; if he hurried, he could get Margot something else before the secondhand shop closed.

*Strange,* thought Jean, as he went back to the car with the pin still in his hand a second time. Mimi was famous as a caretaker of France's displaced children. Was she too bound up in that to see how much her own little girl needed her?

Then something nagged at him that he couldn't ignore as he put the key in the ignition. If Mimi had left with her parents, she'd be in Canada now. And this child might be a happy one. *He* was the reason she'd missed the plane. And then she believed he had died in the synagogue explosion. Overnight and in the middle of the war, she was left without family because of him. She had stayed and fought—and because of that, her daughter was now suffering.

Jean looked again at the pin in his hand. There had to be a way to put it to good use—to bring some of life's magic to that little girl. Without interfering and without giving himself away. But what?

# CHAPTER TWENTY-ONE

## 1962. Paris

*Watch out, Paris, Amanda Cohn is going to make her mark!* she vowed as she stood before the Louvre. An electric thrill ran through her as she looked up at the celebrated palace. Paris was in the midst of a great push to clean up its major buildings. Some worried that the historical sites would lose their stateliness when the dingy facades were gone. But in fact, the cleaned buildings united the old world with the new exciting life of the sixties.

Mama had always talked about the two of them going to Paris together, but it was always postponed because of some pressing problem at the children's home Mimi ran. But here Amanda was at last.

Hard to believe that her childhood sketching had gotten her here. What surprise she'd felt when Marcel, her teacher, told her he had submitted her work to L'Académie des Beaux-Arts in Paris and that she'd been accepted as a student.

"Amanda has an enormous gift," the art

teacher had told Mimi at the school conference.

"She has many," Mimi had answered with a wink at Amanda. "Which one are you talking about?"

Amanda looked away. Embarrassed by her mother's glowing expression. The same one she'd seen when she was a little girl. Praised for being a special big girl. She could tell Mama sensed her discomfort. And, never guessing the cause, reached for her hand and squeezed it. Why did her mother always seem to pick the worst moments to show affection? Right in front of Marcel. Bad enough to have such a crush on Marcel, she could hardly meet his eyes. But to sit here and have Mama treat her like an infant. Then Marcel told Mimi about Amanda's acceptance into the Académie. Her face lit with pride, then she looked mortified.

"But we can't afford—" Mimi stammered. "I mean, if I could—"

Amanda turned away. It was so awkward to see her mother look so troubled. And she hated being the cause.

Then Marcel looked slyly from one to the other. "It seems that someone has paid Amanda's tuition." He waved a receipt.

Mimi and Amanda exchanged puzzled looks. "Does the receipt say whom the money comes from?" Mimi asked.

"No. Evidently the donor prefers to be unknown."

Mimi and Amanda sat in stunned silence for a moment. Then Mimi decided that the money must have come from one of the families she had helped reunite. They were always so grateful that they did whatever they could to support her charities. But this time, someone was helping Mimi help her own child. Amazing! Still, who could it be? And now Amanda would leave Ville de Fabian, like so many people Mimi had loved. She had always thought they would have more time together when her own work was less demanding, but that time had never come. Now it was too late. Amanda was going to Paris.

Sunshine streamed in from the skylight in the room where Amanda sat with the dozen other pupils in her form. Their easels were grouped in a circle around a live model, and their charcoal pencils flew back and forth on their paper. This was a far cry from the tiny classroom in Ville de Fabian where Marcel had plastered the walls with student work—mostly Amanda's.

And her classmates, with their bohemian black outfits and heated, intense ways, seemed such aggressive types; they scared her. When they weren't arguing the death of Surrealism, they were hotly debating world politics—problems in Algeria and in Cuba, and the Khrushchev and Kennedy confrontations. Their opinions, shouted at each other as they waved their coffee mugs in the air, were as simplistic as they were emphatic.

If she had felt confident enough to enter the fray, it would have been to quote De Gaulle. "How can you govern a country that has two hundred and forty-six varieties of cheese?" he had said of the French. She finally understood what he meant. And if one nation's problems were so complex, how could one reduce the answer to the world's dilemmas into one definitive statement?

What little free time she had between school and her waitressing job, which supplemented the generous gift, Amanda spent marching through the museums and galleries.

*Heaven exists and I have stumbled upon it!* She laughed to herself as she walked through the Bernier's Exhibition filled with contemporary masters. Picasso! Ernst! Tanguy and Magritte!

Amanda was so lost in her own world that it took her a moment to realize that the woman at her side was speaking to her. A dark, slim young woman whom Amanda had seen at l'Académie.

*"Pardon?"* Amanda asked. "Did you say something?"

"I was saying that I think the Surrealists were right when they said Dali's work was window dressing. Don't you?"

Amanda didn't know how to respond. If she had a reaction to the art she looked at, it was simple like or dislike. Through the years she had lived so much in her own head that she was always slightly startled when someone asked for her opinion.

"I really don't know too much about it," Amanda said.

The young woman exploded into laughter, and Amanda was sorry she'd admitted her ignorance. Maybe she should have bluffed something. But in Ville de Fabian, nobody had the leisure to pretend to know about things they knew nothing about.

"An Académie student who doesn't know *everything*!"

When Amanda realized she was being complimented, she smiled. The young woman introduced herself. "My name's Odette Lisse."

"I'm Amanda Cohn."

"I know who *you* are," Odette said. "Everyone does, who has M. Montel. He's always using your work as an example."

Amanda felt her face redden. She knew she was good, but she hadn't heard it from a fellow student since she'd come to Paris. They were all too competitive to praise anyone else. *But Odette is certainly different from the brooding bunch,* Amanda thought as they finished seeing the exhibit together.

When they were ready to leave, Odette said, "How about coming back to my house for tea? My boyfriend, Armand, will be stopping by. I've been telling him about your work."

Amanda felt torn. She would have loved to

spend more time with Odette. And to go to a real home—instead of to her tiny room above a tobacco shop—sounded great. But it was already four.

"I begin work in an hour," Amanda said, a note of sadness in her voice. "I have to go home and get my uniform."

"I'll walk you there," Odette said. "Uniform? Hmm . . . either you work with the police, or you're a Playboy bunny."

Amanda laughed. How good it felt to be with a new friend. Her first friend in Paris. "Actually, I'm a waitress."

When they turned off place St. Michel, Odette pointed to the Lisse gallery. "Come inside and say hello to my dad."

Odette's father owned Lisse Fine Arts! One of the most elegant galleries on the Left Bank. Amanda's face lit as she peered through the window at the lovely gallery, and a quick tour reinforced her happiness. Sunlight streamed over exquisite paintings hung on clean white walls. Among other fascinating works were a Picasso pastel and a Degas ballet dancer.

They went into the second room, where M. Lisse, a tall patrician man with gray hair and silver-blue eyes, was advising his helper Hubert on the placement of a picture. Odette kissed her papa on the cheek. "This is the sketch-class star of I've told you about. Meet my friend Amanda," she said.

M. Lisse shook Amanda's hand. "Sorry

we're so frenzied now. We have an opening of Georges Fontenoy's work tomorrow. Why don't you come see it? Please, I insist. From what Odette says, you'll be showing your own work soon. Might as well get used to the business."

Come back to this paradise? Too bad she ever had to leave! "I'd love to come for the exhibit," Amanda said with a big smile. Then she turned to Odette. "But I must hurry now."

"Bring Amanda for supper," M. Lisse said as they left. "If we get on her good side, maybe she'll exhibit with us."

*Un coup de hasard*, a stroke of luck, Amanda thought happily as the new friends raced through the Paris streets. Lovely Odette, her kind father, and his gallery all in one day.

"No wonder you're so slim," Odette grunted comically when she reached Amanda's room on the fifth floor of the building. But Amanda had a feeling the dilapidated place troubled Odette. And when they reached the bleak café where she worked, Amanda was again aware of Odette's attempt to hide her negative reaction. "How many hours do you work here?"

"From five to ten weekdays. And noon to ten on weekends."

"How do you manage to get your assignments done?"

"At lunch and after work." It was true that Amanda worked long hours, but she didn't mind. She was determined to make something fabulous of her life. And if the schedule was tough, so be it. A small price to pay for the success she would one day create.

"After work!" Odette gasped. "You must be up half the night! Do you work Friday nights, too?"

Amanda shook her head.

"Come home with me this Friday for a Shabbat supper. If you don't mind me taking up your only night off."

The comfort of the Lisse flat in a lovely section of Paris charmed Amanda so, she instantly determined to have a home like this someday. Antiques were everywhere she looked, and china vases were filled with the most elegant flower arrangements she'd ever seen.

The Lisses observed Shabbat with candles and prayers—something that she and Mama never did, because ritual had never been important to Mimi. Then there was a scrumptious dinner of roast chicken and noodle pudding with raisins. Afterward Amanda rose to clear the dishes as she always did at home.

"What are you doing?" asked Odette.

"Aren't we going to wash the dishes?"

Mme. Lisse scolded Odette for laughing. "It's lovely of Amanda to offer." She turned to Amanda. "Colette will take care of the dishes, dear."

Amanda's face reddened. She had watched the Lisses carefully for clues to how one acted in a cultivated environment. She noted which fork was used for which dish. After getting through the evening thinking she had begun to master the protocol of refined society, she had shown herself to be a country bumpkin. Never would she make such a fool of herself again.

Odette's room was as splendid as a movie set, with lace curtains and a pink Persian carpet. Posters from New York and London shows were on the walls. She had stacks of records from America: Chubby Checker. Bob Dylan. Elvis Presley. And on the dressers was a picture of Odette riding a horse, and another in which she wore a tutu at a ballet recital. Someday Amanda would have a home like this. And someday she would give her daughter a life just like this.

The next Monday Odette caught up with Amanda after her art history class. "My father needs someone to help out in the gallery part time. Feel like a job change?"

Amanda's face radiated joy. She loved the Lisse gallery so much, she would have worked there for free. "When do I start?"

"Wednesday afternoon. But there's just one drawback." Odette paused for effect. "My dad will have to double your café wages."

Amanda sighed in mock sadness. "That is going to be very hard to cope with, but I'll give it a whirl."

# CHAPTER TWENTY-TWO

Amanda reached across the mahogany reception desk of the Lisse gallery and picked up the ringing phone. "Lisse Fine Arts."

"Happy Hanukkah two days early, Lisse Fine Arts," Mimi teased on the other end of the line. "*Comment ça va*—how are you?"

"*Bien!* Fine! And happy pre-Hanukkah to you, Mama! I thought you'd be here for our luncheon by now?"

"Parking is always so hard in Paris, but with the snow today, it's unbelievable. We'll be fifteen minutes late."

"Okay, Mama. See you soon."

Amanda hung up the phone and went to check her appearance in the closet door mirror before her mother and Sophie arrived.

What would Mama think of her new short haircut? A few people had said that with her big eyes and high cheekbones, she resembled Audrey Hepburn. True or not, the comparison delighted her. And after Amanda got her first paycheck, Odette had dragged her around

Paris for her new look. Haircut and makeup lessons at the Solange salon. And a down payment on two outfits at Clarissa Boutique. There was not a trace left of the country girl in her hand-me-down clothes.

"Anybody home?" a male voice called from the entrance.

"Be right with you," Amanda said, coming to the front room. Two men in their twenties stood near the door. Neither of them spoke, but she knew they were admiring her. She was getting used to the fact that she was attractive. And since Odette's makeover, a new confidence was taking root inside her.

"I'm Leon Rappaport," said the one in horn-rimmed glasses. "And this is Elie Feld." Leon had a warm, open smile. He gazed at her with shy appreciation.

So the taller one was Elie Feld, heir to the newspaper fortune. His office had phoned to say he'd be there to view the Blum still life. He held his hand out. "And who, may I ask, are you?" A much smoother type than this Rappaport fellow.

"Amanda Cohn," she said, shaking his hand. Elie held her hand and covered it with his other one.

"Excuse Elie for being so bashful," Leon joked.

Amanda smiled and took her hand back. "The Blum picture is in the other room. François will be happy to help you."

"But I want you to help me!" Elie pleaded humorously. Amanda smiled and called to François. As he showed them into the other room, Elie called out, "Please don't go away."

"His folks are sending him to a therapist," Leon said with a smile. "To try to help the poor guy loosen up a bit."

Amanda laughed and went to her desk, feeling both delight and nervousness. Though she liked the new wave of attention, she was uncomfortable with it. The people at the parties that Odette and her boyfriend, Armand, took her to always said such clever things—and she still felt like such a bumpkin. One fellow said that her "mysterious quality" was so interesting. *"Mysterious quality!" It's more like my tongue is tied with self-consciousness,* she thought as she filed the latest invoices.

Suddenly Mimi and Sophie came through the door. Amanda ran to meet them. "You both look great!" she said happily.

After their hug, Mimi looked at Amanda in stunned silence.

"*We* look great?" Sophie exclaimed. "So look who's talking!"

"Amanda, you look so—so Parisian!" Mimi said, smiling.

"She didn't get that haircut in Ville de Fabian. Or that fancy blouse! I'm so happy to see you," Sophie said, now crying.

Amanda got her a tissue. "I missed you, too, Aunt Sophie." She called into the back room, "Going for lunch, François!"

As they started to leave, Elie and Leon rushed in.

"You're leaving!" Elie said.

Leon sighed. "After all we've meant to each other."

Amanda laughed and introduced her mother and Sophie.

"Mrs. Cohn, you have a lovely daughter," Leon sang out.

"Ditto," echoed Elie as the women sailed outside, Mimi and Sophie giggling and Amanda red from embarrassment.

Though the weather was icy, the sidewalks were crowded with shoppers; Paris, decked out in its holiday finery, was like a beautifully wrapped gift.

As Amanda looked down at the menu, Mimi couldn't take her eyes off her. This beauty was the daughter she had brought to Paris in the fall? Her hair, her clothes—they were all new, but she also had a new inner radiance. Those two young men in the shop seemed to have noticed it, as well. Her little girl!

Amanda caught the waiter's attention and ordered the special crepes for all of them, telling him to bring the fillings on a hot plate on the side. How sophisticated and at ease she was. Paris had done wonders for her. Then Mimi felt a pang of guilt. *Wonders that I couldn't do. She's probably so embarrassed by Sophie and me in our country boots and worn coats.*

"Is that skirt velvet?" Sophie reached for the hem.

Mimi pulled her hand away. "We're in Paris, Sophie. People don't go grabbing at each other's skirts in cafés."

"*Excusez-moi!*" Sophie huffed. "What do you call that style?"

"The English 'mod' look," Amanda told her.

"English!" Sophie nodded. "You know what I like? Clothes that don't make you itch. That's my idea of fashion."

Amanda and Mimi laughed. "When she's not crying, Aunt Sophie's actually very funny," Mimi said.

"Try some warm cream on your apple crepe, Mama," Amanda said, holding the pitcher over her mother's plate.

As Amanda poured the cream, she thought, *How unhappy Mama looks. Probably thinks I'm becoming a snooty city type. She probably thinks I should donate my whole salary to her orphanage. Doesn't she know not everybody is a saint like Mimi the legend?* A woman was writing a book about Mimi. What would she call Amanda? A selfish daughter who spent her salary on clothes. As the waiter cleared the dishes, Amanda took two gaily wrapped packages from her bag. "Happy Hanukkah!"

When she unwrapped her gift, Sophie's mouth dropped open. "A beautiful satin— what? What is it?"

"A bed jacket for cold mornings. And it

doesn't itch!" She looked at Mimi, who had finished unwrapping her identical present.

"Beautiful," Mimi said. "I've never seen anything so fine. But you shouldn't be spending so much money on me."

*Of course not, Mama. The worst sin of all is to* faginen—*to indulge*—*yourself,* Amanda thought.

Mimi handed Amanda her present. "From Aunt Sophie and me."

"A scarf!" she said. "And mittens!" The homeyness of the gift warmed Amanda's heart.

"Aunt Sophie crocheted the mittens and I knitted the scarf."

"A woman I visit in the old people's home taught me to knit. But don't look too closely. It seems I can only knit irregulars."

"Well, I love it! Absolutely love it!"

Mimi wished she had brought something different. This present was for her country girl, not for this radiant, sophisticated Paris lady.

# CHAPTER TWENTY-THREE

Amanda felt that her life was so splendid, she was sure a guardian angel was taking care of her. She loved Paris so—especially since she and Odette had taken a flat together. The oak-paneled walls and the antique Queen Anne furniture that they both adored made it a lovely home. And it was on such a pretty tree-lined street, and it had a lift, and there was a concierge who greeted them cheerfully. How had she ever tolerated a minute in her old room?

School was going well and M. Lisse kept giving her more responsibility and more money at the gallery. And then, of course, she was being pursued by Elie Feld and Leon Rappaport. The problem was, she didn't know which one she liked better.

"Most girls would love that kind of problem," Odette said as she towel-dried her hair. It was Tuesday night, the night when they stayed home and did their beauty routines. "Two charming men! Leon, a promising lawyer. Elie, a newspaper heir. If I weren't crazy for Armand du Lac, I'd be part of the jealous crowd."

Amanda sat on the edge of her bed and opened her nail polish. "What made you decide to go steady with Armand?"

"He asked me."

"Be serious or I'll polish your nose Candy Apple Red."

"I feel so *right* with him, Amanda. When I first met him at synagogue, I wasn't very impressed. He would ask me out and I'd keep making excuses not to see him. When I signed up to organize the Purim festival, he kept showing up. He hardly ever spoke, but when he did, he had something to say. Then one day, he didn't show up and I was so disappointed, I called him."

"How daring! What did you say?"

Odette went to the mirror and combed her hair. "I asked him why he stopped coming to the rehearsals. He told me he was getting too attached to me and he didn't want to get hurt."

"What did you say?"

"I asked him what he was doing Saturday night."

"I'm impressed. Then what happened?"

"He was so easy to be with, I figured this must be love."

"Ah, *l'amour*," Amanda said. She blew on her wet nails.

"Let's do something we used to do in school. It's a tie-breaker for problems like yours. Get a pen and paper, Amanda."

Amanda took a pen and a pad from the top drawer of her desk. "Make columns," Odette said. "Looks, personality, chemistry." She bit her lip. "Oh yes. Common interests."

Amanda looked up from her writing. "Now what?"

"On a scale of one to five, what does Elie get in looks? Describe him as if you were giving a police report. Facts."

"Tall, lean, dark curly hair, a dimple in his chin."

"A solid five. Write that down. Now describe Leon."

"Kind of chubby. With glasses and . . ."

"Okay. Leon gets a two."

Amanda started to write, then stopped. "I can't give Leon a two."

"Okay, he gets a three. Now let's do personality."

The concierge rang and the two of them jumped. Odette picked up the phone. "Flowers for Amanda?" She rolled her eyes.

When Amanda opened the box, she was stunned by the beauty of the rare orchids Elie had sent.

"Elie's in the lead," Odette said. "Make a 'gifts' column."

The concierge rang again. Odette reached for the phone. She turned to Amanda. "Another delivery for you!" she said with a groan.

A package from Leon! Amanda ripped off the wrapping.

"A teddy bear!" she squealed.

"That is the goofiest-looking bear I've ever seen. With that silly eye winking, and a dumb beret!" Odette said. She took out her mirror and tweezers and slammed the drawer shut. "And if Armand doesn't get me one exactly like that in the next five minutes, he better find himself another tootsie!"

Amanda hugged her teddy and erupted into laughter.

"Ouch! Ouch! Ouch!" Odette muttered as she began to pluck her eyebrows. "How can you laugh when I'm in pain?"

"M. Volais for you," M. Lisse said, looking impressed as he handed Amanda the phone.

Amanda cradled the phone on her shoulder and ran her eyes over the client list. "Well, of course, if you'd like to review the Girand show early, I'd be happy to arrange it."

When she hung up the phone, M. Lisse beamed. "You even have the tough critics charmed. How did I manage without you!"

Amanda was grateful for his compliment; in the ten months she had been working at the gallery, he had trained her in every aspect of the business. And she had soaked up each lesson hungrily.

"*Merci*, M. Lisse. But you taught me everything I know!"

"You have a magic that can't be taught. Even clients I've been dealing with for years always ask to speak to you."

Amanda knew M. Lisse meant what he said. Each day she felt something wonderful stirring inside her as she crossed the gallery threshold. She felt that she had somehow gained admittance to a magical dimension, rarefied and resplendent! Yes, the surroundings were elegant—more exquisite than any of her old fantasies in Ville de Fabian. And daily she felt a core of assurance inside. She was no longer an outsider at the great party going on in the world. She belonged!

When M. Lisse left, Amanda flipped to the second page of her client list and started on the next batch of exhibit invitations. She was halfway down the list when the phone rang.

"Lisse Fine Arts," she answered.

"Amanda? *C'est* Sophie. Mimi's had a fall. She was up on the ladder putting boxes on the shelf. She's in the hospital!"

"I'm on my way, Sophie. I'll be there as soon as I can."

*Mama! Oh, please, let her be all right!* Amanda's heart was pounding as she dialed M. Lisse at his client's office.

"Just lock up and go to your mother," he said. "If you need anything, Amanda—money, whatever—you let me know. Okay?"

She thanked him and hung up the phone. She could borrow Odette's car, but she was too shaky to drive. She started toward the door, trying to fight the fears that were racing through her. And then suddenly she reached for the phone and began to dial.

"Leon?" she said into the phone. "My mother had a bad fall in Ville de Fabian. I've got—"

Before she could finish, he said, "Stay put, Amanda. I'll pick you up outside the gallery in five minutes."

Each time Amanda felt a shudder of anxiety, she looked over at Leon as they traveled the highway. Though he drove in silence, her heart could feel the strength he was sending her.

"Rest up, Mama," Amanda said, patting her mother's hand. "Dr. Glick said you'll be fine." But to see her mother so frail scared her. Mimi the legend, laid up in a hospital bed.

Mimi smiled at her daughter, as if she didn't want to miss a moment with her. Amanda knew she was trying to stay awake, but the medicine had made her so drowsy, she couldn't fight sleep any longer.

Dr. Glick took Amanda into the corridor. "Your mother may need several hip operations. Like many who lived through the war, she went very long without proper nutrition. Her bones aren't very strong. She may always walk with a limp after this."

"Whatever she needs, please make sure that she has it. I want her to have the best, whatever the cost." But how to pay? Her anxious mind began to click away. *I'll work extra hours at the gallery and at night at the café. . . .*

"I'll help you, Amanda. Don't worry," Leon said, as if sensing her anxieties.

"You're too late, son," Dr. Glick said. "An M. Jacques Lisse from Paris has already wired us to send the bills to him."

M. Lisse! How would she ever repay such kindness?

"How can you think of dropping out of art school, Amanda?" Leon asked as they walked hand in hand along the Seine. "Do you know what people would give to have your talent?"

Amanda sighed. "When I was a child, art was a magical escape. But it's not what I want to spend my life doing."

"If it's about money, Amanda," Leon said, squeezing her hand, "I'll be happy to help you."

"If I could take help from anyone, Leon, you know it would be you. But in one month at the gallery, I made more than I would make in years as an artist. Still, it's not just the money—though I can't say I mind money." Amanda gazed into Leon's eyes. She wanted so much for this dear man to understand what she understood about herself. "The fact is that I feel something more satisfying at the gallery than I do at school. And I'm very good at the business. I adore every minute of my time there. Leon, once I make up my mind to do something, I do it. I wouldn't make this choice if it wasn't the one I wanted."

Leon looked at her. "It makes your heart sing."

"I like that." Amanda smiled. "Yes, it makes my heart sing. . . . Tell me something, Leon. What makes your heart sing?"

Leon took a deep breath and reached into his pocket for a small velvet box. He handed it to her and cleared his throat.

"Amanda Cohn. You make my heart sing. Will you be my wife?"

Amanda felt a surge of joy. She looked around at the other couples along the Seine. Everyone was doing it. She wrapped her arms around Leon and kissed him full on the mouth.

Rabbi Levi looked at Dominique across Mimi's old enamel kitchen table. "Your parents were married that fall. In two years your mama had earned enough commissions to pay M. Lisse back. Then Leon received a superb opportunity with a New York firm."

Dominique smiled. "That part I know. And how Mama started the gallery without even knowing English and made it a success."

"But all of us who knew Mimi over the years know that she always blamed herself for Amanda's dropping out of art school."

Dominique sat up in her chair. "But it sounds as if Mama loved the gallery business more than painting!"

"True. But Mimi still thinks her accident was to blame."

Dominique shook her head sadly, wishing she could dissolve all the years of misunderstanding between mama and Grandmère.

"Your mama always wanted Mimi to move to America. But Mimi couldn't leave Ville de Fabian. Your mama sent Mimi money regularly. But Mimi always sent it back. She was too proud to feel that she was a burden to your mama. She didn't understand that it gave your mama happiness to send her something. Or that she made your mama feel rejected again when she refused her checks."

Dominique sat quietly for a while, letting it all sink in. Then she turned to Rabbi Levi. "Jean sold Grandmère's pin to pay for Mama's school."

"But he could never go back to see Mimi. His scarred face kept him from Mimi and from most of the rest of the world.

"Even as a child, Julian sensed his shame and it pained him so. For such an extraordinary man, to spend a life in hiding! As soon as Julian learned that there was such a thing as a plastic surgeon—a doctor who might be able to help people like Jean—Julian made up his mind that plastic surgery would be his life's work."

*So,* Dominique thought, *I judged him too quickly again. He didn't choose plastic surgery to make a lot of money. But how could he be the grandson of Jean Adler and be such a manipulator?*

*Mine is not to reason why,* Dominique told herself sternly. *Mine is to stop thinking about him. Now!*

# CHAPTER TWENTY-FOUR

Mimi and Dominique walked down the winding driveway toward the car, where the driver was putting Dominique's bags in the trunk. "I'm so happy you were able to visit, darling," Mimi said. "And thank you so much for putting that room back in order. I just wish we had a more exciting life here for you."

*More exciting!* Dominique thought. *What I've heard this week is excitement enough for several lifetimes!* "I loved every second," Dominique told her. The visit had been more satisfying than Dominique could ever have hoped. The strong bond she had with Mimi had grown so much deeper over the last few days. And though she knew she'd feel that bond all her life, it was still hard to say good-bye. "I wish you'd come to visit in New York sometime."

Mimi laughed. "I find it hard to be in Paris! How much harder would it be in a city where they are not speaking French. But maybe you'll find your way back to me soon. Give your parents my love. Tell your mama how much I miss her, too."

Dominique looked deeply into her grandmother's eyes, engulfed by the warmth she saw there. "Of course I will."

Mimi went into the house, back to the bedroom where Dominique had slept. Maybe my darling girl will come back soon. Who knows? On the night table, she found the snapshot of little Amanda. She put on her glasses and looked closely at the picture of the little girl with such sad eyes. Why had she never realized poor Amanda was such an unhappy little girl?

In another ten minutes Mimi was sound asleep on the bed. Then she awakened with a start. Someone was calling from the door. "Come in," she called, crossing through the kitchen.

The door opened and Mimi almost had the shock of her life. Not ten feet from her was a young man who looked exactly like Jean Adler! She had to steady herself.

"Are you Mimi?" the young man said, looking into her face with dark, familiar eyes. "I have heard so much about you."

Dominique sat back in the cab and sighed. After a quick stop at the Paris flat for the rest of her luggage, she'd be on the plane back to Manhattan. She felt a bit guilty for being so relieved that Sara wasn't traveling with her. As much as she loved Sara, she needed time to absorb all she'd learned in Ville de Fabian.

As the car bumped over the country road, she turned for a sweeping look back at the quaint cottages nestled in the lush countryside. Images crowded her head. Mimi and Jean as teenagers, vibrant and totally in love. She smiled, remembering the faded snapshot of the tall, gentle man who had been her great-grandfather. How she would have loved to know him.

Dominique leaned back against the red leather seat. What might have become of Jean and Mimi if her great-grandmother hadn't been so full of her pretentious social striving? The tragedy of losing each other so brutally in the terror of the Nazi occupation. This rustic country road she was now traveling had once been overrun with German tanks! Could she have withstood the awful losses that Mimi had survived? And come through with such a great capacity for love?

Suddenly Dominique felt a strange sensation in her chest. Julian. Would he ever know—would Rabbi Levi ever tell him just how powerfully their histories were intertwined? Dominique took a deep breath. Too overwhelming.

The picture of her mother as a sad little waif came back to her. It was awful that her mother could never know how much Mimi loved her. Since learning all she had about her mother in Ville de Fabian, Dominique felt her own heart had softened. It was clear that Amanda took such ardent control of her life because she never could feel her own mother's caring. A smile came to Dominique's lips. *And oh, Mimi, have I ever been paying for your mistakes!* One thing Dominique was certain of: She wanted to have a better relationship with her mother. *But Mama and Mimi—there has to be a way to get them to heal the hurts between them.* Dominique was absolutely determined to find it.

Mme. Renault picked up the Du Lacs' telephone. "Yes, who is it, please?"

"It's Julian Adler, Mme. Renault. Has Dominique arrived?" He held his breath.

"No, but she's expected soon. Her luggage is still here."

"Thank heaven!" Jean exclaimed. "Mme. Renault, will you give her a message for me? It's important. Will you tell her that I'm in Ville de Fabian and that she must not leave before I get there? Have you got that?"

"Sounds like urgent business," Mme. Renault said.

"It is the most urgent business of my life."

"I'll make sure that she gets it. Don't worry, Julian."

Julian hung up the phone in the small house in Ville de Fabian, hugged Mimi, and raced outside to his car.

Five minutes later Pierre came through the front door of the Paris flat, carrying a bouquet of long-stemmed roses. "Dominique hasn't been here yet, has she, Mme. Renault?"

"No," Mme. Renault said, looking over the note Julian had dictated, "but she should be here soon." She put the note in her pocket. "I've got to check on tonight's roast."

Pierre went into the sitting room and looked out the window. There was still time to patch things up between them. How could he have expected a sheltered girl to understand a sophisticated man like Pierre du Lac? A little more time, a little more patience, and he'd have her right in the palm of his hand.

Mme. Renault came into the room. "I'll have to run to the bakery to pick up some bread for dinner." She was halfway out the door when she remembered Julian's note. "I almost forgot this. Julian said it was urgent to give it to Dominique. I'll leave it for her on the table near the door."

"I'll take care that she sees it, Mme. Renault."

Strange that Julian was sending Dominique urgent notes. Pierre smoothed his hair in the hall mirror.

As the concierge rang to announce Dominique, he picked up the note from Julian. "Don't leave before I get there . . ." it said. What was this all about? Maybe Lizette's suspicions were true. Hadn't she mentioned something about finding Julian and Dominique in the library at the Dragoni estate? And then

287

again at the pavilion, after that bad storm.

Pierre began to laugh. *Julian, you sneaky devil!* All this time Pierre had been thinking how poor Julian was struggling so hard to get through medical school. Working, working, always working! And trying to put the moves on Dominique *and* his sister at the same time. That wasn't very nice of him. Not nice at all. *But,* Pierre said as he crumpled the note into the basket and went for the door, *you're still too much of an amateur to play in my league.*

Dominique looked out the window as she and Pierre rode to the airport in the limousine.

"If I apologize again, Dominique," Pierre said, "you will think I am a fool, *non?*"

"No, Pierre," Dominique said. "I won't. But I'll still think we're better off friends than lovers. Let's just let it go."

"Do not cross me off entirely, Dominique," Pierre said, putting his arm around her shoulder. "There's always next year."

Dominique shook her head, looked at his arm and removed it from her shoulder. "Don't do that, Pierre," she said quietly but very, very firmly.

Julian dashed in and out of the rooms of the Paris apartment. She was gone. The words *too late* echoed in his head. Maybe she didn't get the note. Then he spotted a piece of paper

crumpled on the floor near the hall basket.
Mme. Renault had written the message quite
clearly. And Dominique must have just looked
at it and tossed it there. He set his jaw. Well, he
certainly got *her* message loud and clear. He
tossed the paper in the basket where she
wanted it and headed out the door.

But before the lift had reached the ground
floor, he had decided that whether she wanted
him to or not, he'd find her when he got to
New York.

# CHAPTER TWENTY-FIVE

Leon Rappaport was not a man who cried easily. But as he watched his wife and daughter opposite him on the den sofa, he felt such tenderness, his eyes began to fill. Dominique had only been back from the airport an hour and she had insisted that they all go to Shabbat services that night.

"Why not relax and we'll go in the morning?" Amanda asked.

"I'm just so full of good feelings," Dominique answered excitedly. "I feel like I need to be at some kind of sacred ceremony—to thank God with both of you there. If I don't get to synagogue tonight, I think I'll explode."

"I wouldn't want our daughter to explode," Leon said to his baffled wife. "Especially so soon before graduation!"

But Leon was even more amazed when they got to the service. Dominique had taken Amanda's hand during the singing. Something he hadn't seen her do since she was a child. Whatever had happened on her trip, it was worth a hundred times more than he had paid for it. Even Amanda looked about to bawl her eyes out. And watching them now on the couch was a gift from God.

"I never spoke of Mama's legend," Amanda said, "because she always said she just did what any human being should do. She said it showed how sad a state the world was in, to believe that helping others was heroic. But I guess she was extraordinary."

"You're extraordinary too, Mama," Dominique said. "Your tenacity in going after what you want is awesome."

Amanda turned a radiant face to Leon, shrugging helplessly.

"Don't look at me for an argument, sweetheart," he said. "I'm in complete agreement."

Dominique rose to her feet. "I think I can sleep now. Thank you both, for everything." She hugged them and went to her room.

It was good to be home, but she had a nagging desire to fast-forward her life to the point where she knew what she was going to do with it. If only she knew what her *bashert* was! What had Rabbi Levi said? That it was looking for her as hard as she was looking for it. It just better hurry up and find her before it was too late to back out of the N.Y.U. program. As she lay down, Little Elvis hopped up beside her and headed for the crook of her arm.

On Monday Dominique found Kaitlin and

Sara at their usual lunchtime booth at Sal's Pizza and hugged them both.

"I'm so glad you guys are back," Kaitlin said. "Sara was just filling me in on the lifestyles of the rich and titled!"

Dominique laughed. "Didn't happen to mention how much she loved the museums, did she?"

Sara groaned. "My *corns* have corns from all that walking!"

"Let's all do the Metropolitan tomorrow. They have—"

"Can't. Tomorrow I'm having a major headache," Sara said.

"She's absolutely psychic!" Dominique said in mock surprise. "Imagine knowing about Tuesday's headache on Monday?"

"Better lose your headache before the weekend, Sara."

She turned to Dominique and wagged her finger. "You both better be at the party my sister's giving me and Zach on Saturday."

"Wouldn't miss it," Dominique said. "By the way, how did your parents feel about the engagement? Are they cool?"

Kaitlin picked a pepperoni slice from her pizza and popped it in her mouth. "You know how my mom gets all her advice from Oprah? Well, she had a shrink on who said if you oppose your kids too much, they'll wind up rebelling. Now Mom's afraid that if she riles me we'll elope. *Vive la Oprah!*"

Dominique and Sara laughed.

"Much as I hate to gossip," Sara cooed, batting her lashes, "I have a juicy scoop about Lizette and Julian!"

Dominique's heart skipped a beat. So weird how she still felt so connected to Julian. She would just have to evict him from her mind. The last thing she needed was to hear about how he and Lizette were doing. She stood. "I've got to run."

"But this is really a major headline!"

"I think I'm going to miss this installment. I've got to make an appointment with Mr. Altman in the guidance office. I've got one more week before the deadline. He's got a visual arts program he wants me to visit."

"Sounds great, Nik!" Sara said.

*Sounds great,* Dominique thought as she waited for the light to change on the corner of Eighty-fifth and Lexington. *But will it make my heart sing? That is the question.*

*Will it lead me to the kind of life I want? A life as meaningful as Grandmère's. A life as challenging as Mama's.* Then she made a solemn vow: *Dominique, granddaughter of Mimi, daughter of Amanda, you will find a career, a life that counts!*

Zach unwrapped the last engagement present. "This is great. *The Jewish Gourmet Cookbook!*" He waved it in the air. "Quick, Kait, without looking, what if I had an urge for *latkes*?"

*"Latkes?"* Kait paused to concentrate. "Cholesterol city! Do yourself a favor, hon, and order a baked potato."

"Aren't they cute together?" Sara asked Dominique.

"They are. Absolutely." Dominique smiled.

An hour later, waiting for a cab outside of the party, Dominique was consumed with loneliness. *Everyone's paired off,* she thought with a sigh as she got into the cab. *Everyone but me.* She gave the driver her address and leaned back in her seat, closing her eyes. Unbidden, Julian came into her thoughts. She remembered the kiss they'd shared in the deserted old chapel. *If only* . . . Dominique thought. *If only* . . . The last thing Dominique was aware of before she lost consciousness was a frightening jolt and the loud crunch of metal as the Gracie Square Deli van, accidentally running a red light, rammed into the taxi.

Dominique had made her feelings—or lack of feelings—for him clear by leaving the Paris flat before he arrived. But Julian couldn't let things end like that. The magnetic pull he felt for her was just too strong. When he got to New York, he had gotten as far as walking past her towering apartment building. She came from that elegant world where people knew the right words. And he was so clumsy with words. All he knew was that he loved her and

295

that he had to find a way to see her again.

When his beeper went off, Julian put down his hospital schedule to answer the call at the nurses' station. "Dr. Shearn is asking for you in the emergency room," the operator announced. "A young woman was just brought in. A car accident." But when he opened the door and saw the red hair the nurse was pulling back from the young woman's face, Julian's heart stopped. Seeing her like this was almost too much to handle.

Then Dr. Julian Adler took over. His medical training had never been so important in his life. "Get Dr. Shearn to E.R. right away! She's obviously had severe trauma to her head."

Leon waited outside Dominique's hospital room for Stan Morris, the Rappaport family doctor. To his weary eyes, the fluorescent lights seemed to make an aura around the nurses' station in front of him. His heart broke as he looked toward his beautiful child, her face in bandages, Amanda beside her, whispering loving words.

Dr. Morris stepped off the elevator. "I'm so sorry, Leon."

"What can we expect, Stan?" he asked in a shaking voice.

The doctor grasped his shoulder. "We've known each other too long for anything but the truth. She was pretty badly injured, and her recovery will take time."

"How much time?" Leon asked in a hushed

tone, staring off at the elderly woman who was being wheeled down the hall, gasping into the oxygen mask on her face.

"It's hard to give an exact answer. After she recovers from the surgery, she'll need extensive physical therapy. But she's young and strong. And I think we can be hopeful that she'll be back on her feet in three to six months."

Leon took a deep breath. "What about her face?"

"She was a very beautiful girl, Leon." Dr. Morris sighed. "Shearn, the head of plastic surgery, says that the doctor used a new grafting technique that's supposed to ensure quicker healing. Not many people are familiar with it here yet, but this young French resident had seen it many times in Paris and was able to assist him expertly. Shearn calls him the French genius. But she was pretty badly banged up. When the bandages come off, no one can guarantee she'll be as beautiful as she was."

Leon looked away. How could life be so unfair? His beautiful little girl, with everything wonderful in life ahead of her, was now mute and still in that cold, gray room. How could his precious child's destiny be so altered in the course of a ten-minute cab ride? But, he told himself, she was alive. Thank God she was alive.

# CHAPTER TWENTY-SIX

Dominique dreamed she was a little girl sitting in Grandmère Mimi's lap. Grandmère was singing "La Clara de la Luna." Dominique smiled. It was such a nice dream. When she opened her eyes she was confused.

"Grandmère?" she said sleepily. "I was having a dream—"

Mimi squeezed her hand. Then she turned to the hallway. "Amanda! Leon! She's awake! Dominique is awake!"

Dominique tried to sit up, but her body felt so heavy. Something was weighing her down. It was a cast. And her face, something was on her face. She was startled to feel bandages instead of her skin. And then pain began to throb in her head. Then she remembered. The party for Kaitlin and Zach. And then the cab ride. That awful jolt that nearly knocked her through the other side of the taxi.

Her father—love beaming from his face. Her grandmother and mother together! They were holding on to each other and crying.

"So many tears!" she said in a happy fog. "And no Sophie?"

Amanda and Mimi burst into laughter.

Dominique stared into the mirror, wishing she had a clue about what she would see when the bandages came off. Her dad had told her that Dr. Morris had said no one could predict what she'd look like. But she was lucky to be alive. Yes, she was. Still—what would it feel like not to be beautiful? For so long she had felt that her looks were a barrier that kept people from getting to know who she really was. And yet . . . what would it be like *not* to look like beautiful Dominique?

A knock on the door suspended her musings. "It's us!" Kait sang out from the doorway. Zach and Sara were right behind her.

Zach held up a pizza carton. "Yo, cuz! Can you stand a present from Sal's with the works?"

"Everything but anchovies!" Dominique answered.

"It's so good to see you," Kaitlin said, cutting the pizza into small pieces.

Dominique felt like smiling. But her face under the bandages felt numb and frozen. The bandages cut off some of her vision, but she could see a doctor in a white jacket in the hall.

"I see you're have a party, Dominique," he said.

*Julian?* She recognized the husky voice before she could comprehend that the face belonged to Julian. *Julian Adler!*

Sara began chattering away a mile a minute. "Julian! I hear you assisted with the surgery. Everyone's saying you were great. Oh, have you met Zach and Kate?"

Julian assisted with her surgery? Dominique's brain was reeling. And now he was beside her, smiling his head off.

"I wanted to see how you were feeling, Dominique," he said.

When she could find her voice, Dominique answered. "I'm not up for the marathon, but I'm doing okay."

He touched her face lightly. "Feel any pain?"

She shook her head.

"You're still numb. But you're coming along very well. You've been through an awful lot, *oui?*"

"*Oui.*" Dominique smiled weakly, wondering again if she was dreaming.


"What kind of pitcher you making?" a childish voice asked.

Dominique looked across the solarium to see a boy, probably about seven, with curly dark hair. He was on crutches. She held her pad up for inspection. "Flowers. What do you think?"

He nodded. "What happened to your face?" he asked.

"Car accident," Dominique answered. She had been so intent upon her drawings that

301

she'd forgotten all about the bandages. "Do you want to draw something?"

The boy slid into the chair beside her. "Can you show me how to make a mean, scary monster as big as the sky?"

Dominique looked at the boy as he slammed his crutches away from him. He was obviously angry. Whatever his physical problem was, she knew the little guy might feel a bit better if he could see that monster right in front of him, on paper, where he could control it. "One mean, scary monster as big as the sky, coming right up!" She held out her box of colored pencils. "What's your name?"

"Joel Jakes." He looked through the colored pencils.

"I'm Dominique," she said.

"Your name is too hard," Joel Jakes said. He pulled a green pencil out of the box. "But you draw good pitchers."

Odd how certain sounds were very easy to recognize in the busy hospital: Julian's footsteps as he got off the elevator. The older nurses at the desk flirting with the handsome French doctor, and his joking response. The sound the stiff material of his lab coat made as he entered her room. Each time the elevator doors opened, she cocked her head and listened, hoping to hear him.

And then he kept popping up wherever she went in the hospital. Sometimes when she was in the physical therapy room, doing her leg lifts, she'd feel an extra surge of power. As if her leg were suddenly stronger. She'd look up and see Julian standing in the doorway, giving her the thumbs-up sign. It was almost as if there were a healing current between them. *Too many corny old movies,* she said to herself, *have turned your brains to mush.*

Little Jennifer asked, "Can my cat be purple?"

"Sure can," Dominique answered.

Jennifer dipped a wet brush into the purple paint.

Five-year-old Sabrina held up a page of colorful scribbles. "Do you like mine? It's a real letter."

"Great, Sabrina. What does it say?"

"I don't know how to read yet. Tell me what it says."

Dominique studied the scribbling hard, trying not to laugh.

Julian leaned over her shoulder. "I know why you're having a hard time reading it. It's in French! Maybe I can read it."

"Dr. Julian's going to read my letter!" Sabrina announced.

"My goodness! It's the French national anthem." He began to sing solemnly.

Dominique perked up as she heard Julian's footsteps approach.

"Dominique," he said, as he poked his head

through the door. "There are some people who want to meet you. Is now a good time?"

"I'm due to pitch for the home team in ten minutes, but I can postpone it," she said.

Laughing, Julian led a couple into the room. "Mr. and Mrs. Jakes, I want you to meet Dominique."

"We didn't know your name," Mrs. Jakes said. "But we wanted to thank you. We're Joel Jakes's parents."

"He's a great little guy."

"You're all he talks about. Working with him on the art really turned him around," Mr. Jakes said. "He's happy and doing better than he has in weeks."

"I've had a wonderful time with him, too." Dominique felt a smile behind her bandages.

Julian swiped two apple juices from the hospital cart and sailed into Dominique's room. "A toast to the mademoiselle of the Kids-Art project. So many of the children you've been working with are telling their parents about you, the hospital's been flooded with requests to start an official art program. Dr. Sandler's going to speak to the board about it. And guess who would be in charge of running it?"

Dominique shook her head in disbelief. This was work she loved! This was what made her happy. To use her art and see the faces of those kids light up with delight.

"Julian, do you really think they'll do it?"

"Don't know how they can refuse. Dr. Savitsky's working with pediatrics to set up a schedule."

She looked down and realized he was holding her hand. She felt the electricity of his touch. He was behind her one hundred percent to get her program launched, to make her dreams come true.

Suddenly Julian's beeper began to sound. Julian jerked his hand away, as if he'd just realized they'd been holding hands.

Dominique laughed. "Duty calls."

"See you later," Julian said. Walking backward out of her room, Julian bumped right into Sara and Kaitlin.

"Whoa," Sara said as he nearly knocked her over. "I hope you look where you're going when you're doing surgery."

"That is one major babe, Dominique," Kaitlin said as soon as he was gone. "Wouldn't it be great if he could coach Zach into speaking with a French accent?"

"Yeah . . . Too bad he's taken," Dominique said with a long sigh, forgetting for an instant her vow to keep it straight in her head that he was her friend, doctor, and comrade in the Kids-Art program.

"Taken?" Sara said, flopping down on Dominique's bed. "Who took him?"

"Lizette, you dope," Dominique snapped impatiently. "You know that as well as I do."

Sara shook her head. "Niki, they aren't

going out. And what's more, they never *have* gone out."

"What are you talking about? You were in Paris with me. You heard—"

"Lizette made the whole thing up, that's what we heard. She wrote me a long letter about it when I got back. I tried to tell you that day at Sal's, but you wouldn't listen."

"I don't get it," Dominique said, her heart pounding in her throat.

Sara groaned. "The romance between Julian and Lizette was all in Lizette's head. After the slew of guys she'd been throwing herself at, Julian was the first who didn't take advantage. He was the first one who treated her like she was more than a silly tramp. All the time he spent with her, he was trying to get her to learn to respect herself. Lizette was so confused by his kindness, she turned it into a love story in her head."

Dominique looked down at the way Julian was holding her hand as they walked through the hospital corridor after she had made her presentation to the board to get the official stamp of approval on her Kids-Art program. She could feel the electricity of his touch moving through her. How could it have turned out that they were together and in love? She smiled to herself. But after all that intertwined history, how could it not have turned out this way?

As soon as the truth about Julian and Lizette was out of Sara's mouth, Dominique had called Julian's beeper and they had both blurted out their stories.

"And when I found the message I gave Mme. Renault crumpled on the floor, I thought you were the one who threw it away," Julian told her.

"I never got the message," Dominique cried. "But even if I had, I probably would've thrown it away, because I thought you belonged to Lizzie."

"Can you keep this straight in your head from now on—that I belong to you?" Julian had said, kissing her head and holding her against him. "I never want to lose you again."

And now they were together. Finally. Where they belonged. *Bashert,* thought Dominique. Destiny. She thought about the fate of Mimi and Jean. And how fortunate she and Julian were to be able to be together.

"When are the bandages coming off my face?" Dominique asked, looking up at him.

"Part will come off on Tuesday," Julian said. "It'll be another six weeks before the rest can be removed."

His beeper began to sound. "I love you," Julian said, kissing her hand.

"Ah, *l'amour!*" She grinned as he went to the phone.

# CHAPTER TWENTY-SEVEN

Dominique looked around her living room at Julian, her parents and her grandmother. It had been a wonderful Rosh Hashanah dinner at Uncle Nathan's. It was great that Zach and Julian hit it off so well; they seemed like old friends already.

How could so much *life* have happened since Passover, when she didn't know where she was headed? And now there was so much to look forward to. She had Julian and the Kids-Art program, which had received the approval of the board; she couldn't feel more blessed. And in the fall she was entering N.Y.U. with a dual major in child psychology and art administration.

"So the thorn had a big rose," her father said.

"What do you mean, Papa?"

"When something bad would happen, Bubbe Sadie would say, 'You always have to be careful because beautiful roses have thorns. But sometimes you think you've only got a thorn and *voilà!*—it comes carrying a beautiful rose.' It was an awful accident, sweetheart. But out of it came something wonderful."

Dominique nodded. "Many wonderful things!"

"But," said Julian, "now we've got another problem. Now we need to find space for the Kids-Art program, and the hospital says they just can't figure out what to do."

"Best problem this family has had in ages!" Mimi said.

"I wish we could build some space onto the hospital. But that would be impossible," Dominique said with a sigh.

"Why not?" Amanda said with a clap of her well-manicured hands. "We know every person in New York with money. Let's make them to part with some of it, *oui*? Let me just get my Filofax."

"A benefit at the gallery?" Leon said.

"Rappaport Fine Arts will have a benefit to build a room for the art program, *non*?" said Amanda.

"*Oui!*" Mimi beamed. "To help the children."

Dominique was overwhelmed at the efforts her parents and grandmother made for her hospital project. Two days before the benefit, they had assurances of a packed house.

"Three stubborn women," Leon Rappaport said with a laugh as he watched them on the telephones at the gallery. "There won't be a dollar left in anyone's pocket the night of the benefit."

Dominique smiled to herself. Whatever gave her the idea that something was wrong with having money? How else could you build hospital wings?

*          *          *

The day before the benefit the family sat together in the hospital as Julian prepared to remove the rest of Dominique's bandages. He looked around at the faces of her parents, her grandmother, and Dr. Morris.

"Julian," Dominique said, "I'm afraid to see what's underneath the bandages."

"I already know what's underneath the bandages, Dominique. Someone who will always be beautiful to me no matter what anyone else's eyes see."

*Sounds wonderful,* Dominique thought. *But what if*— "Hurry, Julian," Dominique said. "Let's get this over with."

She could feel the eyes of her family and Dr. Morris on her. But she kept hers focused on Julian. And when he snipped the final bandage from her face, she saw what she needed to know. The fact that his expression hadn't changed at all said it truly made no difference to him what she looked like.

She turned to her parents and grandmother. Their faces were full of relief. The operation had been a success.

"Beautiful as ever," Dr. Morris said with a big smile.

"Congratulations, darling," Julian said, dancing with his wonderful Dominique, who was elegant in a green silk gown that matched her eyes. Because she was in his arms on the hotel ballroom floor, he hadn't even minded the formal attire that he had always hated before tonight. "We've got enough pledges to build your art wing. I'm so proud of you."

Dominique nestled her head against his shoulder, smiling at her parents and grandmother, who were sitting at a table just off the dance floor.

"There's one more thing I have to do," Julian said. "One final test." He bent and kissed her cheek. "I'll have to check your face for numbness." He kissed her again. And again.

"Julian," she scolded in a loud whisper. "My parents! Grandmère Mimi! Please, try to control yourself!"

"*Pardon,*" Julian said, looking around the room.

The people around them on the dance floor . . . the ones she had always thought of as shallow phonies, the ones whose generosity had assured her program's success, smiled in their direction.

"*Pardon,*" Julian said again as he stopped dancing and looked into her eyes before he put his lips against hers. In full view of the room. In full view of the world. The band stopped playing as everyone in the room erupted into spontaneous laughter and applause. But they were nowhere near loud enough to block out the sound of Dominique's heart singing.